THE
WATCHER

THE WATCHER

A Novel

JENNIFER PASHLEY

CROOKED
LANE

NEW YORK

Copyright © 2020 by Jennifer Pashley

Published in the United States by Crooked Lane Books, an imprint of The Quick Brown Fox & Company LLC.

Crooked Lane Books and its logo are trademarks of The Quick Brown Fox & Company LLC.

Library of Congress Catalog-in-Publication data available upon request.

ISBN (hardcover): 978-1-64385-442-7
ISBN (ebook): 978-1-64385-443-4

Cover design by Nicole Lecht

Printed in the United States.

www.crookedlanebooks.com

Crooked Lane Books
34 West 27th St., 10th Floor
New York, NY 10001

First Edition: September 2020

10 9 8 7 6 5 4 3 2 1

For my mother, who told me I wouldn't understand
her until after she was dead.

Many are the deceivers.

—*Anne Sexton*

ONE: KATERI

MONDAY, OCTOBER 16

He warned her in the dead of summer, when the heat blew over the trees like a dry lick of fire, that nothing happens here. Until it does.

It's the same stuff over and over up here, Hurt told her. Drugs. Robbery. Domestic. Child abuse. Animal cruelty.

She'd cut her teeth as a criminal investigator in Syracuse. But after her own run-in with the law, she'd come to Spring Falls as a plea deal.

She hears Hurt call her name before he appears in her doorway. "Fisher," he says, and then leans in, hair and pants misted from riding his bike in to work. "I need you on suspicious activity."

"Where are the deputies?" she asks, and pushes her chair back. In truth, she's happy to have something to check out, a reason to get out of the office, even if it's just a task.

"Everyone's out on the Lenox Ave fire," Hurt says. Six months side by side and he is still awkward around her. He comes no more than a foot into her office and seems to look anywhere but at her. She folds her arms over her chest.

"All the deputies are at a fire," she repeats, disbelieving.

"It's a meth fire," Hurt answers. "Blew up a motel room."

She nods. She heard the call earlier. Twelve-room motel on Route 8, heading into the mountains. Everything a loss. Kateri stands and attaches her duty belt, and Hurt watches the wall behind her.

"Where?" she asks.

"At the edge of Silver Lake Park." He hands her a report. The address is only a space—Hidden Drive, Space 17. Hidden Drive, a winding road that leads into acres and acres of forest.

Before Spring Falls, Kateri herself was found on the edge of a park. Covered in blood, throat cut and embedded with glass, unconscious. It was a cop who found her. It was a cop who sent her here. Hamilton County had expected a promotion from within, and instead they were sent an outsider, a woman, from a city. One who'd arrived after a forced leave of absence, and with a mysterious scar.

Kateri looks at the report. "Did they find something?"

Hurt shrugs, then sighs. "People get panicky about a dead smell in the woods," he says, but adds, "It's probably nothing. It's probably a deer."

* * *

She drives out in her own car, a Subaru she bought when she left for the North Country. Winters were already bad in Syracuse. What awaited Kateri up north seemed like a nightmare of snow and ice, stretching from October to May.

Her other car, a small, smart Jetta, was unsalvageable. She was lucky: no one else had been involved. Just Kateri and a brick wall at the edge of Thornden Park, her Jetta crumpled like a wad of paper. She didn't remember leaving the bar or getting behind the wheel. The whole night, a blackout. She woke up in the hospital with fifty-two stitches under her chin, a broken wrist, and two cracked ribs. They had her on the addiction rehabilitation floor.

She was given a six-month unpaid leave of absence. After her grandmother died, she sold her childhood home, filed the final divorce papers, and moved to Spring Falls with nothing but a small suitcase. Things were falling away from her. She needed a change. She needed a town where no one knew her.

"How will I know where to look?" she asked Hurt before leaving. He gave her a paper map of Silver Lake Park, dotted hiking trails, camping areas, parking lots. He circled a blank spot in the trees— Space 17.

"There's one residence," he said.

"Inside the park?"

"On the edge," Hurt said. "There's a house. You'll see it. The Jenkins own half of it."

"Half of the house?" Kateri asked.

"Half the land," Hurt corrected. "The park isn't as big as it looks. A lot of the land is private, and most of that belongs to the Jenkins."

She imagined a mansion, dilapidated and old, guarding the entrance of the forest.

"I don't even know if it's still occupied," Hurt said before she left. "They're dirt fucking poor and crazy," he added.

She was just beginning to glean the importance of some families in Spring Falls. The Nelsons, who owned the credit union. The Parrys, who were on the school board. The Sullivans, who made up two-thirds of the law firm.

"Who are the Jenkins?" Kateri asked.

Hurt looked at the wall behind her, a habit she disliked. "Almost as bad as the Metzgers," he said. They'd arrested the senior Metzger last week on weapons charges and child endangerment. He was sitting at county, waiting for arraignment.

*   *   *

She parks at an entrance called Blue Bell, a field of grass and flowers near a picnic pavilion, a public bathroom, and an opening into the woods marked WHITE TRAIL. She can just make out the house through the trees. It's gray and low, with a sloping porch. A dense vine grows over the sides and roof, stitching in around the front door, like the woods are trying to take it back.

She would have guessed it was vacant. It doesn't look livable. But a box fan runs in one window, a small, quiet sign of life.

Her first patrol cases were rural, calls where she went along with a senior partner, checked the welfare of children and animals. She's seen suicides by hanging and by gunshot and her fair share of DWIs. When she moved to criminal investigation, she worked a rape and murder by the lake, a child rape case, and drugs. Drugs are everywhere.

A jogger enters the trail with a spray of pebbles, his feet hitting the ground with a hollow thud. He startles Kateri, and Kateri surprises him, standing there in her work clothes and belt. She sets her mouth and waves slightly at him while he picks up the pace, his brow furrowed and his cheeks puffed with exertion. He doesn't stop, and Kateri watches the backs of his calves as he climbs the trail, his ankles paper-thin above his sneakers.

She thinks for a minute about Joel Hurt, the shape of him next to her in the squad car. She knows he runs out here as well, his body lean and working. He's never completely still. He's like a compressed spring.

Who didn't come with her.

She draws her weapon and keeps it low, approaching the house with her head cocked and listening. The woods are loud with birdsong, chattering squirrels, the creak of branches, the crunch of her own feet, the sharp caw of crows.

She can smell it from the porch. The iron tang of blood and a warm, rotten smell underneath it. The house is dark inside, closed up, close, ripe. Slow, fat flies buzz in the windows.

Kateri pulls her sweater up over her nose and takes shoe covers and latex gloves from her pack. The air inside is too thick to breathe.

In the front room of the house, there's the largest flat-screen TV Kateri has possibly ever seen. It must be six feet wide. The screen, turned on, shows nothing but the quad of security cameras, pointed into the woods, out at the road. One shows the chairs around a fire pit in the yard, another a sliver of light on the trail where Kateri appeared moments ago, the jogger rushing past her.

A large pool of blood collects in the kitchen, the edge smeared from the pull of the body. It drags over the linoleum and onto the wood but disappears. Someone has wiped the path to the doorway. Blood spatters the cupboards, the counter, up onto the ceiling in a particular pattern. Nothing but the floor has been wiped.

On the cluttered counter are bottles of oil, homemade infusions, spices poured into jars and marked with careful handwriting. A row of herbs grow in small pots on the windowsill—basil, mint, oregano. A magnet on the wall holds a collection of old but good-quality knives, a pair of kitchen scissors, a cleaver. The blood is heavy in concentrated areas, caused by blunt force, not a spray from gunshot. From the amount on the walls, she imagines a head wound. From the floor, maybe a stabbing. The cleanup is sloppy and compromised. Whoever was attacked likely fought back.

Kateri glances down the hall to two open bedrooms, a bathroom, and a locked utility closet. She pulls her sweater up over her nose, breathing through the wool, and steps away from the kitchen, eager for fresh air and anxious to call Hurt.

"What'd you find?" he asks.

"A lot of blood," she says, "but there's no body inside the house. Looks like a struggle."

"How fresh?" Hurt asks.

"Sticky," she says. "With spatter, but not from a gunshot. Looks like blunt force, possible stabbing."

*   *   *

Kateri's grandmother died quickly, within four months of her diagnosis. She declined treatment, accepted pain management, and stayed home with Kateri in a hospital bed in the living room, where they watched TV together, her grandmother drinking tea, Kateri whiskey.

When it happened, Kateri leaned her head onto her grandmother's arm, and she said, "Honey, you have to let me go."

She left the house for two days while a team from hospice removed all the medical items. She had her grandmother cremated at her request. When her friends called for a memorial service, she couldn't answer them. She turned her phone off, let the battery die, didn't return messages. She stayed in, closed the blinds, left the TV going and the bottle open.

When the accident happened, right before Christmas, Kateri herself spent three days in a hospital bed, her arm in a cast and her jaw stitched up. After, she went back to the same rooms, the same TV, and tried to live as she had before, minus the whiskey, minus the woman who'd raised her, minus even the husband she'd held on to for a few short years in her youth.

The yellow walls, the plaid furniture, her grandmother's things, an owl figurine, a sprawling spider plant, told her it was time to go. Time to sell, to let new, different life into the house. She lit a candle, barely believing, but asked her grandmother to send her a sign.

The next day, the sheriff offered her a transfer from Onondaga County out to tiny, rural Hamilton County. They'd had a criminal investigator retire. At best, it was a lateral move.

"I'm not terminating you," the sheriff said.

It still felt like an ending.

* * *

Kateri asks for backup and a full forensics team, who come in hazmat suits with bright lights and packets of baggies to gather evidence. She looks into each of the rooms, one packed with clutter, clothing, books, candles. There's a half-blackened sage stick beside the bed and a long cord with brass bells hanging in the window.

In the other bedroom, there's a twin mattress on the floor, boys' sneakers and a flannel shirt, a stack of cracked-spined paperback books next to the pillow.

"House belongs to Pearl Jenkins," Hurt says in the hallway, where they stand side by side in regular clothes while a bevy of suited forensic technicians work around them. "But it was recently transferred to her son, Shannon," he adds.

"Why?" Kateri asks. She knows that any transfer of property, like any large life insurance policy, is never a great sign. At the least it signals money trouble. The worst, coercion.

"The house was about to be seized for back taxes," Hurt says. "I'm sure it was a work-around."

"How old is the son?" She watches Hurt as he watches the quad screen of surveillance.

"Let's pull footage from this," he says to a tech. "He's an adult," he tells Kateri.

"With a record?" Kateri asks.

"Not the kid; just the dad," he says. "Park Jenkins was put away for years."

"For?" she asks.

"Arson," Hurt says.

Behind him, two techs pull samples from the blood and snap pictures of the spatter on the walls, the cabinet doors, the ceiling. They have pulled all the knives and bagged them. They begin opening drawers, careful not to disturb but looking for more evidence of a weapon. It would have to be a heavy object to cause that trajectory of spray.

"Detective Hurt," one of them says.

Between the potted herbs, another tech finds a single molar, a tiny bit of dried gum still clinging to the soft curve of exposed root.

"Bag it," Kateri says. "There's our ID."

She watches as they pick up the tooth with tiny surgical tweezers and place it in a bag. Behind them, investigators comb through the bedrooms, bagging clothing, hairs, dusting for fingerprints, shining bright lights into dark corners, revealing mouse turds and cobwebs.

"Ma'am," a tech calls, her voice sharp and panicked. "Ma'am."

Kateri thinks, here it is. They've found the body, or what's left of it.

The only female tech on the forensic team stands at the utility closet door, a heavy lock cutter in one hand, the other on the doorknob.

Kateri meets her eye before she pulls the door open, bracing herself for the worst: A dismembered corpse, hacked into pieces. A trash bag filled with parts. More blood.

But what she sees isn't in pieces, or dead at all.

A small girl sits in a pink beanbag chair. The closet is empty except for her and the cushion. She has her knees bent up under her chin and her hands clamped over her eyes. Her hair is a mess of fire-red curls, her clothes spattered with more blood.

On the wall at the back of the closet is a stick-figure man, the kind a kid draws but out of proportion, his arms and legs too long and creepy, his body in black crayon. His eyes in the middle of his big circle head are bright blue, and his mouth is painted on in dried blood.

Kateri looks over her shoulder at the tech, who has paled and tells her to be quiet, even though she hasn't made a sound. Then the tech says it again, louder, to everyone else in the house. Kateri sees Hurt look in and hears him mutter an obscenity.

"Get everyone out for a few minutes," Kateri says to him, and he starts rounding people up, waving his arms, speaking in a harsh whisper. Flashes go off, and Kateri holds up her hand to block the light. The closet has one dim bulb on a pull chain and no window, no outside light.

She hears the team start to shuffle out, and the house settles to an eerie calm, just the tick of the clock, the quick patter of a leaky faucet. Kateri crouches in the closet, close to the child but not touching. She watches as the girl parts her little fingers, peeking out. She has light eyes. Greenish, like seawater.

TWO: SHANNON

AUGUST

Every town has one. A loner. An outlier. A stranger who doesn't belong, someone who blew into town, disconnected from the people who have been there for generations. Sometimes the stranger stays and learns to fit in, and after years, no one thinks of them as strange anymore. Sometimes you try to keep them, like catching a young deer, still wobbling on his spindly legs. But at some point, you know they have to go. At some point, you stop holding on so tightly, and the deer follows his instincts. He does what he was born to do.

* * *

The last time I saw my father was through safety glass. It took three tries over two days. The first day I walked in there and went through security, I left all my belongings in the car, even the keys, so there wouldn't be any hitches at all. And the guard said, "No visitors."

"I'm sorry, what?" I asked him.

"Park Jenkins. No visitors," he repeated.

"I'm his son," I said. I was there on my own, without my mother knowing. I'd driven three hours to look him in the eye. Even if I didn't say anything to him, I wanted to look him in the eye.

The guard tried to look past me. He was big. Six inches taller than I was and about three of me wide. I saw him blink.

"Come back tomorrow, kid," he said.

* * *

I knew what my father looked like from pictures. I remembered living in the farmhouse, but I didn't remember living with him. We moved into the woods when I was three, when the farmhouse burned down. When my father, Park Jenkins, set it on fire and tried to kill all three of us, himself included. What I knew was the story my mother had told me, about the falling beams, about the staircase on fire, about crawling out to the front porch, which was crumbling above us as we went. I remembered her story but not the event. I carried the trauma on my body in the form of scars. As if trying to kill me wasn't enough. I had damage anyone could see, anyone could feel with their hands. A scar on one shoulder that spread over the blade and up onto my clavicle, the skin wrinkled like a wadded-up piece of paper. It was mostly covered in a T-shirt.

I didn't remember the pain. Or the hospital.

My mother got out with a permanently damaged back. A beam had fallen on her, burned the skin and broken two of her vertebrae. We lived with my grandparents after the fire, when Park was in prison and while my mother got better. And when my grandfather died and my grandmother moved to Vermont to live with my uncle Jimmy, we lived there alone.

My mother never stopped taking the pills. Or she would, for a time, and then she'd flip out, sweaty and panicked, and go back on them. She was only twenty when the fire happened. She never worked after that. She'd barely worked before. She'd left high school when she had me. Then we holed up in the woods and she got disability, she got food stamps and public assistance, and she got painkillers. That was our life. Until Birdie was born.

* * *

Park wouldn't look me in the eye. We sat a couple of feet apart at a table with thick plastic between us. I held the phone to my ear, but he didn't say anything for a long time. Time was limited. I studied his face, his shoulders, the way he sat, the way his spine curved forward. I kept my eyes on his, waiting to catch them. We didn't look alike. I looked like my mother. We didn't seem alike at all, but I felt it, that fear in my gut that I was just fucking like him, which forced me into a situation I didn't want to be in. The only way out would be death.

"What do you want," he said.

"Nothing," I said. "I don't want anything from you." Except, I thought, maybe for you not to have tried to kill us. For you to have been around. Maybe not, though. If it hadn't been the fire, then what?

"Well," he said. "Good talk." He was about to hang up the phone. I was alarmed by the hollowness in his face, how old he looked for forty-two. He was missing a bottom tooth. His eyes were deep set and dark green. His hair, buzzed down to a silvery shadow. On his thick forearm, he had a pentagram with a deer's head that I knew my mother had drawn in high school and that my uncle Jimmy had tattooed on him. They were all cousins.

Park put the phone back to his ear for a moment.

"Tell your mother I know everything," he said.

"What?" I said, startled at the rasp of his voice again, at his directness.

That's when he looked me in the eye. "You heard me," he said. "Tell her I know every goddamn thing she does," he said, and hung up. When he stood, the guard was right behind him, took him by the elbow, and walked him away from the visitation room.

I hung up my phone without making a sound.

That was two years ago.

*   *   *

Our town had misfits. There was Junior Savage, who ran the diner. His whole family was from Spring Falls or just north of it. He didn't quite medically qualify as a midget, but he was only four foot nine. He was missing a finger on his left hand. He let me work at the diner and paid me cash every week so I didn't have to report it against my mother's welfare.

There was Sally, the lady who ran the flower shop. She was willowy and about seventy, and her flowers were exquisite and delicate, but she would sometimes leave the counter in the middle of a sale because she heard the baby crying. She'd hold up a knobby finger. "Let me just check on the baby," she'd say, and then disappear, usually for the rest of the afternoon. There had never been a baby as far as anyone knew, but Sally would appear in the windows of the apartment above the shop, pacing, like she was walking an infant to sleep.

There were the Metzgers. They were trashier than we were. A whole family of boys, a dead mom, a dad who started drinking cheap beer at breakfast. I'd gone to school with two of them. I was often mistaken for the youngest, Kyle. We had a similar slight build, blond hair—two flannel-wearing, cigarette-smoking, truck-driving losers in the same town. Except that Kyle was hopelessly straight and dumb as a box of fucking rocks. My mother bought oxys and benzos from him. Nobody in town knew how they even made it, but I knew for a fact that my mother gave Kyle a hundred a week for pills.

And there was my mother, Pearl Jenkins, who rarely went into town but would drive in to pick up her prescription or to get things from the farmers' market in the summer. She dressed like a crazy hippie. Most of the time her hair was dirty and she smelled. In the summer, she was always barefoot. People knew her as paranoid and disabled, even though she got around okay. We lived in the woods, surrounded by security cameras. People would say her husband tried to kill her and their son.

* * *

The cairns on the side of the road were what stopped me. They might have been there all along, but the day I noticed them, it was like they'd grown overnight. A balanced pile of rocks that seemed impossible, a bigger stone on top of all the rest, touching at only a narrow point. It was two feet high, visible from my bike as I whizzed past. I skidded to a stop a few yards ahead and backtracked.

There were two. One close to the road, and another, similarly precarious, a few feet in. They marked the edge of a narrow dirt trail that followed a line of pine trees along Mill Road, where I rode my bike every day on the way home from the diner.

I looked off down the path. It led into the woods in such a way that I thought it might cut right through to my house. I'd been biking my way down Mill Road to Hidden Drive all this time, riding for miles around the edge of the woods.

It wasn't dark yet, so I got off the bike and walked it beside me, following it alongside the trees and then deep into them, the woods cool and completely shaded, heady with pine needles, like the floor was spun with gold. Not far in, a ravine sloped off to the right, and people had dumped tires and old appliances down it. A whole washing machine lay on its side between tree roots and rock.

And behind it all, slid down the dirt, was an old Pontiac, crashed against a tree trunk, like someone had driven it over the lawns and between the trees sixty years ago and left it there, doors flung open, and run.

I stood with my mouth open. "Holy shit," I muttered.

I had never been back here. I'd covered the trails all around our house, but they'd never connected to anything that led here. I gauged the terrain between where I stood on the narrow path and where the car lay. If I put the bike down, I could probably make it. I glanced at the sky, still light enough, and went for it.

The inside was a masterpiece, covered in leaves and dotted with water spots. The steering wheel was huge and part chrome, the seats black leather with white piping. I pulled on the door that I imagined had been rusted open for years, and it creaked, but it shut, heavy, full steel, like closing the door on a vault.

My heart raced; my skin pricked in my armpits.

I knew there was strange shit in the woods. People always said that somewhere there was an old refrigerator with the body of a little kid in it. I'd never seen it. But then, I'd never seen the car either. People also said that if you went far enough north off trail, you'd find a cabin, and that an old fur trapper still lived there, eating the animals he skinned, living on gamy meat and berries and melted snow.

There was no cell service once you turned the corner on the way out of town. Much of the woods hadn't been mapped. It was just dense green, filled with chasms and secret waterfalls that froze half the year.

After I got out of the car, I kept looking back at it—from the other side of the ravine, from the trail as I wound in with my bike. When the path curved to the left, the car was out of sight, and so I stepped back, making sure I hadn't imagined the whole thing.

It flashed into view all at once, and my heart skipped a little. I noticed from this vantage point that another cairn stood on the edge of the cliff, five rocks high. I could see the lights of town from up here: the lit-up football field, the parking lot at the IGA, the new houses being built way up on the opposite hill.

It seemed like a magic spot, a secret. Tomorrow after work I'd bring a book, and some cigarettes, and maybe something to drink, and I'd hide out while the last light came through the windshield, safe, in a steel vault.

By the time I got home, it was dusk, the woods purple and close. Our house was lit with one lamp in the living room, but I knew I'd find the TV on as well. My mother never turned the surveillance cameras off.

They were asleep already. My mother, sweaty from a pill, was out cold on her back with the baby crooked in her arm.

Except when I looked at the baby, and the length of her four-year-old body alongside my mother, I thought, she's not a baby anymore, and realized, looking at the muscle tone of her arms and legs, naked on the sheet, that this baby, this sweet little pudge of a girl with fire-red hair and the temperament to match, might someday rise up against us.

*   *   *

The following day was payday, and I gave Junior Savage money back from the cash he paid me to go across the street and buy me a small bottle of whiskey.

I could buy my own cigarettes, but at nineteen, I had to finagle liquor.

He did it without hassle. He brought back a flat plastic bottle of Canadian Club, and I left the restaurant at three thirty and headed straight to the car.

I had an old paperback with me. My mother would grab them from the library trash and bring them home. Sometimes they were too moldy, but lots of them were fine. Old dime-store pulp titles that had once sold for sixty cents. I had a copy of *Giovanni's Room* with yellowed pages and tiny print. The spine turned to dust where it cracked open. It was hard to see in the dim light inside the woods, inside the car, but I loved just the smell of it, the feel of the brittle paper in my hands. I drank, and smoked, and read while I could, stuck in the dream of the story until a stranger appeared alongside the car, looking in at me.

I was too scared to scream.

His face appeared in the passenger's side window, watching me smoking and drinking with the book propped open in one hand. My mouth went dry and my heart took up all the sound in my own head, pounding. It sounded like the ocean.

I thought, I'm going to die.

He waved. One hand raised, moving slowly.

I couldn't believe I'd been so stupid.

*   *   *

I was a kid who was used to getting in trouble. Getting yelled at for cutting through people's yards, getting suspended from school, having the cops called on him. There wasn't anything in me that believed this wasn't something that would get me arrested, beat up, or killed.

The stranger was wearing a soft button-down white shirt and gray pants, and his outfit was trim to his body like it had been tailored for him. His hair was blue black, cut like an old-fashioned movie star's, and swept up off his forehead.

"I'm sorry" was the first thing I said when he opened the door and stood there looking in at me.

"For what?" he asked. He slid in but left the door open, one foot still outside in the leaves. His shoes, even, were shiny black leather.

I couldn't look at him. "Am I on your property?" I asked.

"You are," he said.

"I'm sorry," I said again, and went to open the driver's side door and get out. Run. He put his hand on my arm, his finger on the part of the burn that wrinkled the underside of my bicep.

"Don't," he said.

He held me like that, stock-still, for longer than I would have thought possible. He kept waiting for me to look at him. When I did, his face was unusually kind, with a soft mouth and bright blue eyes.

He let go of my arm and fished a pack of cigarettes out of his shirt pocket. Lucky Strikes. He lit one with an old flip-top Zippo.

"Is it your car?" I asked.

"No," he said.

"I didn't—" I stammered. "I thought I could cut through the woods to my house."

"You can," he said.

"I've never done it," I said.

"You did it the other day," he said. He smiled.

"You saw me," I said.

"I was watching," he said.

I thought for sure I had never seen him in my life. I'd gotten used to everyone in town—everyone who came in and out of the diner, who worked in town, who went to the school. I would have remembered. I asked him if he was new.

"I'm just here on business," he said. He blew out a straight line of blue smoke.

"I've never seen you," I said.

"You've just never noticed," he said.

It left me with just one response. I took at drink from the bottle and offered it to him. "But you've noticed me," I said.

He smiled again, his eyes narrowed, and he took the bottle from my hand, brushed my fingers. "I know who you are," he said.

I asked him his name, and he told me people called him Baby Jane, a name I'd never heard, didn't understand, and didn't question. I said it back to him. It felt like uttering a magic word. Like learning to say Rumpelstiltskin.

I said my name was Shannon.

"I know," he said.

THREE: KATERI

"My name is Kateri," she says, making herself small, lowering her hips to the floor by the little girl. "What's your name?" The girl has on jeans and little hiking boots, a sweater that's caked with mud and what looks like blood.

She raises her head and peeks out through her fingers. Her hands and face, too, are speckled with spatter. Her fingertips, deeply stained.

"It's okay," Kateri says. "You're safe with me." She pulls her own sweater down, concealing her weapon and her cuffs. "May I sit here with you?"

The girl nods. When she takes her hands down, her little face is gaunt, hollow under the eyes, which makes them look huge. She has a round, turned-up nose and chapped lips. Over the bridge of her nose and across the tops of her cheekbones are a smattering of light freckles.

"I'm supposed to wait," she tells Kateri.

"For what?"

The blood on the girl's hands is so dark, it's like ink, seeped into the creases of her skin, her fingerprint whorls, her cuticles. Her eyes are wet with tears, and she pokes her tongue at the worst crack in her lip so that it glistens with fresh blood.

19

"Sweetheart," Kateri says. She hears Joel Hurt's voice from the yard, directing techs to look farther along the trail. "What's your name, honey?" she asks.

"Birdie," the girl says, and Kateri says it back to her.

"Birdie, did someone put you in the closet?"

Her face is blank until Kateri asks her again. "Birdie, who were you waiting for?"

"Him," she says.

Kateri waits.

"The angel," Birdie says. "The angel was coming to get me."

＊　＊　＊

She doesn't appear to be a flight risk, so Kateri lets her sit where she is, on the beanbag in the closet, with the door open, and goes to get her a cup of water and to step outside to find Hurt.

"I need medical," Kateri says when she sees him on the edge of the yard. Hurt takes his phone out to begin, but Kateri stops him. "I'll call," she says.

＊　＊　＊

She had a case with two young sisters. One had been killed. One had survived. Both had been raped. They were little girls, ten and twelve. It was the ten-year-old who survived. When they sent the ambulatory unit, with lights flashing and sirens screaming, the girl flew into a panic. She thrashed and reopened a wound on her belly. Her vagina was bruised and still bleeding. Kateri was covered in blood trying to keep her still. She ended up restraining the girl the best way she knew how, from behind, with her arms crossed over the girl's and the girl's head bashing backward into Kateri's face, giving her a fat, bloodied lip. The medics were all men. The girl was traumatized all over again. All those blank faces. So many big hands. The roar from inside the moving medical unit, barreling down a highway to a hospital she'd never been to. Her sister, dead in a separate van.

Kateri was twenty-five.

She remembers the estranged father of the two girls, living like her own estranged father in a dark, dirty apartment thick with smoke. He had a ponytail. Was never without a lit cigarette. Sometimes he had two, one in the ashtray, one in his mouth. His eyes went from top to bottom and lingered at Kateri's chest.

"Little-girl cop," he said. "Give me a fucking break."

*   *   *

Dispatch sends a small van, marked, but without its lights going, and two medics, a wiry woman in her fifties and a younger man, baby-faced and soft around the edges. Kateri meets them between the trees. The deputies have put police tape around the house, fluttering.

"Detective Fisher," she introduces herself. "She may be in shock," she tells the woman medic. "She's almost certainly a witness to something brutal, quite possibly a murder," Kateri says, "and she may be a victim as well. I can't tell what condition she's in, physical or mental. She might be badly hurt."

She looks at the woman's badge.

"Maggie," the woman says. "This is Rick."

"She goes by Birdie," Kateri says.

"How old?" Maggie asks.

"No more than five or six," Kateri says. "She's small. She still has baby teeth. Please," Kateri says, though she knows she doesn't have to, "be very, very gentle."

Kateri watches while Rick stays in the doorway and Maggie practically crawls through the gore of the kitchen toward the girl hiding in the open closet. She hears Maggie speaking slowly, quietly, like she's luring an injured animal.

Birdie comes out with her eyes blank. Kateri is afraid of a potential fight, that she will protest being taken anywhere, will wail for her mother or thrash when touched, will need to be restrained or even sedated in the van. But she does just what Maggie asks her to do. She comes out and gets on a small stretcher that Rick brings forward, and she lies back, her little brown hand gripping Maggie's wrist. Between Birdie's fingers, Kateri notices a small blue tattoo on Maggie's wrist, a crescent moon. Rick covers Birdie with heavy cotton blankets, tucking the sides in.

"I'll meet you at Mercy," Kateri says to Maggie. Her throat tightens and she's afraid for a moment that she'll spill. Girls are so tough, she thinks, watching this one, covered in blood, clinging to a moon tattoo on a woman she doesn't know.

Behind the house, deputies have upturned rocks and carefully scattered leaf piles. Kateri sees the shape of some of them moving, far off in the trees, the shine of their lights, the flash of a camera. Hurt comes and stands beside her, watching the stretcher load into the van.

"She mentioned a him," Kateri tells Hurt. "She said she was waiting for him."

"Who?" Hurt says. "The son?"

"I don't know," Kateri says, but shakes her head as if she does. "She called him an angel," she says. She looks past Hurt at the activity in the woods.

"Go," he says. "I'll let you know what we find here. You belong with her."

She hesitates, because from someone else, it would feel patronizing, telling her to look after the child. But Kateri thinks he's right.

*   *   *

Our Lady of Mercy Hospital is thirty miles away, in the next town over, Mount Snow. It's just big enough to have a community college and a tiny women's school, Creveling College, a Walmart, a Wendy's, and a small Catholic hospital. When Kateri arrives, the girl is in triage in the ER and there's nothing to do but wait. She can't sit still on the plastic chairs in the waiting room, surrounded by sick or injured people waiting to be seen, so she walks.

She spends time in the art deco lobby, looking at the high windows and the inlaid quartz in the floors, the dark wood, the giant chandelier that hangs in the center. And then once she's walked the perimeter, she ducks into a door that says CHAPEL.

It isn't her thing. Even with her saint's name and her Catholic grandmother, she doesn't feel any truth to it. Her mother rejected the faith, and what Kateri knows at all was gleaned from her grandmother's things, her little portraits of the Blessed Mother, the crèche she put out at Christmas, her *Lives of the Saints*. It all feels like a faraway myth. The room is dim and red and smells like candles and incense, like warm wood and spice. Kateri dips her finger into the holy water and crosses herself as she was taught.

She sits on one of the six pews, lulled by the warmth and closeness of the room, and feels herself welling up with discomfort and want, with an ache in her core.

She distinctly remembers sitting on one of the ladder-back chairs in her grandmother's kitchen, having her hair brushed the morning of her mother's funeral. It was November, and she wore a dress she hated, and stockings because it was too cold to go bare legged and her grandmother said it was disrespectful.

She liked the feel of the brush, pulling from underneath. It was eight in the morning on a Saturday, when Kateri wanted to be sleeping.

"I am never having kids," she announced.

Her grandmother stopped brushing and let Kateri's hair fall, smoothing it with her hands.

"I know you feel that way now," she said.

"Ever," Kateri said.

She'd lost both parents in four years, between twelve and sixteen. Heart attack, drug overdose. Her mother just didn't wake up. They'd been watching TV, and when her mother passed out, which wasn't unusual, Kateri went to bed.

In the morning she was in the same spot, cold.

Her immediate feeling had been rage. It took her years to feel any sadness or grief at her mother's death.

Her grandmother kissed the top of her head. "It'll change," she said, and Kateri snorted in disapproval and rolled her eyes.

Now she makes a steeple of her hands and presses them against her face, breathing through them. The room is lined with alcoves of saints, most of them women. Both the hospital and the women's college were founded by nuns. The stained-glass window behind the altar is a blazing immaculate heart, flowers laced between the swords.

She stands, woozy from the warmth of the room, and makes her way down each side of the chapel, stopping at each image. Bridget with her bowl of fire and reed cross. Monica, an old woman, the mother of St. Augustine. Bernadette, the girl saint in her grotto.

*   *   *

Kateri remembers that the sisters she failed slept on cheap blow-up pool mats instead of real beds. The two of them side by side on the living room floor, a string of Christmas lights hanging above them.

They'd been attacked by their mother's boyfriend.

She remembers her own mother's boyfriend grabbing her by the wrist and leaning close to her face with beer breath. "You could make a million fucking bucks," he said, "with those tits, if you just had blue eyes."

Kateri lights the candle underneath the girl saint and lets the red glass glow.

She doesn't ask for anything. She doesn't know how. But she stands for a moment, thinking of little Birdie, with her red hair and her green eyes, and waiting for the ache inside her to go away.

*　*　*

They admit the girl, settle her in a room on the pediatric ward, and give her a sedative. Kateri meets the attending in the hallway. He says the child is in shock.

"She doesn't have a great grip on reality," he says, and then adds, "which is difficult to tell sometimes in a child so young. We'll run a full psychiatric evaluation tomorrow," he says, "in addition to some further physical testing. She would not let us do a pelvic."

Kateri's eyes narrow. "Is there something that makes you think that's necessary?"

"Well, if you want to rule out sexual assault by an invader," he says, as if Kateri ought to know.

"I don't know that there was an invader," Kateri says, "and if there was, I don't know that the crime was sexually motivated. And what do you mean, she wouldn't let you, if you'd sedated her and she has, as you said, a poor grip on reality?"

"She bit a nurse."

He's still in his twenties, she thinks. Gingery, with a face that will always look younger than his age. She tries to imagine him someplace else, out at a bar, running. He is attractive, and that annoys her further.

"We tried," he says. "But she thrashed. If she was assaulted, we are required by law to do a rape kit."

"I'll decide that," Kateri says. "In the meantime, wait until it's requested. It's invasive. I don't know that it's necessary."

"Well, it's evidence," the attending says. "And I would think that anyone who fought the kit that hard had likely been assaulted. It's not like she didn't know what we were examining or looking for."

Kateri looks at her fingernails and not at the doctor. "Could be," she says, and then shrugs. "She's what, five? She may have been taught to fiercely guard her privates. She doesn't know you. You're a strange man to her." Kateri's lips are tight when she looks up at him. "All your rape kit proves," she says, "is penetration within the last forty-eight hours. And nothing else if there's no semen left behind. I'd like to speak with her."

"We're going to need ID and parental or state consent," he says. "Who did she say she was?"

"Her name is Birdie."

"That's a pet name," the doctor says.

"You don't know that," Kateri says.

"Her mother?" He asks.

"Is likely dead," Kateri answers.

"Is there a guardian?"

"None specified," Kateri says. "This is an active investigation."

"I understand, Detective." He looks off down the hall, low lit, where people walk by in pairs or push carts and announcements come on overhead. In a Catholic hospital like Mercy, the day begins and ends with a recitation of the Lord's Prayer. "I sent her clothing to the lab as you requested," he says.

"Thank you."

He looks quick over his shoulder and then says, "Can I ask you something?"

Kateri crosses her arms over her chest. "Of course," she says.

"Do you think she's responsible?"

"For what?" Kateri asks, her eyes suddenly wide.

"The murder," he says.

"Why would you think that?"

"Detective," he says. "She was covered in blood. She was very close to the crime. Very close," he says again.

She feels a headache begin behind her eyes. "Doctor, we have not recovered a body," she says. "This girl is what, forty pounds?"

"I'm just telling you what I saw," he says.

"Maybe we can concentrate on our own roles in this," Kateri says. "Unless you want me to conduct the medical testing? And you can investigate the crime scene?"

He sets his jaw.

"When can I talk to her?"

"Tomorrow," he says, cold. He takes a step back from Kateri. "She's resting," he says. He clips his pen onto his coat pocket. "Good night, Detective Fisher."

She watches him disappear down the hall, walking into the light, tall, thin, like a skeleton wearing clothes. She takes her phone out and calls Hurt.

"We haven't found anything," he says. "I shut it down for the night. It's getting dark. We'll resume at first light. How's the kid?" he asks.

"Covered in blood," Kateri answers.

"Injured?" he asks.

"Nothing apparent."

"Interesting," Hurt says. "If she were older, we'd arrest her."

"She couldn't have locked herself in that closet," Kateri says. "It was locked from the outside."

"I'd like to know what she saw," he says.

"Me too."

Before she goes, she asks the nurse if she can peek in on the child they have labeled Jane Doe. An officer has come to stand guard by her room. A kid, she thinks, just out of training.

"You are?" the nurse asks.

Kateri shows her badge. "I'm the lead detective," she says. "I won't disturb her," she adds.

The nurse goes ahead of her and opens the door, as if it was locked, and stands in the doorway while Kateri goes in to the girl's bedside. She sleeps sound, small in the bed, tucked in, her hair around her like a halo. The nurse waits. In the hall, a clattering cart goes by, but the girl doesn't stir. Kateri lays her hand on the girl's head, her skin cool, her hairline damp, and then leans in to peck her forehead.

"Try to remember," she says.

FOUR: SHANNON

TUESDAY, SEPTEMBER 5

I tried to remember when it was better, when anything was normal. I longed to live somewhere where no one knew who we were. Where no one made jokes about the tiny homemade tattoo on my mother's face, a blue crescent moon where her widow's peak met her forehead. Where the cops didn't come question me about a barn set on fire.

"Arson's my father's crime," I'd tell them. "Look it up." And when they finally accepted that I'd been where I'd said I'd been, at work, at home, or nowhere near whatever it was that had burned, they'd give me that flat look of unwilling acceptance. Just checking.

Everything changed with the baby. My mother didn't tell me, and I didn't know for a long time. But when I started to notice, it was unmistakable. The swell of her belly. The way she walked like her hips were unhinged.

"Listen," she said to me on the porch.

"Have you been to a doctor?" I asked. I was fourteen. I thought I knew everything important, and honestly, her body grossed me out, the way it was blossoming, the shape of her hands and feet as she changed.

"No," she said. I watched her twirl a long lock of hair around her fingers. "He can never know," she said to me.

"Who?"

"Your dad."

"How would he know?" I said. "I can't even remember what he looks like. It's not like I go see him on the weekend," I snipped.

She pressed her lips together. I thought she was trying. She had seemed less high most days. But I didn't know what she did while I was at school.

"I'm sorry it's your burden," she said then.

"Yeah, me too," I answered.

"You can't tell anyone."

I didn't have to tell anyone. Everyone in this town already knew who we were. That my dad was in prison for trying to kill us. Sometimes I told people he was dead, that he'd died in prison years ago instead of living on, cared for with meals and books to read and card games while we had to figure everything out on our own.

My mother rubbed her belly in a circle, and the light caught her tattoo, and I thought she looked like some kind of medieval witch sitting there in a long hippie skirt.

"Are you going to keep it?" I asked.

"Her," she said. "And yes."

"How do you know if you haven't been to a doctor?" I asked.

"Don't question things you'll never understand," she said.

*   *   *

I never knew what kind of agony she went through in deciding to keep her, because she never told me. We accepted each other as who we were and didn't ask questions. She assumed I wasn't interested in women having babies or why or how, and she was right.

I was already taller than her. She put her hands on my arms and gripped her fingernails into my skin while she squeezed her eyes shut with pain. We had lived all this time like adults, even when I was little, like equals. We didn't have shit. She was terrified of Park getting out of prison. Every week, she counted out cash for me so I could pay the bills in town, riding my bike to the grocery store service counter. And whatever was left was for food.

"I need you to help me right now," she said through her teeth. She stopped breathing for a moment, holding her breath, gripping my arms. And then it seemed like a wave passed and she started again. "Help me," she said.

She had me get towels and water. She had me place a cold cloth on her head.

"Do you know what you're doing?" I asked, stupid, but I didn't know. It seemed like we needed a doctor. Or maybe a wise woman, but my mother was the wise woman. I guessed if anyone could do it on her own, my mother could.

We had no phone at all by then. I wasn't old enough to get my own cell phone, and my mother wouldn't get one for herself. She didn't want to be tracked. The landline had been shut off years before that.

It was the middle of the night in her bedroom, in November, and my mother stripped herself naked in front of me, her body blooming itself inside out like some kind of weird night flower, reds and purples and things I'd never ever seen before, and wouldn't again. Her belly moved from the inside like she was possessed. She was sweating, her deep-red hair down around her shoulders and stuck to her face. For a while she got down on her hands and knees and lowed like a cow, rocking back and forth, her head hanging down.

I could see her muscles working. Could watch the contractions as they tightened her lower back, the scar from her surgery like a dark seam in her skin, writhing. They came quicker and quicker. And then it got so painful she couldn't speak.

I had been born at Mercy Hospital when my mother was seventeen, and Park was signing paperwork when the nurse came out and told him he had a son.

When Birdie came, my mother had candles lit, and sage and sweet grass burning, and bowls of salt water in the corners of the room.

"Come here," she said, and I got down on my knees in front of her and held her hands and she pressed her sweaty forehead to mine, her shoulders round and slick with perspiration, her breasts already milk-engorged and standing out from her rib cage.

"Mother Mary," she muttered and stopped. Breathed and stopped, like something strangled her from within.

Then she told me she needed to be alone.

*   *   *

The baby was fat and gray skinned until my mother toweled her off, rubbing her to get her blood going, to turn her skin to a pinkish brown. My mother put on a loose nightgown that was black and covered in stars and made her look like a fortune teller. She wound her hair up on top of her head and stuck the baby on her nipple. When the baby was done drinking, my mother handed her to me, wrapped tight in a pink towel.

She was heavier than I thought, and smaller, like a dense little bean. I rubbed at her hair because it looked bloody, and I thought it was still caked from birth, but that's just the color it was. My mother wafted sweet grass around the room and then rubbed a small spot of sandal-wood oil on the baby's head.

"Sparrow Annie Jenkins," she said. Her face was beaded with sweat, and her eyes had a glaze that I'd come to know. She'd loaded up on oxys after the birth. I couldn't really blame her—I'm sure she hurt like hell—but I wondered if she could do what she needed to take care of the baby.

"I can't promise you that we won't just run," she said to me.

"Run?" I said. The baby made a gurgling sound, and I jostled her in my arms. "What about me?" I asked her.

"You're his," she said. "She's mine. That's just the way it goes sometimes."

"What if I don't want to be his?" I asked.

"You don't have to be," my mother said. "You just have to be you." She closed her eyes and swayed on her feet. She'd stay the next week in her bed with the baby, sweaty and under with fever and so much blood, the baby just nestled into her, drinking when she wanted.

"I have to protect her," my mother said. "At all costs."

After, she never left my mother's side. She lived her life on my mother's hip, or in my mother's lap, and she was a big, fat sass of a baby with a wicked laugh and hair like copper springs.

I loved her.

But every day, my mother and I seemed to just check on each other, to see if the other was still there. I left school and I started working, and I'd drive my mother's truck out to Walmart to buy diapers with cash. Where no one knew to ask me who I needed them for.

*   *   *

Baby Jane never asked me anything. He just let me talk, so much that sometimes I felt like I was unraveling.

I asked him everything. What his real name was. Where he was from. Where he had worked. If he'd been married.

"That is my real name," he said. I didn't believe him.

He was from Georgia.

He worked on cars.

He'd never been married.

I went to the car that first time, then waited a few days to go back. And then the days got closer together until I met him almost every day. I knew it was weird. But some days, having somewhere else to be between work and home felt like a balm.

I told him all the books I'd read and loved and why. I liked the sound of his voice. It was deep and reedy, and there was something old-fashioned about the way he said certain words. I couldn't tell if he had an accent. I liked the smell of his clothes, his cigarettes, the way his hands moved and his mouth when he talked. He was smart like no one else I'd ever known, and something underneath the surface said to me that he was deeply broken, in ways I couldn't imagine.

He told me he'd retired early. If I saw him in town, he'd nod in recognition, but he never stopped to talk to me.

Summer is a brief hot second up north. After Labor Day, the nights got cold. Not long after, the grass was dusted with frost in the morning.

My mother let me drive her truck only if it was raining. Otherwise, I took my bike. She didn't want to be detectable at all, and having the truck parked at the diner was predictable and traceable. I'd throw a flannel shirt on over my work shirt, ride my bike down Mill Street to the shortcut, and duck in, my wheels hitting the trail with a puff of dirt.

I'd sat in the car by myself that first night, and some nights after. But mostly, he knew when to expect me, or he saw me go by his kitchen window. He seemed to like to give me time to smoke a cigarette and have a drink before he walked out through the backyard and into the woods after me.

* * *

I leaned on a pine tree on my way into the car, and my hand was sticky with sap. I sat rubbing it, smoking, waiting. I felt too restless to read, and it was dim in the forest.

When he came, Baby Jane saw me rubbing my hand, and reached for it.

"You need alcohol," he said. "That's the only thing that'll get it out." That was the night I asked him his real name.

He raised his eyes and gave me a look that said I'd never know. I thought he looked different each time I saw him, and I blamed the failing light of fall, the heavy tree shadow, the early dark.

"Baby Jane is my real name," he said, and smiled. I thought his eyes were a blue I'd never seen.

I tried to touch his cheekbone, and he flinched.

34

I thought I would break the seats inside that old car if I could just put my hands on the sides of his face and look at him.

"Can we go inside?" I asked him.

"No," he said.

"Do you live with someone?" I asked.

"No."

I felt small.

But then he asked, "Do you?"

I hesitated. No one ever asked me. My mouth went dry. "Just my mom," I said, and he nodded.

"I have to go," he said after that, his eyes flat. But he waited. He sat there waiting for me to say the last thing. I didn't want him to go. I didn't want it to be over yet.

"How did you know who I was?" I asked.

"I pay attention."

He got out. He disappeared between the pine trees, and his shoes didn't make a sound. I could have followed him, but I sat still, breathing hard, my heart knocking in my chest, thinking I'd ruined something, that I'd broken the spell. And then I didn't see him again for three days.

*   *   *

At home, I woke up to a stranger in the yard. My mother and the baby slept hard, in her closed room with the red curtains drawn. They might have been up half the night. I never knew. My mother had never been an early riser.

I heard the truck, and I heard hammering, and I saw him on the TV surveillance, a big guy, putting a sign in the yard. Sometimes men came through for maintenance, to take care of a downed tree or clear other storm damage on the trails. But this was right in our yard.

I went to the porch, barefoot, cold, and lit a cigarette. "Can I help you?" I called to him.

He was over fifty, with a moustache. His truck had a logo on the side I couldn't quite read from there. He stepped forward and handed me a flyer.

Tax Auctions.

The sign in the yard read PUBLIC AUCTION, NOVEMBER 29, 9AM.

"What the fuck is this?" I barked at him.

"Tax auctions," he said, and shrugged. "You must owe something."

I looked at the flyer. Ours wasn't the only address listed.

"What am I supposed to do?" I yelped.

"I don't know, son," he said. "Call the number. I'm just putting up the signs."

When he pulled out, I took the ugly black-and-yellow sign from the dirt and tucked it behind the house.

My mother had heard me, and she was up inside, making coffee, and Birdie all at once had like eleven Barbie dolls out on the floor, in various states of undress. She had one Ken doll that she called the angel. She would sometimes fly him around the room.

"Who was here?" my mother asked.

"The county?" I said.

She paled so hard she looked green. She clicked the stove on and set the percolator to boil.

I hated conversations about money. I just wanted to make enough to cover everything and never have to talk about it.

"Do we owe money?" I said.

"Oh fuck," she said, and pinched the bridge of her nose.

I stepped past Birdie into the kitchen so she wouldn't hear. My mother rooted around in drawers, in the cupboard, looking for old mail. I paid the bills usually. But everything I paid was utilities. There was no mortgage. My grandparents had owned the house outright.

"Fuck," she said again, digging into the junk drawer that overflowed with matchbooks and balls of string, markers, marbles, seashells and rocks. "Here," she said, pulling out a rat-edged white paper that had the sides ripped off. Behind it were similar notices that hadn't even been opened, letters from the county, letters from real estate companies, hand-addressed to Mrs. Pearl Jenkins.

The notice listed our address, my mother's name, and the auction date, and stated fifty-seven thousand dollars in back taxes.

I didn't know anyone who made fifty-seven thousand dollars a year, let alone owed it all at once.

I watched my mother reach in the side cupboard for a pill and take it without water.

"Have you ever paid the taxes?" I asked.

She only sort of twitched her head.

"I mean, since Grandma left?" Never mind, I said, and left the paper on the counter and walked away from her. Birdie was singing in the living room, above her the giant screen of security cameras from outside: trees, the path to the parking lot, the side yard, and a hiker going by with a dog.

"Shan," my mother called from the kitchen doorway. "We'll figure it out."

"No, we won't," I answered. "I might, but you won't." And I understood all at once what she meant by running, that she'd be gone, with her precious Bird, and I'd be left to figure all this shit out on my own, homeless if I couldn't do it. I watched Birdie trip across the living room floor on her toes, the angel doll flying high and then swooping in to pick up one of the scattered girls and carry her off.

FIVE: KATERI

Kateri has to wait until the next day to see the girl. In the morning, she sends Hurt back into the woods with a search team that includes dogs, and Kateri sits by the girl's bedside, her little body dwarfed in the big bed. In the dull blue hospital light, her hair appears like rusted metal.

Kateri picks up her chart. They have left her name as Jane Doe, date of birth unknown. Estimated age five years. Height 38 inches, weight 38 pounds. No known allergies. BP 90/60. Pulse 115.

Little rabbit, Kateri thinks.

She's on a slow drip that Kateri assumes still contains a sedative. An orderly comes in at seven thirty, and Kateri drops the chart back on the foot of the bed. He has the little girl's breakfast. He opens the curtains, turns on the overhead light, all of it, an assault of brightness and smell.

"Breakfast, sweet pea," he says. He raises up the head of the bed. Her little shoulders swim in the pediatric gown she wears. Birdie's eyes open and lock on Kateri.

"Who are you?" she asks, all at once alert.

"I'm Detective Fisher," she says, "but you can call me Kateri if you like."

Birdie looks at the tray in front of her. They have brought her dry toast and a juice box, a Styrofoam bowl with Cheerios and a carton of milk. She looks away, disinterested, and the orderly puts the straw in the juice box for her. She takes a very tentative sip.

"Good girl," the orderly says, and looks to Kateri, who nods. There has been an officer outside her door all night.

"I was hoping we could talk," Kateri says. "Yesterday, you told me your name is Birdie."

She nods.

"Is that short for something?"

"You mean my real name?" she asks.

"Yes."

"Sparrow Annie," she says.

"Sparrow Annie what?"

"Jenkins," she answers. Then, "Do you know what your name means?"

"Kateri is a form of Katherine," she says. "Which means pure."

"Annie means grace," the girl says. "And pearls are precious and sometimes people rip them out of the shells." She takes a noisy draw on the juice box. "Shannon means river," she says.

"How do you know all this?" Kateri asks.

"My mama teaches me," she says.

"Is Pearl your mama?" Kateri asks.

She nods.

"Who lives at your house with you?" Kateri asks.

"My mom," she says. "And Shannon."

"Shannon is your brother?" she asks.

"Yeah, but he's big, like Mom."

"What do you remember about yesterday," Kateri asks, "when I met you at your house?"

Birdie shakes her head.

"Anything?" Kateri prompts.

She just shakes again.

"When I met you," Kateri says, "you were in the closet. Is that some-place you normally play?"

"No," Birdie says, with a tinge of sassy disbelief. "Unless there's a thunderstorm. Sometimes if there's a thunderstorm, we go in there with a lantern and we wait."

"You and your mom," Kateri says.

"Yeah," she says.

"Why were you in there yesterday? Was there a storm?"

"No," she says.

Birdie picks at the dry Cheerios one by one. Her eyes look far away.

"Who were you waiting for?"

Birdie startles; her head twitches almost unnoticeably.

"You said you were waiting for someone," Kateri prompts her.

But Birdie answers with something else. "My mom cut her hair," she says.

"Did she?" Kateri goes along with it, thinking that if nothing else, keeping her talking about anything, about normal everyday activities, will reveal something important.

"Yeah, she cut it all off."

"Short?" Kateri asks.

"Bald," Birdie says. "She was going to do mine, but I cried. And then I had to hide."

"Why was she going to cut all your hair off, Birdie?" Kateri asks. Her arms break out in goose bumps.

"So they can't find us," she says.

"Who?"

"Anyone," Birdie says.

"Who would be looking for you or your mama?"

"Anyone," Birdie says again.

"Is there someone who was mad at your mom? Or maybe fighting with your mom?"

Birdie's mouth makes a flat line.

Kateri switches gears. "Birdie, did you draw the picture inside the closet?"

"Yes," she says. Her face colors with shame. She knows not to draw on the walls.

"Can you tell me who the picture is of? Is he someone you know? Or that your mom knows?"

Birdie shakes her head.

"No?" Kateri asks.

"No," Birdie says.

"Who is he?"

"He's the angel," she says.

*   *   *

Hurt calls her as she's walking to her car. The day is gray. It rained overnight, and the pavement shines with puddles.

"Any news?" she asks.

"Potential murder weapon," Hurt says. "An ax."

"Where?" she asks, and starts her car.

"A ways into the woods. It's burned," he says.

"Can you get anything off of it? Prints or blood?"

"The handle is almost completely charred, the ax-head itself covered in soot and dirt and some corrosion. But it's suspicious enough," Hurt says, "and it's close enough. And could be what caused that much blood. There's no indication in any of the spatter of gunshot residue. It looks like blunt force."

Kateri nods but doesn't answer.

"You there?" Hurt asks.

"Yeah." She sits with her car running, warming, the lights off, the radio turned down.

"How's the kid?"

She's a little rag doll, Kateri thinks, and imagines picking her up, running her fingers through all that hair.

"She says Pearl Jenkins shaved her head before she had to hide in the closet."

"Any idea why?" Hurt says.

"So people couldn't find them. She planned to do the girl too."

"Did she say who was looking for them?"

"No. She's five."

"Kids know more than you think they do," he says. "Did you ask about the son? Shannon?"

"No," Kateri says.

"Why not?"

"She doesn't seem afraid of him. He's not a source of tension for her at all," she says. "But she keeps talking about an angel. Do you think we'll find a body?" she asks.

"At least we have a weapon. A commonplace item you'd find in a house in the woods. Where an adult male might have killed his own mother. I need you to try again, Fisher."

"I'm coming in," she says. She needs to think, needs to see it mapped out in front of her, not just hear words over the phone. She always works better with a visual.

* * *

They set up a situation room with a map of the woods and photos from the house, including the pool of blood and the spatter found on the cabinets and ceiling. Kateri finds Joel Hurt in there, mimicking the swing of an ax, looking in front of and behind him and up at the ceiling, and making notes with small yellow Post-its on the photos.

"They were victims of a crime before," Hurt says without saying hello.

"When?" Kateri asks.

Hurt takes a black-and-white picture of Pearl from years ago and tacks it up.

"Sixteen years ago," he says. "Her husband—Shannon's father, Park Jenkins—burned the house down with them in it."

"Where's Park?" Kateri asks.

"Clinton." He puts Park's mug shot next to Pearl. His brow is heavy, his eyes deep set, and his mouth a hard line.

"And Shannon's record?" Kateri asks.

"Doesn't have one," Hurt says. "The only picture I have is from his ninth-grade yearbook." He sticks it to the board next to Pearl's. He's a pretty boy with a heart-shaped face, blond hair in his eyes, shy looking. He's not smiling. He looks mildly alarmed. "This was five years ago," Hurt says. "Didn't graduate. Works at the diner in town."

A male tech leans into the room. "Detective Hurt," he says. "No footage on the TV."

"None?" Hurt says.

"It's rigged like a baby monitor, sir. Nothing is recorded. You can only watch."

"Fuck," Hurt says. Then, "Well, they're all pointed outside the house anyway. Nothing was watching what was going on inside." He puts his hands on his hips and turns to Kateri. "The Hub Diner closes at three," he says. "Shannon Jenkins at least needs to be questioned."

Kateri looks at her watch. It's just past two. "I'll go," she says.

"He's clearly not making anything of himself," Hurt says. "Something tells me apple doesn't fall far from the tree."

*　*　*

They part ways. Hurt goes back into the woods to join the team, who continue to comb through the rocks and trees, and Kateri drives into town to see if she can catch Shannon Jenkins at work. At the very least, she needs to break the news to him. She may need him to identify a body. She might have to arrest him.

The Hub sits right in the middle of town, where Center Street curves south toward the river and becomes Route 23. Just past that, the land is cordoned off for new luxury condos and giant houses that seem geared toward someone else entirely. Professionals looking for a winter retreat, a lodge, a mountain getaway from the slush of the city. Out-of-towners who think of the snow as picturesque.

The diner is empty, getting ready to close. She leaves her car haphazardly taking up space in the lot and hurries in to see if Shannon is still there.

A waitress meets her in the doorway, carrying an apron and wearing a pink camouflage fleece jacket.

"Oh, Officer," she says, noticing Kateri's badge, her belt. "We're closed already."

"I'm not here to eat," Kateri says. "I need to ask a few questions. Is Shannon Jenkins still here?"

The waitress shakes her head and comes on more direct than Kateri expected. "Look," she says. "Whatever it is, he didn't do it, okay? What are you, new? Did they send you down here to badger the poor kid?"

"Pardon me?" Kateri says. She takes a step back from the woman and rests her hand on her belt, exposing her weapon.

"They're always out here looking for Shannon," she says. The waitress isn't much older than Kateri but looks it. She's big around the middle, mature in her mannerisms. Kateri would guess she's about forty, with grown kids.

The waitress steps out from under the yellow corrugated-plastic awning and lights a cigarette.

"Is he still here?" Kateri asks, curt.

"No."

"How about the owner?"

The waitress looks at her for a minute, deciding, then makes a frown and shrugs. "Go ahead," she says. "He ain't friendly," she adds. "Especially toward cops."

Inside, the Hub's owner, Junior Savage, has an open bottle of bleach in his hand that he sloshes along the tile kitchen floor.

"Sir," Kateri calls.

"No," Junior answers. He picks up a wet mop and moves the bleach around.

Kateri shows her badge. "Sir, I just need a moment."

He seems small from far away, and she thinks it's a trick of the size of the room, the tile, or the lighting, until he gets closer, and she realizes he's less than five feet tall.

"I just need to get the fuck out of here," he says. He comes up to Kateri's chest and wears a knit fisherman's cap and a white chef's jacket that's filthy with blood. "What'd you find?" he asks. "Break-in? Dead cat?" He pours out more bleach. "I don't know what to tell you." He turns his back again and mops farther away, calling out over his shoulder, "When he's here, he works clean. I don't talk to him. I've never heard him raise his voice. I don't know why your department has such a fucking hard-on for him. Because of Park?" he says. "That guy's a psycho. This kid's all right."

Kateri waits while he ties up the trash bag and pushes the can closer to the door.

"His mother is dead," she says.

Junior lets the bag deflate in the can, his hand still on the knot, and he looks up at the ceiling. Up close, Kateri notices that he has gray-blue eyes, and a roundness to his face she wouldn't have expected.

"Son of a bitch," Junior says. "Drugs?"

"I need to speak with him," Kateri says. The bleach smell is overpowering, burning her nose.

"Do you know where I can find Shannon Jenkins?" Kateri asks.

He shakes his head and leans on the garbage can. His hands are small and stubby, and he's missing a finger. "He hasn't been in," Junior says.

"Since when?" Kateri asks.

"Few weeks."

Kateri raises her eyebrows and waits. "Did he quit?" she asks.

"I offer him hours," Junior says. "He turns them down. He's got better-paying work somewhere. I don't blame him," he says. Then, "I got somebody else."

Kateri pulls out a card that he won't take from her. He just nods for her to leave it on the counter, near the napkins, where somebody has neatly lined up all the salt and pepper shakers.

"Why did you say drugs?" Kateri asks Junior.

He waves his hand. "We all know each other's habits," he says.

"What kind of drugs?" Kateri asks.

"I don't know," Junior says. "Is she on trial? She's dead."

Kateri taps her card on the counter. "I'd appreciate your discretion," she says. "Information has a way of getting to the wrong people. If you hear something, please call me."

He holds her eye contact for a moment and smirks a little when he says, "Yes, ma'am." Then he scratches the back of his head underneath the cap, and he leaves the garbage can there, a barrier between them, and goes back into the kitchen to finish cleaning.

Outside, the waitress has gone, and there are no cars in the lot except Kateri's own Subaru. She sits and waits to pull out, her armpits prickly with heat and embarrassment. She didn't get anything at all from Junior or the waitress, except that Shannon Jenkins hasn't even been showing for work. If anything, she's moved herself further away from the information she needs. She thinks about the signs on the edge of town that read SPRING FALLS GREETS YOU. Not *welcomes*. Just *greets*.

SIX: SHANNON

THURSDAY, SEPTEMBER 7

My mother went about her business as though nothing had changed. I'd never seen someone so capable of shutting down, of taking a pill and going to sleep, of pretending that their house wasn't about to be auctioned in two months. Where would we go? I suspected she had a plan, would run, as she'd hinted, back to her own mother, or to a cousin in Vermont, someplace where she could change her name, someplace Park couldn't find her.

I needed to find out when he was eligible for release.

I needed to make more money.

If they ran and I was stuck with a house taken out from underneath me, with a minimum-wage job, I'd have to go someplace else. I needed a place to live, and in order to get that, I needed more money, or someone to live with. My job alone wasn't going to cut it. I didn't even have a car I could live in. Unless my mother ran on foot.

Sometimes I sat in the truck and screamed, alone on a lonely road, where no one could hear me. Sometimes, on days off, I lay in bed while the sun moved over me, from one side of the room to the other. More than once, I stood on the bridge and looked down at the railroad tracks. The train was never coming fast enough.

I wondered what the inside of Baby Jane's little mill cabin looked like. I imagined it as otherworldly, old-fashioned, like him. A place maybe with books and candles, with an old-timey bedroom set, delicate teacups. A closet full of pressed white shirts and creased gray pants.

I couldn't live in the abandoned car. Not for long. Winter was too harsh. I wouldn't make it past November, and even that was questionable. If the house was auctioned at the end of November, I'd be up against snow and ice already until at least April.

I went to work.

Junior had already given me all the hours he could. Most days it was just him, me, and Terri. If I couldn't come in or I was sick, he had one other guy who filled in, an old Navy man in his seventies. I had tapped that job for about all it was worth. I needed a skill. Which meant more school, or at least more than a goddamn GED.

I wiped down all the glass salt and pepper shakers and filled them. I spent half an hour marrying the ketchup bottles so none of them looked even a little bit empty. Terri had counted her drawer and was out back having a cigarette. My face was flushed. I didn't get paid until tomorrow, and I was ready for a cigarette and a drink myself. Then the bells clanged against the glass door, and a man I had never seen before in the diner, or even in town, came in. He scanned the empty counter, the vacant booths, and me doing closing side work, and asked if we were still open.

"Um," I stalled. I had to try not to stare. "I mean, we're open for another half hour," I said, and knew that Junior would kill me if I walked back there with another order. He was already slamming pans and scraping down the grill. If he got the bleach out, I was done.

The man shook his head. "It's okay," he said. "I'll just have some coffee." He had a folder with him that he laid on the counter.

I wasn't used to serving, but I grabbed a mug from the shelf below and poured slowly from the fresh full pot Terri had brewed for us as we cleaned. I looked at him as much as I could while he looked through his papers, his eyes down until I put the cup in front of him. He sat at the counter and sipped, and I went back to buffing glasses, even though my hands had a tremor. The man had long, honey-brown hair, curled at the ends, green eyes, and a soft mouth. He wore a flannel shirt that looked like it felt like butter. Fine hands, narrow wrists. When the cup was half empty, I picked up the pot.

"More?" I asked.

"Sure," the stranger said, and smiled. His teeth were exquisite. White and straight. I thought, no one passes through Spring Falls. It's on the way to nowhere. I almost dropped the full pot getting it back on the burner.

"Hey, do you have a place I could hang this?" he asked then. He opened the folder and took out a flyer, the kind with phone numbers perforated at the bottom. It read *Handyman needed for light carpentry, painting, installation.*

I took it from him and held it, my fingers damp and wrinkling the edges. "Are you hiring someone?" I asked.

"Yeah," he said, "Do you need the work?"

I let out a nervous laugh and looked behind me, through the window into the kitchen, where Junior was letting the oil out of the fryer.

"There are all these construction workers in town," I said.

"That's not what I want," the stranger said. There was something feline about his features, the way his eyes crinkled, the sharp points of his canine teeth.

I kept looking at the flyer. His name wasn't on it, just a number, repeated at the bottom.

"Did you just move here?" I asked.

"I did. I have things that need attention at my house." He tilted his head, thinking, and started to smile at me. "Is that something you do?"

"Yeah," I said, lying. I didn't have any actual experience.

He pulled out a stiff, plain-white card with just his name on it and a number different from the one on the flyer.

"Bear," he said, and held out his soft, fine-boned hand.

"Shannon," I said. My voice was just my breath. I was aware of how rough my hands were from the dish soap and hot water.

He cocked his head. "We both have weird names," he said, and then pointed at the card. "That's my direct line." He took the flyer from me and crumpled it.

I started laughing again. "You're not going to interview anyone else?" I asked.

He shrugged. "No need," he said. He arced the wadded-up flyer into the trash can behind the counter. Then he took a ten-dollar bill out of his pocket and left it next to his empty cup.

"Coffee's only a dollar," I said.

"Call me," he said. And he took his keys out and left.

I slid his business card—BEAR MILLER—into my back pocket and picked up the cup he'd left behind. I held on to it the way he had, with the handle in my right hand, and leaned it into my lips, lining up the invisible prints. And then Terri came in the back door with a slam, her apron off, and I dropped the mug onto the rubber mat, where it didn't break but just rolled way under the counter.

"What in the hell are you doing?" she asked, and laughed. "Clean up," she shouted, shooing me. "Get out of here."

I rushed the door and then walked out slow, looking. Bear Miller was gone. I wished I'd seen what he was driving or how he'd gotten there, if he'd walked, which direction he'd gone, where he had possibly come from.

* * *

I rode my bike through the woods, whizzing down the trail past the car, because I needed to get home and charge my phone. When I came out on the other side, my mother's truck was parked in the lot next to a Volvo that looked like it cost more than my entire life. A woman had two rambunctious pit bulls in the field, one black, the other a silvery blue nose. She wore a white jacket. The dogs barked at each other and wrestled, rolling over the ball. I slowed to a coast and circled around the lot before I crossed over to the entrance where our house was.

I didn't know the woman, but I thought she was probably somebody's wife, someone's mother, someone I knew from school. She looked at me like she was going to ask me something but stopped herself. So I got off the bike, walked it past her, and opened up the truck, looking inside to see if there was a pack of cigarettes. When she kept looking in my direction, I poked my head up over the door.

"Is something wrong?" I asked her.

The sun was filtered, hazy, low over the field and the wrestling dogs. She pointed at the entrance to the woods that led to our house.

"I just—" she started. "There was a little kid earlier," she said. "And I just worried because it seemed like she was by herself."

My heart hammered. "A little kid?" I asked. "How little?" But I knew, I knew it, before she even said it.

"Maybe five?" she said. She held out her hands in protest, or guilt, or explanation. "I just have never seen her," she said. "And I know these kids. I teach kindergarten. I've seen all the five-year-olds in town. Not her."

"Huh," was all I said.

"She came right out here and talked to me," she said. "She asked about my dogs."

"She did?" I asked.

"Yes, she was friendly, and quite bright," she said. "Talkative."

That was Birdie, I thought.

"And then she took off into the woods," the woman said, "and I didn't want to run after her because of the dogs. I didn't want to scare her. But . . ." She started laughing. "Now I'm wondering if I saw a ghost." She laughed harder, and my eyebrows went up in surprise.

"A ghost," I said.

She shrugged and threw up her hands. "Crazy. I know," she said.

I looked off into the woods. There was no movement, no sign of them outside, no smoke from the fire.

"Have you ever seen her?" she asked.

"No," I said, and only after thought maybe I should have said yes, that maybe saying yes would have drawn less attention to the little girl who might not even be real. "But I'll keep my eye out," I told her. I added, "I'm here all the time."

I'd started to walk away when she said, "She told me . . ." She hesitated, and then went on while I waited.

"What did she tell you?" I asked. I stopped and went back to her at the back of her Volvo, where she stood with the gate open, trying to herd the dogs back in.

"I asked her if she was alone, or if she was lost," she said. "Like, if she was looking for someone."

"Yeah?" I asked.

"She said she was looking for the angel."

I blinked, hard, unbelieving.

"I know," the woman said. She laughed again and shook her head. "You're just a kid yourself, and I'm a crazy woman telling you about a little girl looking for an angel, but . . . you know how sometimes you just can't tell what's real?"

I thought about the beautiful man sitting at the counter, asking me if I did any handy work. I felt for his card in my back pocket to make sure it was still there, to reassure myself that he was real and not something my mind had tricked me into seeing.

"No," I said. "I know."

* * *

Inside the house, the kitchen was quiet. No fan, no ticking from the loud clock on the stove. And then I noticed that the TV was off, the screen blank, flat gray and dusty.

I flipped a switch on the wall. Nothing. No hum from the refrigerator. And it was getting dark inside.

"Mom?" I called out.

She was asleep on her bed, her hairline telltale sweaty. Birdie sat beside her, in the crook of my mother's bent legs, which both my mother and Birdie liked to call The Nest. If she stayed in The Nest, she was safe, but apparently she hadn't.

She held two Barbie dolls, one male, dark haired, in a black jacket but no pants.

"Bird," I said. "What's going on?"

"The TV went off," Birdie said, "but Mom was asleep."

"How long has she been asleep?"

Birdie shook her head. She didn't know. She had a poor concept of time. Two hours might have felt like days to her. Sometimes it did to me.

On the floor beside the bed, Birdie had half packed a pink backpack with pairs of underwear, a sweater, and a different doll, and in the front pocket a whole handful of rocks, crystals, and river stones, different colors and shapes. Just like Mom, I thought.

"Were you going somewhere?" I asked her, kicking at the bag.

She held up her arms to be picked up, and I indulged her, swinging her onto my hip and smelling her hair. I carried her out to the kitchen to get her a glass of water, but when I turned on the tap, nothing came out.

"There's no electricity or water?" I said to Birdie, only half asking. I was trying not to shout. But it wasn't her fault.

She shook her head.

"There's a big poop in the toilet," Birdie said. "It won't flush."

I let out a groan.

I tried to remember the last time I'd paid bills. Usually they came in the mail while I was at work and my mother set them aside, then gave me the cash to take to the Big M so I could pay at the counter. I thought back a week, two weeks. I'd been going to Baby Jane's after work. More than once, I'd slept in the car, waking stiff and cold in the morning but getting back on my bike and riding back in to work.

I didn't even know where my mother kept the cash. I used to. I had dipped into it before, but now she moved it every few weeks. I was ready to tear the house apart looking for it.

I looked in the cupboard and found one last juice box for Birdie. She wagged her feet back and forth, sitting on the counter.

"Were you outside today?" I asked her.

Her eyes darted over to the left, a sure sign she was fibbing.

"Without Mom?" I added.

"No," she said. I watched her cheeks get hot and bright pink.

"Bird," I said.

She crossed her arms over her chest.

"You can't go out," I told her.

She looked at me, point blank, with her big light eyes and her jaw tight.

"Why not?" she asked.

I didn't have an answer for her. I stalled, and I heard my mother snoring.

"It's like you're Mom's favorite doll," I said. "And she doesn't want to share you."

She got to the bottom of the juice box with a loud, rattling suck.

"You can go out," she said to me without looking up.

I smiled a little. "I'm not her favorite."

I thought it would make her laugh, but she started to cry, just a little at first, her lip wobbling and her eyes filling up, but then it roiled into a full-blown sob and she needed to be held, rocked in the living room with her head on my shoulder.

"Bird," I whispered.

My mother slept through all of it.

56

When Birdie settled, she lay still on my lap. I raked her hair off her sweaty, damp cheek.

"It's not fair," she said.

"It's not," I answered. I patted her back, no longer the round curve of a baby but still just the width of my hand.

"You should be a favorite too," she said.

SEVEN: KATERI

Kateri checks her phone in the parking lot of the Hub while she watches the waitress get in her own car and leave, the lot a mess of potholes and gravel. She has a text from Hurt that says *Remains. Please call me.*

She tries, and it goes straight to voice mail each time. Hurt phones her finally from outside the park. "There's no service in there," he tells her. "I didn't think there was any point in waiting. They're bagging and bringing everything to the morgue."

"You couldn't wait for me to get there?" she says.

"It's just bones," Hurt says.

Kateri looks to the heavy gray sky, as if she can tell time by the passing of clouds. "That's advanced decomposition," she says. "She hasn't been dead that long. The blood was fresh."

"The body was burned," Hurt says.

"How far into the woods?"

"Quite a ways, and way off trail. We found some clothing," he says. "Some articles that we'll need to confirm but I'm sure are Pearl's."

It's possible, she knows. You can burn a body in the country, in the woods, in a way that you can't in a bigger town or city. There are fires all the time, especially in the fall. Bonfires, burning leaves; rural folks still burn trash.

The team continues to dig, and Kateri follows Hurt to the county morgue. The building has been built into a hill, the back of it accessible from a lower parking lot below where ambulances and hearses can pull into a garage to collect or drop off a body.

Hurt waits for her in the parking lot, next to his own car, which she rarely sees him drive, a pine-green Honda Element that she thinks he probably also uses for camping. There's a round sticker on the back that says ADK46er. He paces the lot in khakis and hiking boots.

"It's one of those days," he says, "that I wish I still smoked."

She pats her own bag. Sometimes she has a pack stashed. She tried quitting when she moved to Spring Falls, but she finds herself picking up a pack more often than not. She still savors a cigarette with her morning coffee. After a meal. And when she's stressed.

"Me too," she says to Hurt.

They meet the coroner, Elise Diaz, inside. She's a tiny woman, no more than five foot two, slim with a sleek bob, and exquisitely dressed in a black pencil skirt and a silk blouse. She wears four-inch heels and she's still shorter than Kateri.

Hurt introduces her as his partner, Kateri Fisher.

"New," Elise Diaz says, and appears to size her up.

"To the area," Kateri says, her hackles up. "I've been a detective for seven years."

Dr. Diaz raises her eyebrows at Hurt. "Well, Detective Hurt and I have been working together for decades, haven't we, Joel?" she says.

"I wouldn't go that far," Hurt says. His smile looks like a grimace. "I'm not quite as old as you are," he jabs.

Diaz lays her hand on the back of Kateri's arm. "Good to have fresh blood," she says. She leads them down the hallway, her heels clicking, her tiny ass barely moving. She walks, Kateri thinks, like she's the first lady, giving a tour of the White House.

In the exam room are bones on a table. They've been discolored from the fire, charred and cracked in ways that most likely occurred postmortem. There's a slender curve of spine and, disconnected, only half the ivory butterfly of a pelvis.

"What can you tell us?" Hurt asks Diaz.

"It's undeniably female," she says. She pulls on gloves and points at the faint pits in the bone. "Parturition scarring. Due to a vaginal delivery." She tucks her hair behind her ear and looks up at Kateri.

"Do you have children, Detective Fisher?" she asks.

"No," Kateri says, looking at the bones.

Diaz laughs lightly. "Probably for the best," she says.

"These were nearby," Hurt says, and pulls a plastic evidence bag for Kateri to examine. There's a bag with a shoe, a soft-sided suede ankle boot caked with mud and blood, and in another bag a braided bracelet, laced with beads and caked in part with blood.

"How close were these?" Kateri asks.

"Within ten feet," Hurt says.

"Only one shoe?" she asks.

"Yes."

She turns the bracelet over in her hands, examining the yarn, the little silver beads. There are tiny bells where the bracelet latches, and she thinks of Pearl, beaten, bleeding, being carried or dragged through the woods having lost a shoe. Her wrist tinkling with the sound of bells as she went.

The bracelet gives Kateri a cold wave of nausea, creeping up her neck, underneath her ears. She's seen so much in past cases: blood, gore, body parts, brains. But the bells on the bracelet, ringing, she imagines, as the body dragged, seem particularly delicate and grim to her. She feels green. She needs to get outside.

"Thank you," she says to Dr. Diaz, and excuses herself to the back parking lot, under a sky that is so heavy she swears she can feel it resting on the top of her head, a mantle, or a cold, dead hand.

Hurt appears at her side. "You okay?" he asks.

"What are we going to do with the kid?" Kateri asks.

"Well," Hurt answers. He looks down at the ground. "Foster care."

It hits Kateri like a thud in the middle of her chest. "Let's see if we have a match to the blood in the house," she says, and Hurt nods. "And if there's anything at all we can extract from the burnt bones."

She walks with Hurt to where their cars are parked side by side.

"Is it enough?" she asks, and knows that it is; it just seems so paltry. Where has the rest of it gone? It takes a long time to burn a human body, she thinks, without the aid of a crematorium. She thinks of the bare pelvis, with its clear markings of childbirth, the way motherhood leaves its trace on you long after you're dead.

"If the blood matches what we pulled from the house," Hurt says, "and we can match that to Pearl Jenkins—she has no DNA on file," he adds, "but we can test the type against her children—then yes," he says.

She wants to ask, "Who would do this?" But she knows. Murder is almost never anonymous.

* * *

They didn't send her to rehab after her accident. She spent a few days on the rehab floor, drying out, but a facility was never mandatory. It might have been court mandated, but there was no court. There were no charges. The county sheriff decided to keep it quiet. It would have been completely different if she'd hurt or killed someone, or even if another vehicle had been involved. But it was just Kateri and the wall.

They'd asked her—not the chief, but a department psychologist, very delicately—if she was suicidal. She never said the word *suicide* or *kill*. But she asked Kateri a lot of questions about feeling overwhelmed, about how she was dealing with it all.

Kateri wasn't suicidal. She did remember having the vague thought that if she died, well, it would be okay. But she wasn't about to take any action.

The sheriff unofficially demanded that she attend AA meetings and prove her presence. She went. A few times, while her face healed, while she figured out what to do with her grandmother's house.

In the months before the accident, her grandmother had declined and died. She was the only type of parent Kateri had had. After, Kateri went home to the empty house on Allen Street every night. Every night she felt unmoored and raw, like she would claw the walls to get out, and so she left. She picked a different bar every night, and for a while a different man. She knew it was dangerous. She left her badge, her sidearm at home. She went out unfettered.

When she crashed, the sheriff asked her how many fingers of whiskey she'd had.

"To be honest, sir," she answered, "it was more like hands." But she didn't remember. That was the worst part—or the best part, depending—the nights that were completely gone to her. Which sometimes meant waking up in her own bed, or on the couch, or in someone else's bed, or in the worst case, in a hospital bed.

The sheriff put her on leave. He asked to see her every two weeks, with some documentation of the AA meetings.

And then the house on Allen Street sold and Kateri hired a cleanout team to come take everything that wasn't already on her body or in a small bag. There was nothing left for her. Her father had died years ago, alone in a shitty high-rise on the south side. Her mother, dead when Kateri was sixteen.

She had died on the couch. Only thirty-one to Kateri's sixteen. Her toxicology report proved what they already knew. She had taken a deadly combination of alcohol and painkillers and benzos. It wasn't a night unlike other nights. It was just the night that killed her.

When Hamilton County called with a second interview, the wound on Kateri's chin had healed to a thin pink slice you could see only if she tilted her face up. She'd been to six meetings, where she rarely talked, just listened to the same confessions over and over, another face, another accident, another car crash, and more tears. She might have died on the couch the way her mother had. Instead, she bought a different car, she put a few things in the back, and she moved up north. She felt spared.

*   *   *

By the time she gets to Mercy, it's getting dark, and the rain has come, saturating, steady. It feels like it will never end, that this is the world now, wet and shining. The parking lot runs with sheets of water, moving toward the gutter.

She walks past the nurses' station and down the empty hallway. When she doesn't see the officer, she assumes they have taken the girl for some testing. The tests have been extensive: hearing, eyesight, brain scans, chest X-rays. They haven't found anything wrong with her. And not a hair on her has been harmed.

But she finds Birdie's room empty, her bed stripped. It catches Kateri so off guard that she just stands there in the doorway, looking in at the generic room, all signs of any patient gone. When they took her for testing before, everything was left behind: blankets, her chart, a pitcher of water. This room is now sterile.

Kateri goes back to the nurses' station.

"Jane Doe," she says. "Sparrow Annie Jenkins," she repeats. "In room four-four-oh-six?"

"Discharged," the nurse says.

"When?"

"This morning," she says. Behind her, the phone rings, stops, and then rings again so that the nurse has to hold up a finger, asking Kateri to wait.

She takes the call, and an attending doctor comes by with files. Another nurse slips in behind the desk to pull up information on another patient.

"To whom?" Kateri asks the first nurse.

"I'm sorry?" she asks.

"To whom was Jane Doe released?" Kateri asks, her voice rising. "And what happened to the officer outside her room?" She feels the heat creeping up her neck, her hair tingling, the metal taste of shame and fear on her tongue. "The child is a witness in an active investigation," Kateri says. "She can't leave without my knowing."

"Were you here?" the first nurse asks the other.

The second nurse nods, chewing a piece of candy she's taken out of the crystal dish on the counter. Behind them on the wall and along the edge of the counter, they've put up Halloween decorations, smiling vampires and skulls.

"Guy from the county," she says. "Appointed legal guardian."

"And the officer?" Kateri asks.

"The overnight guy," she says, "Officer Dillon." She blushes when she says his name. "He left at eight," she says, "but no one came in to replace him. He said they were notified of her transfer instead."

"I was not notified of her transfer, see?" Kateri says, her fingers pronged out on her breastbone. "That's the problem. Who was the man from the county? From DSS?" she asks. "Did he show identification?"

"He was tall," the nurse says, "and wearing a suit." As if that helps, Kateri thought. "He signed," the nurse says.

"May I see the signature, please?" Kateri asks.

The nurse riffles through the files from the day.

"This is an active investigation," Kateri says again. "That has become a murder investigation. In case you want to ID me," she adds. She unfolds her badge.

"Oh, Detective," the nurse says, and laughs. "We all know who you are."

"What did he look like?" Kateri asks, and fears that she sounds as desperate as she feels.

The nurse shrugs and grabs a second piece of candy. "Sorry," she says then, "this is my dinner." Then she adds, "Tall, dark hair." She frowns a little, self-deprecating. "Super good-looking."

"How old?" Kateri asks.

"Old," she says. "I don't know, like forty?"

Kateri pushes her tongue between her front teeth to keep from clamping down.

The second nurse pulls the folder and opens it to show Kateri but won't hand it over to her. The signature is illegible. A long flourish, its tail like a comet dragging off to the right.

*　*　*

Kateri calls the Department of Social Services from her car in the parking lot at Mercy while it pours on her windshield, the rain on her roof like a jackhammer.

"Kateri Fisher," she says to the case manager she spoke with yesterday, Emilia Ward. "Who checked out Jane Doe? Sparrow Annie Jenkins," she says, "from the Jenkins investigation. From Mercy Hospital."

"No one," Emilia says. "I have a caseworker from Catholic Charities coming to meet her tomorrow."

"No," Kateri says. "Someone picked her up."

"She is still admitted," Emilia says.

"No," Kateri says, louder, over the rain, trying as hard as she can not to start yelling. "She is not admitted," she says. "I am at Mercy Hospital right now. She is gone," Kateri says. "With someone who says he was her legal guardian."

There's a long silence on Emilia's end.

"Can you check with your caseworker?" Kateri asks. "To see if maybe he got the days mixed up?"

"It's a woman," Emilia interrupts her. "The caseworker is a woman. And she wouldn't have checked her out."

"Is there any chance someone else from your agency might have thought she needed to be picked up?" Kateri asks.

"There shouldn't be," Emilia says, "but I'll check. I'll also check with the officials at Mercy," she says. "I don't understand how this could happen."

"Me neither," Kateri says, but she tries to picture a man, any man, who might have come to sign out Birdie. Shannon doesn't fit the description in any way, and he certainly isn't forty. The man Kateri pictures looks like a movie star. Something unreal. She thinks of the drawing in the closet, the tall man in black, with a circle head and no face, and she hears Birdie's voice in her head. He's the angel.

She calls Hurt.

"Officer Dillon was at Mercy overnight guarding the girl's room," she says as soon as Hurt says hello.

"Yes," he says.

"Can you find out who was supposed to replace him?"

Hurt is at his desk. She can tell by the quiet around him, the click of his fingers on his keys.

"Craig O'Neil," he says, "was on at eight this morning."

"No he wasn't," Kateri says.

"Well, who was?"

"No one," Kateri says. "The girl is gone. She was checked out by someone who said he was her legal guardian."

"Shit," Hurt says. "Really?"

"Can you find O'Neil?" she asks.

"He should still be there," Hurt says. "He's scheduled until six. Hold on." She can hear him rolling his chair. "Let me have Dawn call his cell," he says.

She listens while he gives the instruction, waits while Dawn dials, and gets nothing.

"His phone is off," Hurt says.

Kateri rubs at the back of her head where her hair is tucked in and loosens it; the pull of the bun is giving her a headache. "We have a missing deputy," she says. "And a missing child."

She hears him sigh. "Are you sure?" he asks.

"Hurt," she says. "I saw her discharge papers. Fuck. Would you ask someone else if they were sure? I'm sure."

Hurt breathes. "Let me do some searching," he says, and hangs up.

EIGHT: SHANNON

FRIDAY, SEPTEMBER 8

I bypassed the car. It was later than I usually arrived, and I couldn't see well on the trail, much less off it. I thought I knew the way blind but kept stopping; the creak of the trees, the movement of deer and raccoons in the brush, every noise freaked me out. I thought I felt breath on my neck. I thought I heard whispering. When I came out the other side of the woods, Baby Jane's backyard was lit with a yellow square from the kitchen window.

I had told Birdie to say I was taking care of it. "When Mom gets up," I'd said, "tell her I went to take care of it." I told her not to worry. I lit a candle inside a hurricane glass and put it up on the counter so she couldn't knock it over. I hoped my mother didn't sleep through until morning. All I could picture was Birdie alone in the dark house, her body curled next to my mother, who was dead to the world.

It would be better if she were dead, I thought.

* * *

I went to the back door, off the kitchen, or maybe the cellar way, and knocked, hoping that Baby Jane wasn't sleeping. It took him a few minutes, but I heard his feet shuffling inside and saw a light come on in another room. When he answered the door, he was fully dressed, like always, even in shoes. His hair was mussed, down over his forehead, the longest locks down to his chin.

"Shannon," he said, holding on to the side of the door, leaning out. "It's late."

"I know," I said. "I'm—I have a situation."

I noticed that his knuckles were white and his hand trembled. The wind blew in the yard. Behind his house was a perfect line of pines, planted more than a hundred years ago in a straight row, seven of them. The branches in the wind sounded like voices, hushing.

"Are you okay?" I asked. I saw him unclench his jaw.

"Yes," he said. But he didn't move.

I tipped my head. "Can I come in?" I asked. "I have a problem," I added. "I need an adult."

"Yes, yes," he said, and moved then, letting me into a black-and-white kitchen with a big enamel sink and a pink counter top. I watched while he turned his head and wiped his forehead with the cuff of his shirt sleeve. He had a tattoo on his forearm I had never noticed, the face of a pocket watch, with the chain wrapped around his elbow.

"I've never seen that," I said, pointing.

He sniffled, and pulled at the waist of his pants, which I noticed were too big. "I have another," he said.

"Can I see it?" I asked.

He pressed his lips into a flat line. "No," he said. "It's late," he said again. "What's wrong? What's the problem?"

I tried to look him in the eye. His top lip was beaded with perspiration. He needed to shave.

"Did you take something?" I asked.

"Like what?" he said.

"Like a drug. Are you on something?"

"I'm not on anything," he said, suddenly frank and sharp.

But I detected something. I knew my mother had two different kinds of sweats, one when she had just dosed and another when she needed to. I couldn't tell what this was.

"Really?" I asked.

He laughed a hard, unjoyful laugh and turned from me to walk into the living room.

The living room was a small square. Off of it were one small bedroom, lit with a milk glass lamp, and a bathroom, tiled in pink and black. In the bedroom the bed was made and there was no detritus of living, no books on the nightstand, no socks or shoes on the floor. Nothing that wasn't put away, dusted, straightened.

"What's your problem?" Baby Jane asked me.

"There's no water or electricity at my house," I said. "And the county is auctioning it for back taxes."

He motioned to a squared-off, avocado-green sofa. "Please," he said. When I sat, he asked, "How much do you owe?"

"A lot. Like more than the house is even worth."

He sat next to me, his leg crooked, his body turned to face me. He leaned his face on his hand, watching. "What about the utilities?" he asked.

"I don't know yet," I said.

He pushed his hand up so that it held back his hair. He had a darkness under his eyes I'd never noticed in the car, and his cheekbones seemed sharp. I thought he'd lost weight. I inched closer, looking intently.

"Baby," I said.

"It's just not a good day," he said.

"Is there anything I can do?"

"For me?" he said. "No. You can stay if you want." I thought of Birdie sitting on the bed in the dark with my mother.

"It's not just me," I said.

71

His eyes went dark. "Your mother made these choices herself," he said. "She can figure them out."

"She can't," I said. "She literally cannot. If I leave her to it, she will just sit in that house without electricity or water until they auction it."

"How is that your problem?" he asked.

"It just is," I said. Her name formed behind my lips, but I couldn't say it. I couldn't break the seal on the secret.

"You can stay," he said again. "On the couch."

I looked at the green velvet sofa and felt the corners of my mouth sink. It looked more comfortable than my twin mattress at home. It wasn't what I wanted. I wanted to rattle him, shake him up. Push him down.

"Put the house in your name," he said then.

"How?" I asked.

"Is there a mortgage?" he asked.

"No."

"Have your mother sign it over to you. It's the least she can do."

"Why?" I asked. It seemed like that would make it mine and mine alone.

"Because then you can take over the utilities," he said, "and start from zero, and maybe you can do that with the taxes too. It'll buy you time," he said.

"How do you know this?" I asked.

"I'm really good at buying time," he said.

He walked into the bedroom and left the door open. I saw him untuck his shirt, unbutton it, lay it across the top of a ladder-back chair. And then his shoes, his pants. Out of my sight line, he changed into pajama bottoms but left his shirt off, his chest and stomach thatched with dark hair and his back covered in a tattoo of a sword that ran down the length of his spine and two wings that sprouted from his shoulder blades.

"Wow," I said from the doorway. He brushed his teeth, and leaned over the sink to spit.

"Are you staying?" he asked.

"Yes," I said.

He took a chenille bedspread off the bed and got in between cool blue sheets. "Turn the light off," he said. "There's a blanket on the back of the couch."

"Can I lie down?" I asked.

"On the couch," he repeated.

"With you," I said quietly. I leaned in the doorway to his bedroom, the light still on. He was covered up to his armpits, his arms out and folded over his chest. When he closed his eyes, I tried not to think of him lying in a casket, in blue satin instead of blue cotton.

"Please?" I said.

He snapped open his eyes and breathed in sharply. I was fidgeting with my fingers, creeping into the room.

"On top of the covers," he said.

I laughed. "Are we in middle school?" I asked.

"Take it or leave it," he said.

I took my shoes off and lay on top of the blanket next to him. I didn't dare touch him. He seemed stiff, like his whole body was on guard against me lying there. "Where were you before this?" I asked.

"Jail," he said.

I didn't jump, but the hairs on my neck stood up. "Why?" I asked.

"You don't want to know."

"Have you killed someone?" I asked.

He turned on his side to face me. "Yes," he said. "But not in the way that you think."

I looked into his blue, blue eyes.

"Go to sleep," he said, and closed them, and I lay there for a long time, clenched and awake, watching him breathe. I didn't know if he was sleeping, but he didn't move, and at some point I fell deeply asleep, curled on my side with my forehead touching his shoulder.

* * *

When I woke up, he was gone.

I looked in the bathroom for anything personal. There were razors and shaving soap that you lathered with a brush. Witch hazel and alcohol. A bottle of aspirin. Nothing with his name on it, nothing that wasn't also completely generic.

In the kitchen there was no coffee, only tea, and only black. There was bread, and whiskey, and in the refrigerator, some eggs and cheese.

On the little metal table in the kitchen, where there might be a bowl of fruit or a bouquet of flowers, were still lifes of bone. A piece that was flat and curved, like a shoulder blade or a hip, and another that was a circular section of spine. Beside them, a white glass vase. Instead of flowers, there was a bunch of feathers, black and brown ones, striped ones, like from a hawk. More delicate than flowers and sturdier, I thought. They wouldn't lose their beauty. They wouldn't die. Neither would the bones. What was already dead couldn't die again.

*　*　*

I went back to the house at first light, roused Birdie, and walked her out to the public bathroom in the park. My mother had gotten up in the night, eaten an entire box of gingersnaps, left a mess of crumbs and a broken plate in the kitchen, and then gone back to sleep. Beside her, I found a bottle of Rebel Yell, tipped over and empty. At six, she was still sleeping it off, so I covered up Birdie and kissed her head, took the keys off the hook, and drove the truck to work in the same dirty clothes I had slept in.

At the end of my shift, damp with dishwater and sore, I asked Junior if I could use the house phone. "Okay if I?" I said, picking up the receiver. I knew it would be, but I also knew I should ask first, because I couldn't always predict Junior's pan-throwing moods.

I almost hung up.

I held the stranger's card in my hand. He'd asked me to call. I went over the conversation several times. I'd said I could work. He'd said he would hire me. He'd thrown out the flyer right in front of me. I pictured the pixie smile on his face, the curls of his hair, the way he'd wadded up the paper and lobbed it into the trash can.

"Bear Miller," he said on the other side. The way a man with an actual profession answers the phone.

"Hi."

I instantly felt stupid. Like I was back in school. A kid, trying to sound grown-up. I knew something had to change. I'd felt it deep in my sleep beside Baby Jane. The notion that everything was ending. That I would learn to do something else. That I could push my body to a limit it hadn't known. Work an eighteen-hour day, sleep, work again. Get everything in order.

"Um, it's Shannon," I said. "We met at the diner?"

"Of course," Bear said, smooth. "I'm so glad you called."

"I'm happy to work," I said. "I need to work. Could we talk about it? When could I start?" I asked.

I held the card so tight I bent it. I had worried all its edges soft and fuzzed.

"Where are you?" Bear asked, at once more direct and more intimate than I'd expected.

"At the diner," I said.

"Are you done for the day?" he asked.

"Yes."

"Stay there," Bear said, and hung up.

"Okay," I said, embarrassed that it had all happened so quickly. "Thanks," I said, and "Bye," into the dead phone before placing it back on the hook so it sounded like a normal conversation. I felt my face fold in, threatening to cry, from everything: Birdie, the house, the whiskey, Baby Jane. I started coughing and excused myself from Junior, who wasn't paying attention anyway.

I went into the bathroom and scrubbed my hands. They were permanently dry from the hot water and bleach in the kitchen. I washed my face with the cheap pink soap that Junior stocked the place with and dried off with rough, brown C-fold towels. I pushed my hair off my head with my fingers. It didn't matter. It was dirty, dark at the roots. A cowlick was sticking up in the back that wouldn't go down until I washed it. It needed to be cut. The longer it got, the younger and girlier I looked. My whole body was sore and tired, gritty under everything. I took three butter mints from the register and hoped I didn't smell from a distance, or that if I did, it was only like bacon, or the grill.

Bear showed up in a dark-green Land Rover with caramel leather seats. He shook my hand tight, with full palm.

His face was like something I'd only read about. High cheekbones. Green eyes. His hair was pulled back in a loose bun near the top of his head. His jeans looked expensive, dark and slim but not tight, and his leather boots looked so soft I wanted to rub my face on them.

"You want to come see the house?" Bear asked.

"The house?" I said. My gut spasmed in panic, and I felt like my heart was beating outside my chest.

Bear smiled. "Where you'll be working," he said.

I glanced at my mother's shitty little truck, slightly crooked off its frame and parked with the front tire in a deep puddle. On the way out of the park this morning, the fuel light had come on.

"I'm pretty dirty from work," I said.

"Why don't you go home first," Bear said. "Shower and change, and then meet me over there."

So logical. So normal. And so ridiculously impossible that I started laughing. I was afraid I sounded hysterical. I wiped at my eyes, and my lips pulled down in a hard, uncontrollable frown.

"Whoa," Bear said, when I had hoped he wasn't paying attention. "What's going on?" he asked.

"Oh." I waved my hand. Blinked my wet eyes. "It's more than you want to know," I said.

"Tell me," he said.

I took a rough breath. "The water and electric were turned off at my place," I said.

"Okay," Bear said.

"So, I need to work," I said. I tried to keep my eyes on the clouds behind him and not on his beautiful face. They were heavy clouds, the kind that bring snow. The air, even though it was warm, had a bite to it.

"Are you hungry?" Bear asked.

"I mean, I'm not in a commercial with a swollen belly and a fly on my face," I said and laughed, bitter.

"I meant right now," Bear said, and he smiled. "Not chronically."

"Oh." I blushed hard, and I felt my heart again, pounding. "Yeah," I said.

He got into the Land Rover then and pushed open the passenger side door from inside. "Get in," he said, and after a second of hesitation, I did. I got in and sat on the buttery leather seat that was warm from the sun, or maybe from a built-in heater.

"I'm pretty sure I can get you what you need," Bear said.

NINE: KATERI

Kateri's phone rings in the early hours, before the sun has come up. In her deepest sleep, she struggles to recognize the chirp of her phone. In her dream, a cricket as big as her hand climbs the wall, its copper wings making the sound of her phone ringing.

"Fisher," Hurt barks as soon as she accepts the call. "I need you out at Mercy."

Her heart starts and she draws a quick breath. "Did they find the kid?" she asks.

"No," he says. "Come now."

His call has her immediately on alert. Still, she stops at the twenty-four-hour Stewarts for coffee before she drives the two-lane highway out to Mount Snow. She watches the sun in her rearview mirror, leaking yellow over the horizon, lightening the black trees, spreading gold over the pavement. By the time she gets to Mercy, there's a circle of seven trooper cars, lights going, an ambulance, Hurt's Honda, and a petite buff BMW that, turns out, belongs to Elise Diaz.

The car is submerged in deep reeds in a swampy patch behind the way back of the parking lot. Kateri watches as a tow truck pulls out a small, nondescript Nissan, water pouring from the doors, from the trunk. The waiting seems to take forever, but it's Hurt who finally goes over and instructs the mechanic to unlatch the trunk, and there is the

79

missing officer, Craig O'Neil, bound and gagged in his own trunk. In the water, the hands have turned puffy and blue. The head leans back at an unnatural angle. Elise Diaz is in the swamp water up to her ankles in rain boots. Cameras go off. Radios sound.

"Craig O'Neil," Hurt says.

"The cop," Kateri says. "He never made it inside."

"Not from the looks of it."

"Rookie?" Kateri asks.

"Twenty-two," Hurt says.

Elise sloshes her way out of the cold marsh and approaches the detectives. "I estimate time of death between seven and nine yesterday morning," she says. "I'll give you my decision on a cause," she adds.

Hurt looks at the sky, squinting. "Everything's gone," he tells Kateri. "Badge, cuffs, firearm."

"So we've got an armed and dangerous," Kateri says. "Willing to kill a cop. With a five-year-old girl."

"That's what it looks like," Hurt says.

Diaz pats Hurt on the arm. "Meet me at the morgue?" she says, an eyebrow arched.

"I wish that didn't sound like a standing date," Hurt says.

Kateri watches as Elise peels off her gloves and hands them to a young male assistant. The stretcher comes away from the water and is loaded into the back of the ambulance. Radios are loud with messages and static.

"We're going to have to go public," Hurt says. "And there's bound to be a frenzy."

Kateri rubs her face. All she did was wash and dress, wind her hair into a ponytail, and rush out. She remembers that she's still tired.

"Ambushed rookie cop," Kateri says.

"I can do the press conference if you want," Hurt says.

"Why would you? Why wouldn't I?"

He looks off behind her. "Look," he says. "Anything that goes wrong with the case . . . anyone not caught or who, God forbid, strikes again . . .

they'll come right back to you mishandling it, if yours is the face they associate with it."

"They won't do that to you?" Kateri asks. She feels her jaw tighten up into her ears and the beginnings of a headache.

"Come on, Fisher," he says.

"Come on what? Because I'm a woman? Elise Diaz is a woman."

"She's sixty," Hurt says. "You're . . ."

"I'm thirty-two, Hurt. I've been in the force for twelve years."

"You look young to people," he says. "And . . ."

"What?" Kateri asks.

"Attractive," Hurt says, deadpan.

Kateri laughs outright.

"I'm not saying it's right," Hurt says. "I'm just telling you how it is. If we put you on TV associated with this case, it's going to put you in an uncomfortable spotlight, and if people go digging . . ." he says.

"Digging?" she asks.

"Into your past," he says.

She lets her hands fall to her sides and stands with her shoulders square, looking him in the eye. "I didn't realize anyone was already digging," she says.

"We were all curious."

She turns around to walk back to her own car. "Then ask me," she calls out over her shoulder. "Fucking ask me." She has to try not to slam the door.

*　*　*

On her way back into Spring Falls, she finally catches sight of Shannon Jenkins. It startles her and she pulls across two lanes of traffic into the Stewart's parking lot.

He wasn't at work when Junior Savage said he should have been. The multiple times she tried his phone, it appeared to be off, with no voice mail or text messages received.

It's the morning rush at Stewart's, and she's in danger of losing him. His height, his slight build, the way he shrinks his shoulders make him easy to miss. He ducks through the crowd and into the store, and he disappears for a minute.

When he comes back out, he picks up bags of firewood and throws them into the back of the blue Toyota truck she's been tracking. In the front seat is a black, pit-ish mutt with a square head and a white blaze. Kateri parks by the free air pump and gets out.

"Shannon Jenkins," she calls, and he jolts, his arms raised like a startled baby or an electrocuted man. The crowd at Stewart's is enough to swallow her voice. She's in plain clothes, in her own car. No one else there notices her.

Shannon puts a hand to his chest and then to his belly, calming himself.

He's just a kid, she thinks. So was Craig O'Neil.

"Kateri Fisher," she says up close.

"I know."

"I need to talk to you," she says. "You've been hard to find."

"I'm—" he starts. "I'm not staying at home."

When the sun catches him from behind, his hair lights up like a ball of amber. Kateri suspects it's prettier than he knows.

"I need you to come to the morgue," she says, "and I need you to come in for questioning."

"The morgue?" he says, and pales.

"I need a next-of-kin identification," she says.

From inside the truck, the dog gives one warning bark to Shannon.

"For?" Shannon asks.

Smart, Kateri thinks. "An adult female," she says.

His chest seems to give way, to cave in.

"Now?" he says.

"I've been waiting," Kateri says, "so yes, now would be good."

She goes around to the other side of the truck and pets the dog through the open window. He's a big baby who laps at her open hand. "Who's this?" Kateri coos to the dog, and while she waits for Shannon to answer, she gets the address off the dog's collar. It's Burlington. She thinks he cannot possibly be staying that far away and driving back and forth. She also cannot have him leaving the state.

Shannon looks at her through the cab of the truck.

"You can drop him off first," she says, testing. "Then you can meet me, and we'll go together."

Shannon looks down at his feet, and Kateri sees the muscles in his jaw set. There's a chance he'll bail. He'll say he's taking the dog home and will never show, and she'll lose track of him again for days, or for good. He's got friends, she thinks. He has someone protecting him. He's not alone.

"Where?" he asks.

"Meet me at the station," she says. "In thirty."

She waits while he pulls out and goes left, the opposite way from his own house, up toward the new construction. The dog pokes his muzzle out the window, sniffing and appearing to smile. He has the loose lips of a hound. But not the soft mouth.

* * *

At the station, both Albany and Burlington newspeople approach her on her way in. Behind them is a truck from a Syracuse station.

"Detective!" the reporter calls. She's a young woman with that gloss of TV news: perfect hair, shining lips.

Kateri holds up her hand and shakes her head. She ducks in before they can barrage her with questions about the murdered cop.

Inside, Hurt and the chief are working on a statement. There's very little they can actually say, but they need to confirm publicly that yes, a young deputy has been murdered. And yes, they are also working on the disappearance of local woman Pearl Jenkins.

"We need a DNA sample from one of the kids to match the blood at the house."

"I'm taking Shannon Jenkins to the morgue," she tells them. The chief stands over Hurt's desk.

"Did you arrest him?" Hurt asks.

"I don't have anything to arrest him for," Kateri answers.

Chief Whittaker rubs his face with his hand. Everything about him, Kateri thinks, is a square. His head, his crew cut, his hands, his torso.

"I know you have urban training," he says to Kateri. "But things are pretty simple up here," he tells her.

"I'll decide that," she says. "I can't connect him to the crime yet." She smiles by way of a frown and leaves them to collect files from her office before she takes Shannon Jenkins to the morgue.

She smokes half a cigarette on the sidewalk beside the building, watching the road. She remembers the direction he drove off in, the make and model of the truck, the sight of the dog. But she waits, tapping her shoe, smoking too quickly. It gives her a head rush. She thinks, I shouldn't have let him go. She watches every car that goes by, every car that's not his. He didn't have the look, she thinks, that look that says *run*. Something about him seemed resigned.

His blue truck, empty of the dog and the firewood, pulls in on time and parks in the back of the station where the employee cars are. She watches him sit in the driver's seat for a moment, ruffling his hands through his hair, looking down at his lap, probably at his phone. She sees him take a deep breath and try to relax his shoulders before he gets out.

She drives him out to the coroner's office in a squad car and not her own. He doesn't talk on the way there; he just picks at his fingers. His nails are bitten down and ragged. She notices that his hands are soft and not rough from dishwashing the way she would have thought.

They enter through the front, not the way Kateri and Joel Hurt came in to identify the bones. In the lobby, the receptionist sees Kateri and picks up her phone, announcing, "Detective Fisher and a guest to see you, ma'am." She hangs up and nods at Kateri.

The office is dark. Black tile floor and walnut paneling. There are two leather chairs that it seems unlikely anyone ever sits in. Elise Diaz comes out in a sharp, conservative suit, completely changed from the way Kateri saw her early this morning, in a rain jacket and rubber boots.

Dr. Diaz shakes Shannon's hand and then holds it and feels the edge of his sweat shirt, the hood of which is up around his neck like a cowl. He swallows. In his left hand, he grips his keys on a short woven lanyard with a print of bears. Dr. Diaz takes that hand, notices the keys, and tells him he can relax. Kateri watches as he tries to release his fingers. He puts the keys in his jeans pocket.

"Thank you for coming," she says. She walks him down another black-tiled hallway, shoes clicking, and stops outside a wooden office door with her name on a matte-gold plaque.

"Come in," she says, and ushers them into a warm room with a beautiful, intricate Persian rug and black-and-white photographs of trees. Shannon sits on the edge of a leather chair, facing the desk. He's pale and, Kateri thinks, brittle.

But pretty well dressed. Both his hoodie and his jeans are clean and fit well, and they seem both new and of good quality. She wouldn't have guessed he's been living in poverty in the woods.

Diaz has paper bags, and inside them, evidence in plastic bags. She takes the bags out one at a time, and Kateri notices a wave a nausea or panic wash over Shannon. He swallows and rubs his throat.

"I have some articles," Dr. Diaz says, "that I'd like to see if you recognize. These are pieces of clothing or personal effects," she says. "Nothing gory or scary. Okay?"

"Okay."

She pulls out a small bag first. "Shannon," she says. "Is it okay if I call you Shannon?"

He looks for a moment like he can't fathom what else she would call him. "Yes," he says.

She reveals the bracelet. "Is this familiar to you?" She lays the bag on the table between them.

"Can I?" he says, reaching for it.

"Of course."

He picks up the bag and looks closely. "That's my mother's," he says.

"How do you know?" Kateri asks.

He points at the stones woven into the braid of the bracelet. "These are rose quartz," he says, and shrugs. Then, "She made it herself."

Kateri nods encouragingly and hands the baggie back to Elise Diaz, who pulls out a larger bag.

It contains the suede boot, caked with mud along the bottom from the woods and stained on the top with blood spatter.

"That's my mom's," he says. Then, "You don't have both."

"Only one was uncovered," Kateri says.

"It's from Walmart," Shannon offers, and Elise checks inside to confirm.

"Thank you," Dr. Diaz tells him.

"That's it?" he says. "Those are just things." He looks at Kateri. "I thought you said there was an adult female."

"What we have," Diaz says, "is not fit for public viewing." She tilts her head down, knowing, but still gentle with him. "I can show you a photograph if you'd like, but I don't recommend it."

"What is it?" Shannon says, suddenly shrill.

Kateri presses her lips together. "It's bones."

"Bones," he repeats. "What happened to her?"

"That's what we're trying to find out," Kateri says. "It'll help if you submit a DNA sample. It's not mandatory, but"—she nods at Elise—"it will help Dr. Diaz make a definite match. Your mother doesn't have any DNA already on file, so the best we can do is match her to next of kin."

The shadow underneath his cheekbone is deep and greenish. He looks gaunt in the light of the office.

"What kind of bones?" Shannon asks.

Kateri looks at Elise Diaz. A sort of heavy resignation has settled over Shannon's face, his lips sinking, his eyes hooded.

"What kind of bones?" he asks again.

Elise folds her hands on the desk. "There's an intact pelvic bone," she says. "And most of a spine."

"That's it?" Shannon says.

"That is all that has been recovered to date," Kateri says. "Forensics are still digging."

"Where would the rest of it be?" he asks.

She's alarmed by his seemingly matter-of-fact questions. He hasn't broken down. He has shut down, weighted, lingering in a dark logic.

"In the woods?" Kateri says. "Animals do the most damage."

He swallows.

"I mean," he says, "what makes you think she's dead?"

Elise raises her eyebrows at Kateri.

"Shannon," she says, "when is the last time you were home? At the house on Hidden Drive."

He shrugs. "A few days, I guess," he says. "A week?"

"Where have you been staying?" Kateri asks.

"With my friends," he says.

"Around here?" Kateri asks, and he nods, but offers nothing else. "When is the last time you spoke to your mother?"

"When I was home," he says. "She doesn't have a phone."

Kateri straightens and drums her fingers on the file folder she has brought with her.

"Just tell me," Shannon says.

"There's a significant amount of blood inside the house," Kateri says. "That indicates an attack, with blunt force. The remains we found, however, were yards away from the house," she says. "And near these other items that belonged to your mother."

She watches him breathe through his teeth, biting down on his tongue.

"Are you okay with giving a DNA sample?" Kateri asks.

"Yeah," Shannon says. "Of course."

"We can complete that at the station," Kateri says. "There are some other questions I need to ask you, and Dr. Diaz has quite a bit of work to do."

Diaz stands and reaches for Shannon's hands.

"I'm so sorry for your loss," she says.

Shannon bows his head, letting her hold his hands. "Thanks," he mutters.

Diaz nods toward the lanyard that hangs out of his pocket. "I'm quite fond of bears," she says.

"Oh," he says, and blushes hard and sudden, his face flared hot pink. "Me too," he says.

Outside, the wind has picked up and blasts across the parking lot. Shannon hunches up his shoulders, but his ears and cheeks remain hot.

"I thought I had to see her," he says inside the squad car. "I thought there was a body."

Kateri shakes her head. "There are only pictures and things," she says. "I'm sorry, I should have told you."

She had no intention of telling him. She wanted to see how he reacted to the possibility of seeing the body. He has remained quiet, ashen, and pinched the entire time. Except for the blush, she thinks.

* * *

That afternoon, Hurt appears on the TV news in a black suit and a black-patterned tie. He looks taller, slightly older on-screen, his hair darker, his face more serious.

88

He announces that they have uncovered the body of a young deputy and that they are looking into possible foul play, with a suspect at large, who should be considered armed and dangerous. In addition, he says, they are investigating the disappearance of Pearl Jenkins and the connection to recently discovered remains inside Silver Lake Park.

"This is an ongoing investigation," Hurt says, without mentioning the missing girl. "I'm unable to take your questions at this time."

He steps away from the podium, and Chief Whittaker waves his hand to the crowd, dismissing them, and leans into the mic to say, "Thank you, Detective Hurt."

In the hallway, he caves in a little. Kateri watches him as he closes his eyes, his spine curved forward like he's folding inward.

"Joel," she says, approaching.

"What time is it?" he asks her.

"Three thirty," Kateri says.

"I need a drink," Hurt says, and eyes her, tentative.

"I can handle a drink," she says.

TEN: SHANNON

SATURDAY, SEPTEMBER 9

Bear Miller's house was a mock Italian villa on the edge of town, one of the new houses going up in the luxury tract. In fact, his was the only house on its street, and empty lots in various stages of construction sat around it. They were all huge, five thousand or more square feet, Bear's house with an in-ground swimming pool, a tennis court, a three-car garage.

It sat alone at the top of Fountain Street, the way my house sat alone at the bottom of Hidden Drive. Around it, poured-cement basements. No streetlights. Few trees, except where the woods began to encroach from behind.

He could kill me, I thought, and just have me poured into the foundation of another home. No one would ever know. I wasn't even sure when someone would start looking.

The upper room in the front of the house had a wrought-iron balcony. A bigger balcony spread across the back of the house and overlooked the pool and the tennis courts. And beyond that, the dense woods.

Bear parked in the middle garage spot, and the door opened automatically with a whisper. Inside were a kayak, a mountain bike, and a tiny yellow roadster with round mirrors on the sides and the top down.

"How long have you lived here?" I asked.

"Not long," Bear said, and pointed to the boxes lined up near the door.

A dog came bounding from the backyard to greet us.

"Watch out," Bear said before I opened my door, and I flinched as the dog approached, barking "He's exuberant," Bear laughed. "And he likes men."

The dog was mostly black with a white blaze and white paws. He was part pit bull, with a big square head but long legs and a thin, athletic body. When I opened my door, he jumped right on me, front paws on my shoulders, licking at my face so eagerly that he hopped on his back feet.

"Buddy," Bear said, sharp. "Down."

"Is that your name?" I said to the dog. "Who's a good buddy?"

"He's a rescue," Bear said. "He's head shy."

The dog circled my feet in the garage, openmouthed and panting, his tail thumping.

"What do you mean?" I asked.

"He's been hit," Bear said. "If you raise your hand," he said, and demonstrated, lifting his hand near the dog's face, and the dog cowered, wincing, his eyes squinted shut, his shoulders braced for what he thought was coming.

I got it. I was head shy myself. My mother didn't hit often, but when she did, she meant it. I remember my ears ringing from one thump when I was still really little. She'd caught me with matches. I was just sitting on the porch lighting one after another, sometimes pressing it into a dry leaf and watching the bright edge curl and snuff out, fascinated and thrilled. She clocked me from behind. "Don't ever," was all she said.

I crouched down to the dog's level, and he leaned into my chest like a hug.

"He likes you," Bear said.

Inside, there was an open kitchen with slate-gray stone counters and light birch cabinets. It looked out over a giant room where the ceiling was the full height of the house. A wall of windows faced the backyard, uncovered. The floors were dark and sleek.

I felt filthy. I leaned and wiped my hands on my jeans, and was afraid to come very far into the house.

"How long has the water been out?" Bear asked.

"A few days," I said.

"Look," he said, "I don't want to make assumptions about what you need. But the bath is down there." He pointed to where the hallway curved around the back of the living room and into a large master suite. "Why don't you take a hot shower, and . . ."

"I don't have any clean clothes," I said, and stopped myself short. I sounded like a brat, but I couldn't stand the idea of getting clean and then putting on the same greasy things. I'd rather stay dirty.

"I'll give you something while these wash," he said, as if it were obvious.

We had an old washer and dryer set in the basement, and I hated going down there. I'd wear jeans twenty times before I washed them.

The hall was marble floored. To the left was a spacious office with a heavy dark desk and walls lined with bookshelves. Along the ceiling was dim, recessed lighting. In the bedroom, just the edge of a big white bed was visible.

I started laughing, from nerves, from embarrassment. "Who are you?" I said, and it came out snarkier than I'd meant.

Bear patted the dog's side. "Go lie down, Buddy," he said, and pointed toward a plush Oriental rug in front of the fireplace.

"I'm going to order some food," Bear said.

* * *

He left me a pair of pajamas, tags still on, from Nordstrom, and a soft T-shirt that said Utica Club. I threw my work clothes, which I would rather have thrown out, into a glass-and-black washing machine, and in the kitchen, Bear had an open box of pizza and he handed me a bottle of beer.

I took a long drink. It was amber, a little bitter. "Holy shit," I said on the other side of the swallow. "Thank you."

"My pleasure," Bear said. I bit my tongue, waiting.

"So," I said, leaving the bottle on the counter. "When can I start?" I said.

"Whenever you want," Bear said. "Right now."

I gave a nervous laugh that was just staccato syllables. "Tonight?" I said.

Bear cocked his head to the side. "What do you need?" he asked.

I felt the words jumble behind my lips, my tongue thick and clumsy. "To work," I said.

"You can work as much as you want," Bear said. He leaned against the refrigerator behind him, his eyes a little sleepy from the beer. The light was dimmed just enough to be soft and gold, like it was sunset inside.

I chewed my lip, and he pushed the pizza box toward me. The pizza smelled delicious. It was not a treat my mother afforded us often. I watched as Bear took his wallet out of the front pocket of his jeans and counted out five twenties onto the counter.

"Will this help you for now?" he said.

I swallowed. "I haven't done anything yet," I said.

He took out two more twenties. "I trust you," he said.

The money just lay on the counter between us, molded to the fold of his wallet. He pushed it closer.

"I trust you," he said again, and smiled this time.

I thought I was going to be an indentured servant forever. But he threw my clothes into the dryer, where you could watch them tumble behind a sleek glass door. With the beer empty and another one open and set right before me, I started to feel bold.

"You're going to kill me now, right?" I said, joking. "Now that I'm clean. Prepped," I said. I couldn't stop myself. I drank again and watched Bear's eyes flash. He smiled with his mouth open, showing his perfect white teeth. His hair, in its loose bun, bobbled at the back of his head.

He put his bottle on the stone counter.

"You could just leave me in one of those basements," I said. Truth was, I couldn't think of a better way to die. By someone else's doing. Giving up control in a long, delicious slide.

Bear's laugh was open and warm.

"You're much more use to me alive," he said.

*   *   *

I ended up driving home drunk. I'd certainly been drunker, but I went home from Bear's that night with my head spinning, from beer, from everything. He'd given me a tour of the house, all the empty rooms upstairs, bedroom after bedroom, a vast playroom with skylights that looked out on the velvet night sky. There were bathrooms in between with beautiful, deep, white tubs and gleaming tile. Everything needed painting. All the walls were just primer white. Dry and chalky.

I'd waited until the dryer buzzed with my clothes. "I should go," I said. I had to stop myself from staring. At his clothes, his face. I wanted to bury myself in that long hair. My insides felt tight with desire. Desire that might go somewhere and not lay unresolved, wearing away at me, like it did with Baby Jane. With Baby Jane, it felt like having a crush on the teacher who would never indulge you.

Bear popped the top off another beer and stood looking at his feet. "Call me tomorrow?" he asked, and then raised his eyes to mine.

My stomach flipped.

"Can you drive me back to my car?" I asked.

He laughed. His whole body radiated warmth, like he held nothing back.

In the deserted parking lot at the Hub, I got out, shaken down to the bones. I left before I said anything, before he said anything, before there was any awkward pause where I started to look or act desperate, or tried something stupid, like to kiss him.

Bear rolled down his window to say good-night and waited until I got into my truck, until the engine turned over and was going strong, before he pulled out.

My hands trembled on the wheel. I wasn't sure how I made it home at all, except that it was just like driving drunk, or driving a route you'd know with your eyes closed, or through a blinding snowstorm, just hoping you'll be where you belong on the other side.

I had a secret. And a hundred and forty dollars in my pocket. I gripped the wheel and had to stop myself from driving out to the twenty-four-hour Walmart to buy clothes. I'd been wearing the same T-shirts since middle school. All at once, I wanted a haircut, new shoes. I had a hunger pang for everything to be completely new and different, and a desire I'd never felt before coiled like a snake in my gut. I couldn't let my mother know. And I could never bring Bear home, or tell him about Birdie. I thought about the way he seemed to show his whole self when he offered something or laughed, and I thought I would only ever be able to offer a sliver. It felt like separate lives. Like a partition was going up, and I would have to navigate over the wall for different parts of every day. When I added Baby Jane to that, I thought I was a crazy person, popping up in these vastly different places, with different people. Showing each one of them something different. And never, ever the whole truth.

In the house, my mother was pacing. She had lit candles everywhere, tea lights in jars and pillar candles and tapers. The house was hot and smelled like a bunch of different things, sandalwood and apple, vanilla and trash.

The power was still out. And the water. I had gone to Bear's and had done nothing but take care of myself.

"Shannon," my mother breathed when I came in. "Where have you been?"

It was late. But not later than when I came home from sitting in the car with Baby Jane. If I came home at all.

She got close to my face and narrowed her eyes. "Huh," she exclaimed. "You smell like sex."

"I smell like beer," I said. "And clean clothes. Don't mistake it. Where's Bird?" I asked.

"She's asleep," my mother said. Her hair was a mess, like she'd taken it up and down twenty times while she paced.

I looked in the bedroom, and there she was, curled like a bean on my mother's bed, her arms and legs together, her face round and cool beneath that fiery hair. It was coming to an end. I could feel it. We couldn't sustain it any longer. It was like sneaking in a kitten and not telling your landlord, and then having that kitten grow up to be a full-grown lion.

Or a girl.

*   *   *

She begged me to call the power company.

"It's midnight, Mom," I said. "They're not going to do anything about it now."

"It's an emergency," she said.

"Only to you," I said.

She nodded at me, cold. "Well, I'm glad you have someplace to go," she said. She left me with an open phone book, the number for power outages circled in wobbly, hard-pressed ink.

Everything smelled sour. Someone must have opened the fridge. I wanted to throw the whole thing out.

Or burn it, I thought, and for the first time, I actually got it, the instinct to burn and run, start over. The clean sweep of a raging fire, everything reverted to ash. I just would never do it with them inside.

The line at the power company was automated, so I spoke the address, which was barely an address at all—Hidden Drive, Space 17—

and the computer voice pretended to look up the file, complete with fake papery sounds.

"Report an outage," I said into the phone.

"Fucking get over yourself," my mother said to me.

"I'm sorry," the computer voice said, "I didn't quite get that."

"Fucking hot shit," my mother said.

"Report an outage," I said louder.

I watched as Birdie walked out of the bedroom, with her pudgy bare legs and little brown feet. She rubbed her eye and sniffled.

"Go back to bed," my mother said. "Nothing's wrong."

Birdie looked at me.

I said the address again into the phone.

Birdie's eyes got wider and she looked at our mother.

"It's okay," I said to her, covering the receiver. But she waited for my mother to pick her up and carry her back to the bed, to lie with her and soothe her until she fell asleep.

"Representative," I said to the computer on the phone.

I thought about Bear's face. The way his eyes watched me when I spoke. The way he listened to everything I said, not the way some people will nod and pretend and not actually hear anything. The way his eyes smiled even when his mouth stayed straight, pink, slightly cruel. I felt the money in my pocket, guilty. But not enough to hand it over.

When I heard a person on the phone finally, I saw my mother coming back out, ready to tell me what she thought of me, and I held up one finger to stop her before she said anything.

I covered the speaker and glared. "Do you want me to take care of this?" I asked.

She turned away, and I could hear Birdie singing to herself. Something I knew she did when she was nervous.

"I have an outage," I said to the representative. "Hidden Drive, Space 17."

She repeated it to me as a question.

"Yes."

"It's been turned off for nonpayment," she said.

Shit, I thought. I knew it.

"Okay," I said. "Is there anything I can do?"

"Pay the bill," she said.

"Um, short of that?" I asked. "This is an emergency. It was shut off suddenly," I said.

"You were given notice," the woman said, "posted on your door, ten days ago, stating that continued nonpayment would result in shutoff. Because it's been shut off," she said, "the amount needs to be paid in full, plus a reconnection fee, before we can turn it back on."

"What's the total amount?" I asked. I fingered the bills in my jeans.

"Twelve forty-three fifty-seven," she said.

I heard my phone ding before it started dying.

"Twelve hundred dollars?" I said.

"Sir, the bill has not been paid since January," she said. "The note in the file says the house is vacant."

"Well, it's not vacant," I said. "We still fucking live here."

"You can make a payment online anytime," the woman said.

"Without power?" I said.

"I'm sorry, sir. Is there anything else I can help you with?"

"No," I said, and hung up as the woman was saying, "Thank you for calling National Grid."

The house was hot, and I went to the kitchen to open the window above the sink. It had been nailed shut.

"Mom," I said into the living room. I checked those windows, beside the front door, looking out to the side yard. Everything had been nailed down.

This was a new level of paranoia, even for her. I'm not sure who she thought was getting in, or maybe she was just afraid that something wild in Birdie would cause her to flee.

My mother dropped into the flowered chair that faced the TV. In the candlelight she looked both younger and older. Like she could be sixteen still, in a long skirt and bracelets, her hair down her back. Or she might be ancient. Her red hair some kind of trick she played on your eyes.

"They left a notice on the door," I said.

"I didn't see it," she said.

"Neither did I."

"You weren't even here," she said.

"Mom, I have to work."

"All night?" she said.

"Sometimes I go out."

"With who?"

"It doesn't matter," I said.

"It sure as hell does matter."

"This has to stop, Mom," I said. "You can't keep us both here. You can't patrol who I'm allowed to see or be friends with."

"What do you think you're doing?" she asked me.

"I'm just trying to live my own life," I said. "And not pay for your fucking mistakes."

"You know," she started. She had a look of confidence. It was the calm face she gave me when she knew she didn't have to yell to make a point—when she didn't swear, just spoke the truth. Her eyes were soft, her cheeks settled, her mouth relaxed. "You know that you are just as guilty as I am."

I gritted my teeth.

"It can't go on like this," I said.

"What are you going to do about it?"

"I don't know, Mom. It wasn't my decision. She's not my kid. We're your kids." I felt like I was breaking into pieces. I was afraid I was going to cry, but I was damned if I would do it in front of her.

"Doesn't matter," my mother said. "Your life was set into motion as soon as that fire hit your skin."

"Mom," I said, pleading.

"You feel that?" she asked. "That gnawing inside you that says you want to be free, that you want to live your own life? That's the fire. It's trying to burn its way out."

ELEVEN: KATERI

WEDNESDAY, OCTOBER 18

Shannon asks her if he's under arrest. He has his head down, his hoodie pulled tight around his neck like a cowl. He looks at his feet like a kid who has always been in trouble. Not a kid who's nervous. A kid who's been here before.

"Am I under arrest?" he says.

"No," Kateri says.

"Can I come tomorrow? After work?" he asks.

She hems. He gave her the DNA sample and showed up when she asked him to.

"I will," he says. "I just . . ." He breathes out hard, blowing through his nose.

"It's a lot," Kateri says. "I'm sorry."

"I need to . . . I don't know," he says.

"It's okay," Kateri says. "You need to process. You need to grieve, and that's going to take longer than any interrogation or arrest."

His eyes dart to the side, wet, and he looks off in the distance, behind the station, to the tall trees that have recently gone bright crimson red.

"Do you have a place to stay?" Kateri asks.

"Yes," he says.

"You can't go back to the house on Hidden Drive," she says. "It's a crime scene."

He swallows and then rubs his jaw. "Okay," he says.

"You also can't leave the county. Or the state."

He huffs, annoyed.

"How long do you work?"

"Until three," he says.

"Can you come in at three thirty tomorrow?"

"Sure."

She puts her hand on his upper arm, padded with the sweat shirt and flannel underneath it. He feels willowy, younger than nineteen. She fights the urge to comfort him further.

"If you don't come," she says.

"I'll come," he says.

"If you don't," she says, "that'll read as suspicious. And I'll have more of a reason to pursue an arrest."

"I know," he says.

She holds out her hand, businesslike, and he shakes it, more confident than she might have expected. "I'll see you tomorrow," she tells him.

*   *   *

The day has felt like two days, starting in the predawn with the body in the swamp, the press conference, her trip to the morgue. At home, she stands under a hot shower for a long time, allows herself the luxury of a sweet-smelling, oily body wash, and wraps her hair in a yellow towel after. She's dressed and drinking tea when Hurt calls.

"I thought you were meeting me," he says.

She looks at the time on her phone. She thought he might have forgotten.

"I updated the investigation room," he says. "And I have some details, if you want them."

He's still in the office. She feels a pang of guilt at having gone home, showered, begun to relax. She squeezes the towel at the base of her neck and then again at the top of her head.

"I can meet you," she says. "It's going to take a bit."

He breathes into the phone in a way that makes her think he's smiling. "You don't have to put on makeup for me, Fisher," he says.

"I'll meet you at Sweetwater," she says, droll, and hangs up.

The Sweetwater is the nicest of three bars in Spring Falls. It's a narrow brick building from the 1800s and feels like it belongs in a bigger city. She's gone there before, when she first started, with Hurt and Whittaker for beer and to see if she could throw darts. She can. That night she paced herself very slowly with beer. She hadn't even felt the beginning of a buzz by the time they all left.

It's a cold night. She dries her hair as best she can with limited time, smoothing it out with a paddle brush and the hair dryer, but it's still wet underneath. Outside, she tries to ignore it, but she's sure she saw flurries, floating, not landing in the air outside the bar. The bartender makes her a dark Manhattan, with two deep-red Luxardo cherries. When she takes that first sip, she thinks, I'm back at zero, the way AA teaches you. There's no trophy for the days in between.

Hurt is already there, drinking a gin and tonic. He tries not to look at her regular clothes, her V-neck sweater and jeans, her hair, down and loose and shining. She had not put on makeup. So he looks, and doesn't look, or looks without meeting her eye, trying not to be detected. In the dark bar, the black sweater does a decent job of hiding the fullness of her breasts, but it's not loose. He looks down at his drink and sips.

"Water in the lungs," he says, pulling them back into focus. The dead cop. The missing girl.

The drink immediately makes her face warm, which she's sure shows in pink spots on her cheeks. "He went in alive," she answers.

"Diaz called with cause of death—drowning," Hurt says. "The parents had to identify," he adds.

On the TV behind the bar, a baseball game plays, muted. The cherries in her glass knock around at the bottom like a pair of kids' play balls.

"Probably right after you left with Jenkins," he says. "Long day," he says. "It's why Diaz gets a BMW."

Kateri laughs, not expecting the bitterness from Hurt. "She likes you," she says.

He looks her in the eye. "She tolerates me," he says. "From what I hear, she likes them even younger." He laughs.

So Kateri puts her hand on Hurt's arm. "Meet me at the morgue, Joel," she singsongs, and he swats her away.

It's a small department. Chances are high that they've had some encounter, even though Diaz is fifteen or twenty years older than he is. It happens in small towns. But Kateri doesn't know anything at all about Hurt's personal life. She's not even sure he's straight.

"How'd you leave it with the kid?" Hurt asks.

"He's coming in tomorrow for questioning. He submitted DNA today."

"Good," Hurt says.

"Anything new in the woods?"

He shakes his head but answers. "Burnt wood," he says, "that shows traces of accelerant. Nothing we didn't expect. No further remains."

Kateri puts her fingertips to her lips. She and Hurt sit elbow to elbow, not facing each other, both looking at the line of bottles behind the bar, where a row of tiny white lights behind them illuminates them red, amber, gold. The slow-moving ball game continues on TV. She has teased Hurt before about gin and tonic, that it's a summer drink and this is a winter place. But it's the only thing he likes. She likes the way gin smells but not the way it tastes. On Hurt, the smell is fresh. Something clean, antiseptic.

When the bartender comes back down, she orders another. And so does Hurt.

"Whoever killed her . . ." Hurt says, starting a fresh drink. She almost stops him, but she lets him go, lets him say what it is they've been dancing around. "Knew about the girl," he says. "And took the girl."

She nods into her drink.

"Both of those murders hinge on that kid." He points his finger down on the bar. "So, who knows about her?"

"Shannon," Kateri says. "And maybe people that Shannon knows."

"Jesus Christ," Hurt says. "I hate when there's a kid involved." The way he sits with his arms on the bar, when he says it he wags his hands open and his thumb accidentally touches Kateri's pinkie, and it's a sudden shock, a pop of electricity. Like dragging your feet and touching the doorknob.

"Sorry," he says.

"No worries," Kateri says.

* * *

Whiskey has always been her drink of choice. She's gone through other phases: cheap vodka, beer when she was younger, she's tried wine. What she loves is good American bourbon.

After, Hurt walks her to her car. She's barely eaten all day, and she probably shouldn't drive, but it's too far to walk back to her apartment outside of town. She tells herself there's no one even on the road in Spring Falls. The closest cabs are Mount Snow. There's no Uber in a town this small.

She leans against the side of her car, parked next to Hurt's, and takes a cigarette from her purse. Hurt looks amused.

"You want one?" she asks after she lights it. She loves the first smell of a lit cigarette, the paper burn, the raisiny sweetness of the tobacco.

"No," he says. He laughs and looks at his feet.

"Did you ever?" she asks.

"Sure," he says.

"When'd you quit?"

He looks at the sky, hands in his pockets. "Fifteen years ago," he says.

Tonight, the sky is extra blue black, thick with stars that appear only in the country dark. Kateri feels loose in all her joints.

"You want me to give you a ride?" Hurt asks.

"We both had three drinks," she says, and thinks, he knows about the accident. He knows why I'm here.

He shrugs. "I outweigh you," he says.

Kateri laughs. "No, you don't," she says. There is no way Hurt is any more than one fifty, and Kateri is a solid one forty. He is built like a swimmer, lean, like a runner with bird bones.

"I'm a guy?" he offers.

"A dainty guy," Kateri says. She tilts her head and finishes her smoke, and the light from the parking lot shines on the underside of her chin, and she sees that Hurt notices it. The slice, the scar. The place where she almost lost her own head.

"Come on," Hurt says. He looks like he wants to touch it, and she wants to let him.

"Do you think I'm drunker than you?" she asks. She breathes in the cold air after the cigarette, slow, blows it out through her lips.

"No."

She stares at him for a minute. Part of her wants to break open, to ask him, Do you want to see it? The mark on me from my mistakes? Part of her wants to push him at the shoulders and watch him windmill to catch his balance. Part of her wants to kiss him.

She looks at his mouth when he relaxes it, the release of his lips and his jaw. He looks beyond her.

"Joel," she says, half reprimanding, half taunting.

"Just text me when you're home, okay?" he says.

She drives a little too slow, and she watches every tree, every peripheral movement for deer jetting out in front of her car. She thinks she hasn't had that much. She thinks the Subaru is a safer car. For a length of road right before her apartment, she closes her eyes and lets the road go, feels like flying, like sinking, like waiting to hit the ground.

It's twelve thirty when she falls into bed, still in her clothes. She wakes once, predawn, when the sky is still dark but the trees outside her window are loud with bird noise. It's then that she remembers Joel Hurt's warning and texts him—*home*—but sees above that that she sent him a text at one fifteen that reads *you don't know anything about me.*

He hasn't answered either of them. She rolls onto her back, wide awake, her mouth dry, her pulse quickened, and thinks *back at zero*, and in her mind she sees the speedometer, its needle lowered all the way to the left. Slow enough to stop.

TWELVE: SHANNON

TUESDAY, SEPTEMBER 12

Baby Jane was gone. After I slept on his bed, my head leaning against his bony shoulder, he had disappeared. I didn't see him at the car, and he didn't appear to be home. There were pull shades in the house, all of them tightly drawn. I tried to peek in the back door, into the dark kitchen, but I couldn't see anything at all, and none of the lights were on.

I thought, he could be dead in there.

Could he die that quickly?

I leaned my head against the glass. It felt empty. That was the worst part.

* * *

I had to keep working. I couldn't afford not to. I tried calculating in my head how long it would take me to make $1,300 to pay just the electricity and heat, and felt sick. It was too long. The refrigerator was festering. The toilet had been flushed with a bucket of water, and we had to go out to the public restroom most of the time. I hadn't showered since Bear's. No one else had washed at all.

If anyone found out, they would take Birdie. If they auctioned the house from underneath us, they would take Birdie.

111

Part of me struggled to believe it might be the best thing for her. But it wasn't what I wanted.

They would send my mother to rehab, or to jail, for keeping Birdie captive. They could send me to jail. I wouldn't know how to fight it. My mother, however, had a talent for appearing completely normal in the face of authority. And if neither of us went to jail, we'd be stuck with each other, without a house. And without Bird.

*   *   *

The hill on Fountain Street was so steep I had to get off and walk my bike. I'd tried for the truck, but I didn't feel like fighting. I just wanted to get out. The first thing my mother said was, "What if I need it?" It wasn't an argument worth having. By the time I got to the top of Fountain, my back was sweaty but my face was chapped and cold, my hands dry and red. The house came into view like a giant looming hotel.

I felt like a bomb that was about to go off. I leaned over on the bike in the driveway, the Land Rover parked in the middle spot again, the field out back just a black sea of cattails and brush. I blew out to catch my breath. Second shift, I thought. I hoped there was enough to do to warrant more pay. I kept the money in my pocket. It was the safest place.

Inside, Buddy bounded on me in the hallway. Licked my face, pushed his paws into my arms, jumped on his back feet. Bear nodded his head toward the shower. "Before you get started," he said.

It caught me off guard. I'd always had a job where you had to shower after, a job that made you dirty, where you came home tired and sore and sweaty and smelling like grease or smoke.

He was clearly in the other camp. The shower-before-work crowd. A job where you flexed nothing but your influence.

"If you want," he said, when I didn't answer.

"I left the clothes you gave me at home," I said.

"I have more," Bear said. He grinned.

I stood outside the big white square of the bathroom, my shoulders low. Exhausted, nervous, shamed. I felt so dirty that I needed to be cleaned before I could get dirty again. Like I needed to be decontaminated just to be here.

Bear leaned on the doorjamb, waiting. I wondered if he would stay to watch me. There were clean white towels rolled into a basket on a table. Then he said, "Are you telling me that a hot shower and a cold beer at the end of a workday doesn't sound good?"

"No," I said. "It definitely does. It's just also the beginning of work." I laughed a little.

"It's just prep work," he said.

He shut the door behind him when he left. And when I locked it, I covered my face and thought, I'm never going to get paid. I'm going to keep him company, I thought, and never actually catch up. I looked in the mirror and then opened the medicine cabinet, the way I had at Baby Jane's, but I was acutely afraid of getting caught, of things falling out, of a trap having been laid for me. There was aspirin. Aleve. Hydrogen peroxide. Allergy tablets. Rubbing alcohol. Q-tips. Tom's of Maine natural toothpaste in cinnamon. A silver razor blade and a tube of shaving cream. There were no drugs.

I used the shampoo that was in the shower, which smelled like mint, and a body wash that was a light clear green and smelled like rosemary. The towels were as big as bedsheets, deep and soft. I thought about walking out naked, but on the bed, Bear had left me a pair of forest-green corduroys that were big in the waist and too long, a plain gray T-shirt, and a flannel that, when I checked the tag, was blended with cashmere.

Bear was on his knees in the living room, getting a fire started, blowing with the hand bellows into the big fireplace. Outside the giant windows, it had started to rain, the sky a deep slate gray and the panes slashed with sideways drops.

I didn't want to go home.

I wanted to disappear. Run as fast as I could without looking back. Change my name. Become something else. Become this. I wished he was even farther away. That we were out of Spring Falls. Out of state even.

I wished there was a way to check on Birdie. She'd been fine when I stopped home. Bored, hungry. I made her a peanut butter sandwich, took her to the bathroom, and put her on the bed with my mother, who was sweaty and sleeping, with a book and a few dolls. Birdie gave me a look.

"Why do you get to go somewhere?" she asked.

I kissed her forehead. "I have to take care of some things," I said, which was true. "And I'm an adult," I said. She wrinkled her nose at me.

If my mother died, I thought, would they let me keep her? Could we do it? The two of us alone? It already felt that way sometimes. I didn't want a kid, though. I wanted what was right in front of me.

"Better?" Bear asked, jarring me out of my downward spiral of thoughts.

"Sure," I said. I sank into the understuffed leather couch, which felt like a cocoon I never wanted to get out of. Buddy made himself a space next to me, curled into a spot that was too small for his bulky body but that he insisted on getting into, grunting, turning circles, until he finally settled with a low groan and his chin on my thigh.

Bear came and sat facing me, his leg crooked on the seat, one foot dangling over the edge.

"Tell me what's going on," he said.

The fire cracked and hissed, a roar of energy rising up the chimney. The flannel already smelled like wood smoke and something else, spicy and exotic, like maybe Bear had worn it and not washed it when he left it for me.

He waited, and I felt a nervous laughter creeping up on me. It was too much. Way too much to explain.

THE WATCHER

There was maybe a hairbreadth between his knee and mine. In that space, a field of electricity. I wondered if he'd pick up my hand again. It was hard to look him in the eye, and he was watching very intently.

"Um," I said, and laughed a little. "Sorry, bad habit," I said.

"I've noticed," Bear said.

"We're losing our house for taxes," I said, stroking Buddy's head, just to have someplace else to look. "And the power and the water are turned off right now."

"Is it just you and your mom?" he asked.

I looked out the window. It was dark and wet out there, and nothing was visible in the trees or the sky. Like there was no world at all out there.

I couldn't lie. I'd been lying for five years, and this was the first time I'd felt like I had something to lose. I'd lied to everyone. People in town. People at school, work, the grocery store. People who knew my mom. We never took Birdie out. She'd never been anywhere. Not to a doctor, never in the car. There was no record of her having been born. No hospital stay or midwife. No birth certificate. She spent time outside, but she never ever left my mother's view. And if my mother had to leave her, on the rare occasion she went to the bank or to buy more drugs, she locked her in the closet with a dim lamp and a coloring book. It was the only safe place for her.

"No," I said to Bear. It felt like a dam giving way. There was something—love, guilt, relief—flooding from my heart.

"Who else?" he said.

"My baby sister," I said. It came out in a whisper. I had never said it to another person other than my mom. The baby. Birdie. My sister.

"Your mom doesn't work?" Bear asked. The revelation of the baby was no big deal to him. Lots of people have siblings.

"No," I said. "My mom's on disability. She has been, since I was little."

"Did she have an accident?" Bear asked.

"We had a fire," I said. "She was injured getting out."

"Yikes," Bear said.

"And then she went on pain meds," I said. "And never stopped."

He nodded in silent understanding.

"And your dad?" he asked.

"Started the fire," I said.

I shrugged. I'd practiced my whole life at looking tough, at appearing as though I just didn't give a fuck about the whole thing.

"Where's he?" Bear asked.

"Dannemora," I said.

"Did anyone die?" Bear asked.

"No."

"Were you there?"

"Yeah."

Silence. Then, "He tried to kill you both," he said.

I nodded.

"And your sister?" Bear asked. It felt like a blessing from his mouth, just the word *sister*, said aloud, in recognition.

"She's five," I said. "She's not his." I couldn't say any more. I thought this flood of truth was going to wash me away and kill me.

He waited while I swallowed it down, while I didn't elaborate. In the dimmed light, his eyes took on a gold glow.

"How old are you?" he asked.

"Nineteen," I answered without thinking, and then wished I'd said twenty-one.

"That's a lot," Bear said.

I looked into the fire, at the flame closest to the wood, the hottest blaze, like white gold. I listened to the rush of it, burning up.

"I don't have a choice," I said.

Bear frowned. "Everyone has choices," he said.

* * *

I remembered, on the way home, how much I had wanted to tell people about her, not because I wanted to threaten my mother's safety but because I was in awe of her. I wanted to walk her around town, show her off, take her to the farmers' market and out for pancakes. She should go trick-or-treating and see the Christmas tree in the middle of town. Not just the black-and-white surveillance video on the huge screen in our living room. Not just my mother's bed. And never the inside of a closet.

I needed to make these things happen. For her. And for me.

It didn't feel like a choice.

THIRTEEN: KATERI

THURSDAY, OCTOBER 19

It's not like TV. Nothing in her career has been like TV—not her cubicle in Syracuse, not the slow drive through the rural suburbs at night in a patrol car, not what's happening now in this remote mountain town, in an unassuming brick building with a small parking lot. In some other districts up north, the police stations are no more than a trailer.

The room where she questions Shannon Jenkins is an office, with a cheap desk from Walmart and a blue overstuffed chair, the kind you'd find in an old lady's living room. There's a lamp, and a bookcase filled with odd reference books: a dictionary, a thesaurus, a set of World Book Encyclopedias from the 1960s, three or four different Bibles, and one Reader's Digest Condensed that includes *The Count of Monte Cristo*.

Kateri leans on the edge of the desk and lets Shannon sit in the blue chair. He juts his head toward the book and says, "Funny."

"Is it?" Kateri asks. "I haven't read it."

"It's about prison escape," Shannon says, dry, as if the joke is obvious.

"Can I get you something?" Kateri asks. "Water? Coffee?"

He still has his shoulders hunched the way he did in the parking lot yesterday, a different sweat shirt on today with the hood closed up underneath his chin. She wonders if this is a normal posture for him. Or what he's hiding.

She tries again. "Pepsi?" she asks.

He rubs his eye. "I'll take a Pepsi if you have it," he says.

She opens a small fridge next to the desk and pulls out a cold bottle.

"I keep my own stash," she says. "They occasionally save my life."

Like today, she thinks. She has had a steady intake of Pepsi and Excedrin. Earlier, she ate a bag of potato chips from the vending machine, which she never does. But she's been fighting sweaty nausea all day.

Shannon drinks, and his foot bounces.

"How long have you lived here?" Kateri asks him.

"My whole life," he says, with the tragic flair of a teenager.

"Always in the house on Hidden Drive?" she asks.

"No," he says. "We used to live in a farmhouse on Cemetery Road."

She knows the road. Her apartment is on Cemetery Road, a road that does indeed end in a large nineteenth-century graveyard. The same goes for Mill Road, which leads to the empty hulk of the former paper mill, and Mount Snow Road, which leads to Mount Snow.

She has the information about the fire from his father's file. The house was a total loss, the perimeter doused with accelerant, the framework old, dry wood. It went up fast and hot, and it was a miracle anyone got out. But she asks, "When did you move?"

"When I was three," Shannon says. "After it burned down."

"That's quite traumatic," Kateri says. "Do you remember it?"

"You know all this, right?" he says. "You can see it in the file."

"I know what's in the file," she says. "Since then, it's been just you and your mother." She looks down at the folder. "Pearl Jenkins, in the house on Hidden Drive."

"Yes," he says.

"That house originally belonged to your grandparents?" Kateri asks.

"Yes."

"I grew up with my grandparents," Kateri says.

"Lucky you," Shannon answers. "Does your mother still live there?" he asks.

"No," she says. "My mother is dead. She died when I was sixteen," she says.

"How?" he asks, without offering condolences. She doesn't expect it. In fact, she's more comfortable forgoing it.

"She died of a drug overdose," Kateri says.

"I'm sorry," he says.

She thanks him and looks back at the file. "When your grandfather died, your mother inherited the house, is that correct?"

"Yes."

"And the ownership of the house has recently been transferred to you," she says.

He fights rolling his eyes. "Yes," he says. "I'm trying to catch up on bills."

She switches gears. "Your dad is Park Jenkins," she says.

"Yep."

"Your mother's maiden name is also Jenkins."

"They're second cousins," Shannon says.

"Are there other Jenkins around here?"

"No," he says. "In Vermont. Both my mom and dad have a bunch of brothers and half brothers. They're all pieces of shit," Shannon says.

"How so?"

"Poor," he says. "Stupid. Incarcerated. Dopeheads."

"You're not stupid," she says.

"Thanks," he says, with a sarcastic lilt.

"When's the last time you saw Park Jenkins?"

"Two years ago," he says.

"Where?"

"I visited him in prison."

"Had you visited him before?"

"No," he says. "That's the only time. I couldn't remember him at all," Shannon explains. "I just . . . wanted to see what he was like."

"And what was he like?" she asks.

"A disappointment," Shannon says. "He barely talked to me or looked at me."

Kateri nods. "Has your mother been to see him at all?"

"No," he says.

"Never," Kateri says.

"No."

"So there is no chance Park Jenkins is your sister's father," she says.

She watches his entire body jump, and then he closes his eyes and his face grows ashen.

"I'm sorry?" he asks when he opens his eyes.

"Your sister," Kateri says. "Sparrow Annie. Birdie."

"I don't—" he says, and then stops. He takes a minute to breathe, slowing himself down. He starts to cough, and when he goes to take a drink, Kateri sees what he has been guarding with his hood: a large bluish bruise around his neck. "I don't know what you're talking about," he says.

"We can come back to that," Kateri says. "Do you know of anyone who would want to hurt your mother?"

He chews his lip, looking down into his lap. He sits slumped into the chair, spine curved. "No," he says. Then, "My father."

"Does your father know about your sister?" Kateri asks.

"No," Shannon says.

She watches his lips purse, his jaw tight.

"Why did your mother run surveillance cameras outside the house?" Kateri asks.

"She was afraid," Shannon says.

"Of?"

"I can't answer these questions," he says. "I don't know."

"You lived there. Was she afraid of people finding out about Birdie?"

He puts both his hands to his forehead and rubs vigorously.

"Let me say this," Kateri says. "You are not necessarily in trouble. But I need all the information I can get from you to secure your safety."

He breathes raggedly through open lips.

"Your mother is dead and your sister is missing, and you reported neither of those things."

"I didn't know she was dead," he says. "I haven't been there."

"How long had you gone without seeing her or talking to her?"

"I don't know," he says. "A few days? A week maybe. I got the power back on, and then it was okay. It was fine there."

She allows him to sit in silence, uncomfortable, waiting for him to say more. He bounces his knee, he drinks the Pepsi, he fidgets with something in his pocket. Kateri has moved from Pepsi to water and drinks from a large liter bottle. She's about due for more Excedrin.

"Where is she?" Shannon says then.

"I might ask you," Kateri says.

"I don't have her," he says.

"Where are you staying?"

"I don't know why that matters," he says.

Kateri shrugs, cool. "In case I have a warrant to search for a missing child or a murder weapon," she says.

"Am I a suspect?" he asks, shrill.

She waits, quiet, while he shifts in the chair, sitting up straighter and then rocking back and forth.

"You are not not a suspect," she says. "Of course, we start with those closest to the victim."

"Why?" he cries.

"If there are people who have reasons to want to hurt or eliminate your mother," Kateri says, "wouldn't you be among them?"

"Why?" he says again.

She takes another drink and rests a minute. "Because she forced you to keep her secret," Kateri says. "Because you wanted the girl for yourself."

"Oh my God," Shannon mutters.

She notices that what he toys with in his pocket is a lighter, that he flicks it just short of lighting it, the spark bright inside the fabric. He has no record for fire starting. But she wonders if it has been a habit for him, something that has brought him perverse, dangerous pleasure, a release.

She asks if he'd like a smoke break.

He pats his shirt pocket underneath the hoodie. "Can I?" he asks.

"You are not being held," Kateri says. "Of course."

She walks him down the hall to a side door where he can smoke in the parking lot. She notices, standing next to him, how slender he is, how narrow across the back, with willowy arms and legs that he has hidden inside clothing.

"Were you going out of town?" she asks him.

"No," he says. "Why?"

"The firewood," Kateri says. "I thought maybe you were going camping."

Shannon's lip curls in a bitter smile, showing his teeth. "I've pretty much been camping," he says, "in my own house. Camping is not vacation to me."

"I thought you weren't staying at the house," Kateri says.

"I was," he snaps. "And it was without electricity or water."

"They were both on when I was there," she says.

"I fixed it," he says.

"Where are you staying?"

"With friends," he says. He opens the heavy door and lets in a blinding block of light. He steps into the parking lot with the cigarette already on his lip.

"I'm going to need to know," she says. She's afraid of losing him.

*　*　*

She overhears only part of his phone call. "I don't know," he says, more than once. And then, "I will." She waits on the other side of the door, grateful for a dim place, her foot holding the door propped so it won't lock him out. Hurt sees her like that and gives her a look.

"Smoke break," she says.

"For you?" he asks, shocked, as if she's smoking inside out a cracked door.

"No," she says, annoyed. "For Jenkins."

"He's out in the parking lot?" Hurt asks. When Kateri nods, he adds, "Hope he doesn't run." He looks down at Kateri's shoes.

Shannon doesn't. He comes back in, cowed and nervous, and Kateri starts right in on him, without giving him too much time to think.

"Who is your sister's father?" she asks.

"I don't know," he says.

"No idea," Kateri says. "Your mother wasn't dating, didn't have people around?"

"No," he says, rolling his eyes. "She barely leaves the house."

"Someone in town?" Kateri asks.

His face goes blank, his mouth a straight line. "Do you know any black men in Spring Falls?" he asks.

But Kateri shrugs, nonchalant. "I don't know that she's black," she says, cautious, but it's clear from Birdie's hair and even the tint of her light skin that she is likely mixed race.

Shannon laughs. "Have you looked at her?" he says. "Have you looked at me and my mom?"

"But you don't know who," Kateri says.

"No," he says.

"When did your mother put up the cameras?" Kateri asks.

"After Birdie was born," he says.

"How long after?"

"The spring," he says.

"Is it possible that she's afraid of your sister's father?"

"It's possible," he says. "But he's not the one who tried to kill her."

"Are you afraid of your dad?" Kateri asks.

"No," he says.

Kateri tips her head. "He tried to kill you too."

"It's not the same," he says.

"How so?"

"I wasn't the target," he says. "I was just there."

"Do you know that for sure?" Kateri asks. "You said you don't remember."

His face closes, gray.

Hurt knocks and comes in before Kateri says it's okay. He carries a file folder and a legal pad.

"Shannon Jenkins," she says, "This is my partner, Detective Joel Hurt."

Shannon nods.

Hurt pulls a paper out of the file folder with a phone number printed on it and nothing else.

"Do you know this number?" Hurt asks.

Shannon's cheeks pale. "No," he says.

"Not at all?"

He won't take the paper from Hurt. "No," he says, and he adjusts the hood around his neck. "Whose is it?" he asks.

"It's the number that called nine-one-one," Hurt says, "the day the crime scene was first investigated." Hurt waits. His tactic is more minimalist that Kateri's, which is why they take turns. She builds a narrative. He cuts through it. "It's an untraceable track phone," Hurt tells him. "And it's been disconnected."

"Do you have a cell phone?" Kateri asks.

"You just saw me use it," Shannon says.

"What kind is it?" Hurt asks.

"An untraceable track phone," Shannon says, edgy. He pulls it from his pocket. "We don't have a landline at the house," he says, "and my mother doesn't trust cell phones. This is all I have," he says. "It's forty bucks a month."

He holds it out, an old-style Samsung with a slide-out keyboard.

"How long have you had it?" Kateri asks.

Shannon shrugs. "A year?" he says. "I had a different one before, but I broke it." His foot bounces, and he slouches in the chair.

"How'd you break it?" Hurt asks.

"In a murderous rage," Shannon says, his face unbreakable. He stares at Hurt.

"Is this funny to you?" Hurt asks.

"Not at all," Shannon says.

"Look," Hurt says like he's leveling with him. "Don't take this the wrong way." Shannon huffs. "But you look clean," Hurt says. "You look pretty well cared for and put-together. Not like someone who was living without water or electricity."

Shannon's face is clean-shaven; his hair is clean, shiny, and well cut. His clothes are fresh and neat. He smells like laundry and men's deodorant and, now, like a lingering cigarette.

"Do you have a girlfriend?" Kateri asks.

"Ha," he says with one sharp laugh. "No."

She doesn't know what to make of his reaction, but she needs to find out who has taken him in, or at the very least, who he has been seen with recently.

Hurt leans against the wall. "Do you know Craig O'Neil?" he asks.

"No," Shannon says.

"You didn't go to high school together?" Kateri asks.

"I mean, sure," Shannon says, "but he was older. Chris O'Neil was in my grade."

"You said you didn't know the O'Neils," Hurt says.

"I didn't," Shannon says. "Just because we went to school together doesn't mean I know them."

"Someone bound Craig O'Neil and put him in the trunk of his own car," Hurt says. "The same day that your sister was taken from the hospital."

"When was my sister in the hospital?" Shannon asks.

Kateri holds up her hand to Hurt.

"Why was she in the hospital?"

Then she holds up her hand to Shannon. "Excuse us a moment," she says, and nods at Hurt to the hall outside the room.

Outside, she leans her head against the tile wall, the cool ceramic on her skin.

"He's admitted the sister," Hurt says.

"Yes," she says. "But we haven't gotten very far."

"How much of it do you think is an act?" Hurt asks.

"I can't tell," Kateri says, turning her face sideways.

Hurt smirks. "How do you feel?" he says. "Miss You Don't Outweigh Me?"

"Shut up," she says, and breathes slowly, warding off panic.

"Rattle him," Hurt says. "He'll spill. And let me know if you want help."

They go back in, and Hurt takes the sheet with the phone number from the desk and slides it back into the folder. "Whose dog?" he asks.

"Whose dog what?" Shannon repeats.

"Whose dog have you been riding around with?" Hurt asks.

Shannon looks uncomfortable with the prospect of being watched. "My dog," he says. "Why?"

"Did you have a dog before?" Hurt asks.

"I just got him," he says.

"Where?"

"From a friend," Shannon says.

"Which friend?" Hurt says.

Shannon stumbles. "A kid I know in Mount Snow," he says.

"What's the kid's name?" Hurt says.

"Jake," Shannon says.

"Jake what?"

"Tucker," Shannon says. His whole demeanor has changed since Hurt came in. He cracks all his knuckles and stretches his neck.

Hurt writes it down. "Okay," he says. "I'll be back," he says to Kateri.

She hears Shannon breathe out slowly, blowing through pursed lips, and he leans over like he's winded from running.

"Am I in trouble for having a dog?" he asks once Hurt is gone.

Kateri shakes her head slightly. "Just dotting the *is*," she tells him, but she watches him closely. She guesses he's told her only a small fraction of what he does know. And what he knows probably includes who killed his mother, if he didn't do it himself. With Hurt gone, his shoulders unhunch from his ears and he looks at Kateri like a frightened animal.

"Did you see her in the hospital?" he asks.

"Yes," Kateri says.

His eyes dart, searching, nervous.

"Did you hurt her?" Kateri asks.

His face drops, not fearful, not sly, not a bit sarcastic. "I would never," he says.

"She was fine," Kateri says. "She was physically unharmed."

His hands drop to his sides. He looks exhausted, from work, from the interrogation, from keeping a secret for so long.

"You're not being held," she reminds him.

"I'm not," he repeats.

"No. You're free to go. While we appreciate your cooperation," she says, "you're not under arrest."

"Yet," Shannon says.

Kateri tilts her head and lets him finish.

"You're just waiting for me to say the wrong thing," he says.

"I'm waiting for you to tell the truth," Kateri says.

* * *

Hurt leans his head in after she lets Shannon go. "Kid gone?" he asks.

She nods.

"Come look at this," he says, and disappears from her doorway, down to his own office.

He has a new plant. Weird, because his office has always looked like he is either just moving in or about to move out. Nothing on the walls but a paper calendar, no framed pictures on his desk or his shelves.

"It's nice," Kateri says.

"Not the plant," Hurt says. He points to his monitor.

He has a file open on a recent parolee, Michael Bartholomew Jane, released from Clinton Correctional in May. His parole officer is listed as Robert Ferris, in the Mount Snow office, and his address is given as Mill Road in Spring Falls.

"Recently released," Kateri says, leaning. She's aware that her blouse brushes against Hurt, and she backs away, but it makes it harder for her to see. She squints. "What was he in for?"

"Fraud," Hurt says. He scrolls down quickly, and the blur makes her faintly nauseated. "Racketeering," he says.

Kateri looks again at the file photo. A thin man with dark hair and deep-set blue eyes, a bluish five o'clock shadow, a sharp jaw. He holds his mouth in a hard, straight line, and still his lips are soft looking, pinkish.

"Any indication of arson?" Kateri asks. When she closes her eyes, she sees the pieces of bones, smoked and broken, splayed on Dr. Diaz's exam table. "There was accelerant on the bones," she says.

"I left a message with Ferris," Hurt says. "I'll ask." Then he looks up at her, his fingers still on the touch pad of the laptop. "This address is less than a mile from the Jenkins property," Hurt says.

Kateri's scalp prickles. "Do we have a phone number for him?"

"No," Hurt says. "But I bet it's an unregistered track phone."

FOURTEEN: SHANNON

FRIDAY, SEPTEMBER 15

I couldn't quite look Terri in the eye when I told her, "I can't stay at work today." I hunched up my shoulders to my ears, and when Terri noticed, she put her hand on my back, rubbing in a circle. Terri was good to me. She knew my mom, and for a brief time had dated Park. Her kids were younger than me.

"What's the problem?" she asked me.

"I have to take my mother to a lawyer," I said.

"Today?"

"Yes, at one."

They'd all gone to Jefferson High School together. We never ever talked about it. Not Park, not school, not the fire. But she had escaped what my mother had not. Normal. Unscathed.

She peered into the kitchen through the round window on the swinging door. "I'll tell Junior," she said. "Go if you have to. We'll deal."

* * *

It was a decent-weather day, and there were people at the park with dogs and babies, birders with spyglasses, runners looking at the changing leaves. I tried to see what anyone might see. Why we would try to save this place. The weathered siding. The slanted porch. The camp chairs with cigarette holes burned into them. Beer cans around the fire pit. I hoped my mother and sister weren't outside. I was glad it wasn't summer. Sometimes my mother let Birdie run around naked, in sneakers, in the hot weather. She was a miracle, I thought. I had never felt either that sturdy or that free.

Inside, I found Birdie at the kitchen table, doing letters, a whole line of cursive capital Bs in a row. Her tongue licking her top lip.

"Where's Mom?" I asked her, but then my mother came down the hall in an orange T-shirt that was too small and a long hippie skirt, barefoot. She was dirty—no one had washed much without water—but her hair was braided to one side, and it didn't look terrible.

"Mom," I said, trying to sound light and open. "We can fix the power."

"Oh, Shannon," she said, and clapped her hands together in thanks. I wondered if we looked alike. I wondered if this was what I was headed for, fifteen, twenty years down the road, barefoot in a dirty house, with a tattoo on my brow.

"You have to come downtown," I said.

She looked at Birdie and then paced to the window to look out.

"Are you out of your fucking mind? Is someone here?"

"It's just me. But we need to take care of the house. I need you to put it in my name so I can have everything turned back on."

"Oh," she said, and her arms dropped. "I get it." Her face had a sweaty film that said she was an hour or so out of a high. "I'm just going to put you in charge," she said.

"Only on paper," I said. I heard Birdie scrape her chair on the floor and come to look out the window, but I held her back at arm's length.

"What are we going to do," she said to me, nodding at Birdie, "once it's all yours?"

I wanted to remind her that she'd been threatening to run for years.

"It's just so I can take over the payments," I said.

"You want to make the payments?" she said. "Make them. It's about time you contributed."

I bit my tongue. I had been doing everything for her for years. "They need the payment in full," I said. "I can't pay that much. If I put the house in my name, I can start over again at zero. I can fix this," I said.

She took the edge of her skirt, which had been dragging on the floor and in the dirt outside, and rubbed it on her face, taking away some of the shine.

"What am I supposed to do with her?" she whispered to me.

"I don't know," I said. "What you always do with her."

* * *

I wanted to die, driving the truck with my mother riding in the passenger seat. I thought this had become the picture of my life, me driving a shitty vehicle that wasn't even mine, that sat a little crooked on its axle, like you were sliding off a hill, driving my mother around to appointments I couldn't pay for. I was afraid to open the windows, and afraid not to because I wasn't sure which was worse for the smell of her damp, unwashed body: blowing it around, or closing it up with the vents on. I stared straight ahead, and she sat like a pouting child, her arms crossed over her chest. I fidgeted with my fingers on the steering wheel the whole way there, picking at my nails, pulling off the cuticles until a fat bead of red blood appeared.

There was a paralegal at the table with Dan Sullivan, a young woman who smiled sweetly, but my mother would look only at a fixed point on the wall and refused to make eye contact or acknowledge anyone in the room. We were twenty-five minutes late.

Dan took the papers one by one from the paralegal and explained them to my mother slowly, in simple language.

"I'm not fucking retarded," my mother said. Her brow was dripping, and she snatched a box of tissues from the middle of the table and blotted at her face.

"I just need to make sure that you're in full understanding of each one of these," Dan said, and she signed what was in front of her.

"Can I use the ladies' room?" my mother asked, and I glared at her.

"Of course," Dan said. "Shelly," he said to the paralegal, "would you show Mrs. Jenkins to the restroom?"

My mother stood up, wearing a little velvet bag that hung crossways over her body, over her tiny orange T-shirt. I swear I heard the bag rattle with pills.

"Mom," I said.

"I'll be right back," she said, and smiled a little, like I was the one who was ridiculous.

After that, she looked around the room while Dan went through the rest of the papers. She watched a cat cross the street outside; she focused for a few minutes on the sweep of the second hand on the clock above the archway. She traced imaginary shapes with her finger on the glossy surface of the table. And she started to fall asleep.

I whispered and pinched her arm under the table. "Mom."

She drew in a sharp breath.

"This last one is an affidavit," Dan said, handing her one more sheet, "just stating that you understand."

"Oh my God," my mother exclaimed, and started laughing, her voice like a bell, her mouth wide and wet and happy. "I fucking understand," she said.

I had to sign underneath her on all the pages, as the grantee, and my handwriting looked like a little kid's. Like a boy, forging a man's name.

We left the office at three thirty. It was my job to get my mother out of there before she started asking questions or fell asleep at the table so hard I couldn't move her. I took her outside, where we each smoked a cigarette, side by side next to the truck, and she wouldn't say a thing to me.

I dropped her at home, where she rushed inside to see if Birdie had stayed put, but I backed right out, heading straight for the power company and then the water authority, where I had to show copies of the new deed and schedule to have service reinstated.

"It can take three to five days," the woman at the desk told me.

I thought about standing outside the bathroom at Bear's house. All he had done was touch my elbow, through my shirt; I had felt his fingers go in a circle around the bone. I straightened up at the counter. "It can also be done right now," I said back to her.

I felt a blush spread on my cheeks, and I thought I had never known how to ask for what I needed, but I raised my eyebrows at the woman, and she came back with an approval for turn-on that evening.

In fact, I left both places with the services restored, the water, the lights, and the heat, even though we didn't need it just yet.

* * *

I left them inside, happy for the moment; Birdie needed a bath, and she would get one. My mother was already messing with the TV surveillance. I heard her voice but couldn't make out what she said, and then I heard Birdie's little laugh.

They were fine, I thought. I got back in the truck before my mother noticed that I'd kept the keys on me, and headed out.

FIFTEEN: SHANNON

FRIDAY, SEPTEMBER 15

I pulled into Bear's just past sunset, the field out back black against a purple sky, a few lone, dark clouds drifting above the horizon. Bear turned on the recessed lights in the living room, dimmed them, opened a beer, and then started to work on a fire, a wadded bunch of newspaper going hot and fast underneath the logs.

"Where do you want to start today?" he asked, with his back to me. When he turned and looked me over, I thought I looked okay. I hadn't been at work very long at all. When I'd gone home to get my mother, I'd thrown on one of Bear's own shirts.

I stood stuck in the place between the kitchen and, as he called it, the great room. I was like a rabbit when you come upon it in the woods, when it stands real still like you can't see it. Its eye big, its little heart racing.

He opened the fridge for another beer, handed it to me, a little close. His eyes scanned my chest. "Did you work today?" he asked.

"Not in this," I laughed.

The room smelled like dry, seasoned wood and burning paper, like clean floor and oiled leather, the hint of hops from the beer. Nothing at all like my house. I hoped no one tried to open the fridge tonight.

Behind Bear were open frames on the counter, the kind a regular house would have filled with photos of babies and dogs, family outings, a wedding. There was a slim laptop, plugged in. Everything else was generic, staged in a way that left no trace of personality, just opulence and comfort. I started to feel like I was nowhere, the way it felt sometimes in the woods, in the car with Baby Jane, like the world outside there had disappeared and I was floating and nothing around me was real anymore.

I could feel Bear's breath.

His eyes crinkled with amusement. He licked his lips and pulled the tie out of his hair, letting it uncoil to his shoulders. "Are you going to allow yourself a day off?" he asked.

"It's not really a luxury I have," I said.

"It is if you make it," he said.

He fingered the edge of my sleeve, by my bicep, not enough to touch my actual arm but enough to send a charge through me. I jumped, and reached instinctively for my cigarettes.

"You want it back?" I said, half laughing.

"Not right now," Bear answered.

I started toward the patio door.

"Here," Bear said, and handed me a pack of American Spirits. "At least smoke better while you're here."

I took it, polite, and we stood on the covered patio watching the last of the light fall over the field, the swimming pool. There was a reason I liked my cheap reservation cigarettes. You had to pull like a bitch on an American Spirit to get a good drag.

I looked out at the expanse of yard. "Do you even play tennis?" I asked.

Bear shook his head.

"What's all this for?"

"I'll tell you about it someday," he said.

"Someday when?" I asked.

"When we're not here."

My eyes got wide. It jolted me all at once, like flying apart, arms and legs off, the notion that the world didn't have to be unknown. That there was more than Spring Falls. That I would see other places, maybe live in them. With someone else.

"You don't have to stay in Spring Falls," Bear said.

I'd only ever been across the border to Canada, with my mother, to buy painkillers.

He noticed the way I pressed my lips together hard, the clench of my hand on the beer bottle, and laid his hand at the base of my neck.

"You okay?" he asked, tentative.

I couldn't think of anything greater than the warmth and the weight of his hand, right then, on the back of my neck, touching my skin. The hair up the back of my head felt electric.

Inside, I stepped out of my shoes and went to where he stood by the fire. "The thing I told you, about"—my voice dropped—"about my sister. You can't say anything about that." He looked puzzled and waited.

My shoulders sank. "I can't explain it," I said. "It's just—today has been such a long day."

"Is she yours?" he asked me.

"What? No," I said, and shook my head. "Oh my God, no." I faced the fire, where one log burned fast in the middle, about to give way.

I heard Bear behind me, and without saying anything else, I felt his breath, his lips on the edge of my hair, on the back of my neck. He put his hands on my biceps, and my head got light and woozy, my sight went dim around the edges, and I jumped, hard, nearly off my feet, and Bear's hands sprung off me.

I was afraid to turn around.

I was afraid it hadn't happened.

"I don't know if I get you," Bear said then.

My heart was loud, hammering in my ears. I turned and tried to shrug. "What's to get?" I said. My lips felt tight and my jaw hurt.

But Bear tilted his head and laughed at my attempt to be cool, to be unaffected. I had never seen anyone so comfortable in his own skin.

Please stop talking, I thought.

Bear let his hands drop down at his sides, his chest open, his palms turned out.

"What do you want?" he asked.

"Nothing," I said automatically.

"Nothing?" Bear said. His eyes lit up.

I got out from in front of him so the fire was no longer roaring up my back. "Nothing," I said again. I started to stammer, my stomach knotted tight. "I told you," I said. "I just need to work." I fumbled in my pocket for the cash he'd given me. I was just going to give it back.

"That's not what I'm talking about," Bear said. "Don't give that back to me," he scolded. "That's not what I'm talking about," he said again, "at all."

In the dim room, his eyes looked darker. He got closer, close enough for me to smell his spicy, exotic scent, which I imagined was thatched right into his hair. On his head, everywhere. I pictured an arrow of hair, like a feather, coming together below his navel, and I just about blacked out.

"What do you want?" Bear said again.

I felt my lip twitch in a nervous tic. I tried to look away, out the window, but it was completely dark out there, and all I saw was a reflection of the room, the fire, the couch where Buddy was curled and sleeping, the two of us toe to toe.

Bear took my jaw in his hand and kissed me.

A real kiss. Not a shy peck to try things out, something that might be misconstrued and explained. He started slow, and when I didn't freak out again, he went right for it, his hand on the back of my neck, my lips apart. I felt his teeth and his tongue.

I made a sound like strangling. Like gasping.

"What do you want?" Bear said again, with just enough space for breathing.

I shook my head. My whole core trembled. I was my own earthquake.

He bit my bottom lip, playful, and I felt like I'd collapse, my knees giving way, my body like a pile of silk on the floor.

"I want you to say it," Bear said.

I can't, I thought. I couldn't articulate anything. He had me by the back of the skull, but he let go and tucked his fingers behind my ears. His body curved like a muscular dog, hunched and ready.

He moved just the dry tip of his tongue around the outside of my ear.

"You want me to fuck you," he said.

"Oh God," was all I could say.

"Say it," Bear said. He put his knee between mine, a wrestling move, like he was ready to take me down, onto the soft butter couch, or right onto the floor in front of the fire. I didn't have any fight in me. I wanted it. My voice felt stopped, dry.

"Shannon," he said, his forehead pressed to mine.

"Fuck me," I said, and my knees felt like water.

His laugh was delighted. I thought if he didn't go ahead, I might die right there on the spot. I dug my fingers into his forearms. "Please," I whispered.

*　*　*

I almost ruined it. When we were tangled up on the couch, kissing, and Bear undid his pants and put his hand on the back of my head and my whole body lurched in panic.

"I can't," I said, breathless. Oh my God, I thought. Is this what he's paying me for?

He backed up, hands off. "It's okay," he said. But then he got up, and I thought it was over, that that was as far as it would ever go and I would have to spontaneously combust from shame. But he held out his hand and led me back to the bedroom.

To the master suite, where I'd showered in the massive white bathroom, where there was a huge white bed and another fireplace, this one gas, which Bear flicked on with a remote control. There was nothing over the windows, the panes just wood framed, tall, thin, bare to the outside. Anyone out there could see everything inside. The high ceiling. A sleek, three-blade fan, far above, that I kept my eyes on a lot of the time.

The bed felt like silk, like glass.

Don't think, I thought, but what I meant to tell myself was not to want anything so hard.

Bear put his hands on my neck and told me to relax. He kissed the skin underneath my ear, down to my collarbone.

I thought I wasn't even there, that it couldn't be real, that I was imagining everything and I'd wake up in my twin bed with the power out, with Birdie singing while she sat on the toilet. Or maybe I was the one outside the window, watching a kid who looked like me, with this beautiful man, the hair on his belly just the way I'd hotly imagined.

But he snapped me to, grabbing my hand. "Do you want this?"

"Yes," I said.

He burrowed his face in my neck. "Then stop fighting," he said.

SIXTEEN: KATERI

There are benefits to a small town. Having the bank know you by name when you walk in. Recognizing a lost dog and then knowing where his owner lives. Having one law office.

Kateri goes to the front desk at Bond, Sullivan, and King and speaks to the receptionist. The office is a large, converted farmhouse, the desk in a spacious front hall with an oak staircase leading up to offices. There's a conference room that looks like a formal dining room, and at the back of the house, a kitchen.

The receptionist is a young woman, dark haired and pretty, just out of college or still in. Kateri shows her badge and tells her she needs information on a recently handled property issue.

The girl takes out a pad and starts jotting things down.

"The Jenkins property," Kateri says, "was recently transferred to Shannon Jenkins."

"Uh-huh," the girl says. "I saw that."

"Can you tell me which lawyer handled that?"

"Mr. Sullivan," she says.

"Is Mr. Sullivan in?" Kateri asks. The downfalls of a small town sometimes include a slow pace, long lunches, people getting back to you when they feel like it. "It's urgent," Kateri says, and the girl straightens her back, picks up the phone.

Dan Sullivan meets her in the conference room. It's annoyingly country in there: plaid wallpaper, dried flowers. It smells like apple-cinnamon candles.

"You're aware," Kateri says, "that we're investigating the death of a deputy, Craig O'Neil, as well as the recent disappearance of Pearl Jenkins." She doesn't sit. She doesn't want to give the impression of ample time, of a leisurely pace. She's afraid someone else will end up dead. And that it might be the girl.

"Of course," Dan says.

"Shannon Jenkins had the Jenkins property transferred to his name recently."

"Yes."

"Did he come in here alone? Did he arrange that with you? Pay for it himself?"

"Um," Dan says, stalling. He laces his fingers together.

Kateri holds her palms up, asking. "I need to know who that person was. Shannon Jenkins is a suspect," she says. "I need to reach his associates, to verify his activity and motives."

Dan Sullivan works his jaw, and his eyes drift from Kateri's to the table.

"Do you have a warrant?" Dan asks.

"It's in the works," Kateri says.

Dan nods, curt. "Keep me posted," he says, and then checks his cell phone. "I have a ten o'clock," he says to Kateri. "You'll excuse me." He jogs off up the stairs.

She stands still in the conference room, a little stunned but thinking. She waits until she hears the floor creak above her, the close of a door upstairs. Then she goes back to the desk.

"I forgot to ask Dan," she says to the receptionist, "who handled the expense for the property transfer."

The girl opens a folder and looks at a yellow receipt, handwritten in what looks like the girl's handwriting, round and small. "Um, it was paid cash," she says. Underneath the receipt, there's a pink Post-it with the name *Bear Miller* in a different hand, capital block letters.

Bear Miller is not a name Kateri has heard in town. She nods to the girl as if it's exactly what she expected to hear. "Thanks so much," she says on her way out.

Outside the station, handmade JUSTICE FOR CRAIG signs have gone up on the lawn, ribbons have gone around trees. No one thinks about justice for Pearl.

She finds a landline for Bear Miller and no legal records, not even a speeding ticket. She uncovers useless information, that he went to UVM, that his tax status is married.

She begins to leave a message: Detective Fisher, investigating Craig O'Neil, Pearl Jenkins, and so on, and he picks up, hushed, halfway through her message, and she hears the machine beep.

"What can I do for you?" Bear asks.

"I need to ask you some questions," she says.

"I'll meet you," he says.

"At the station?" she asks.

He chuckles, low and familiar. "How about coffee?" he says.

"Fine," she says.

"I'm free at five thirty," he says.

"Sounds like a date," Kateri says.

*　*　*

At 5:25, as the sun is slipping behind the tallest brick building in the center of town, Kateri waits in front of the closed Center Street Café, not understanding why coffee shops in small town don't stay open into the evening. Where are you supposed to get coffee after five o'clock? she thinks. Maybe in the basement of the Presbyterian Church at the AA meeting. It's the worst coffee in the world.

The sky has deepened to a rosy gray. The spate of cars usually parked in the tiny downtown are thinning out. Bear comes around the corner, tall, lithe. He wears a European-style leather motorcycle jacket and slim jeans with purposeful tears. A slouched knit hat. Kateri thinks his clothes look about fifteen years too young for him.

"Kateri Fisher," she says, and holds out her hand.

"A pleasure," he answers. "Bear Miller." His hands are soft and cold. Strong, but bony. He points at the café. "Well, this won't work," he says. He steps back, half turned toward her, and cocks his head. "What's your preference, Detective Fisher?" he says. "Cheap beer? Or cheap beer?"

"The quietest, please."

She doesn't want to follow him, because he seems to want exactly that, to be followed, to charm the snakes right out of the woods. But she does, her work shoes padding softly on the pavement. She wears her lanyard badge and has her gun on her hip.

Of course, he walks into the Sweetwater Lounge. The other two bars are dives, younger joints with beer in plastic cups, simple mixers, bar nuts.

She blows out a slow breath, and her head makes a familiar *whomp*.

When the bartender comes, Kateri recognizes him, and Bear motions to her.

"I'm on duty," she says to Bear, and then asks for a club soda with lime.

"What would you get if you were off?" Bear asks.

The bartender is a man over fifty with neat gray hair, wearing a slim black button shirt. He smiles at Kateri. She considers telling Bear that she's sober. But it's a lie.

"An old-fashioned," she says, humoring him.

"Bourbon?" he asks.

She smiles. "Well, what I really like is Angel's Envy, but that's hard to find."

The bartender shakes his head. "I don't have that," he says.

It had a different smoothness that she liked. And a bottle draped with the outline of wings.

"Basil Hayden's," Kateri says, and the bartender nods.

"I'll have what the lady would have had," Bear says.

She watches the bartender make it, muddling the orange and pouring the whiskey into the heavy-bottomed glass. It makes her mouth water, the crushed citrus, the color, the pop of cherries.

Bear takes his time. He sips his drink and offers nothing she doesn't seem to ask for twice. She asks him what he does for a living.

"Real estate," he says.

She's never seen his name on a sign. Spring Falls has the same family names on everything. You're either a Sullivan, a Berringer, or a Kurtz.

"Residential development," he says.

She thinks about the string of new houses going up. There's nothing to offer here except the landscape, and even that is harsh, cold, unforgiving, and beautiful. You have to go to the next town for a college. There is just the one small Catholic hospital. Not everyone stays year-round.

"Are you new to town?" she asks.

He nods.

"You didn't grow up here."

"No ma'am," he says.

Kateri puts her notebook on the bar but doesn't open it, doesn't reference what's inside. She may have come armed with crime scene photos that show the awkward bend in Craig O'Neil's neck or his blue, water-bloated hands. Or the burned bits of Pearl Jenkins's bones.

"You have a PO box," Kateri says.

"I don't have a mailbox yet," Bear says. "My house is brand-new. It's the only one up there."

"In the River View tract?" Kateri asks.

"That's the one."

"That's your development," she says.

"It's the company's," he says.

"Your company?"

"My mother's," he says. "Kerpak Industries."

That's when she looks at her notes. Kerpak is developing the land north of the woods, beyond the train tracks and farther, with large family homes, luxury condos, and, between here and Canada, a huge casino resort with a golf course, indoor water park, and trails for hiking and cross-country skiing. The existing property, in the woods, is privately owned. By Shannon Jenkins.

"You're not listed as an employee of Kerpak Industries," she says. When she did a search on him, she found no association with Kerpak. When she looked into the property, the only contact she found was Patsy Kerpak.

"I'm not," Bear says.

"Are you on the payroll?"

"Technically not," he says.

"Are you working on this residential project?" she asks, indicated the map she has of the park, the land Shannon now owns. "Or the casino?"

He gets to the bottom of his old-fashioned, and the bartender strolls down their way. He tops off Kateri's glass of club soda from the gun, then places a fresh lime on the rim.

"Thank you," she says.

He points at Bear's empty glass.

"Please," Bear says. He doesn't answer her question about the projects.

"How do you know Shannon Jenkins?" she asks. She's acting on a hunch, only the Post-it note in the property file at Sullivan's office. She knows Miller is connected; she just isn't sure how. And she's curious to see if he denies it.

"He does some work for me," Bear says.

"For Kerpak?"

"No, for me personally," Bear says. He sips his new drink.

"What kind of work?" she asks, and he holds her eye contact a little longer than she finds comfortable.

"Extra hands," he says.

"How did you find him?"

"At the diner."

"I mean, how did you know he was looking for work?"

"I didn't," Bear says, and laughs a little. "But what nineteen-year-old dishwasher isn't looking for better-paying work?"

Kateri sips and swallows hard, the bubbles caustic in her throat. From the side, Bear's face has something elfin about it, the slant of his eyes toward his temples, the shape of his ears.

"Mr. Miller," she says, and he laughs.

"Please," he says. "Call me Bear."

"Shannon's a suspect in his mother's murder, as well as the murder of Craig O'Neil."

Bear seems neither alarmed by this nor particularly moved at all.

"Do you want my opinion?" he says.

"I think you're probably going to give it to me either way," Kateri says. She thinks he's going to throw him under the bus. Give her reasons why Shannon would have killed his own mother.

"He didn't do it," Bear says.

She watches his face closely for any flicker of warmth, some recognition, a soft spot. She sees none. Instead, he seems particularly homed in on her—his gaze when she talks, the way he moves his tongue. If this weren't an official interview, she'd have thought he was after something else. And she would have taken him up on it.

"Why did you pay his legal fees?" Kateri asks then.

"I didn't," Bear says, putting his drink down and making a steeple of his fingers.

"Really," Kateri says. "Who did?"

"What makes you think he didn't pay them himself?" Bear asks.

Kateri shrugs a shoulder, soft, cool. "That's more money than that kid has," she offers. "You have a vested interest in him."

"He's a kid in trouble," Bear says.

"So what?" Kateri asks.

"I was a kid in trouble," he says, and smiles at her. "A long time ago."

She's found nothing that indicates trouble. Which doesn't mean he hasn't paid his way out of it.

"I don't know," Kateri says. "If anyone had a reason to harm Pearl Jenkins, he did. Have you ever heard him talk about his mother?"

"No," Bear says. "I've barely heard him speak."

"No . . . siblings, or any other family members?" Bear shakes his head. "Do you know where he's staying?" she asks.

"No," he says.

"But he works for you," she says. "You don't know where he lives?"

"I reach him by phone," Bear says.

"Is he a good worker?" Kateri asks.

"Very." Bear leans his arms on the bar. "How'd you end up here?" he asks.

"I could ask you the same," she says.

"You got a place in town?"

"Outside," she says. She watches his eyes, soft at the corners, crow's feet from smoking, but mostly just the whiskey blurring all his edges.

She hadn't wanted to live in town, where she saw everyone every day. Joel Hurt. The captain. The lady secretaries. The younger officers. She needed a retreat. A backyard. To be close to the river, the trees. Where she could lie in bed at night and hear the train, the rush of water. Where it was dark.

At her grandmother's house in Syracuse, even in the city, there were trees. The backyard under a dense canopy. There were birds and squirrels, deer, creeping in from the outskirts, ravaging everyone's flowers.

"How old are you?" Bear asks, and it catches her off guard.

"How old are you?" she shoots back, and he laughs, which disarms her a little.

"Fair," he says. "Older than you," he answers.

"We both have weird names."

She hands him a card, even though she knows he already has her number. "I'd like you to come in for an official statement," she says, and shrugs to soften the sound of it. She knows that coming from a man, that sentence has weight, the kind of request you listen to and comply with. And coming from her, authority sounds like bitchiness.

"We've asked everyone he works with," she explains, but then she also stands with her hand in her pocket, her weapon slightly exposed. She leaves a five-dollar bill on the bar. She asks one more question.

"Is Kerpak interested in the house on Hidden Drive?"

Bear sniffs and looks down at his empty second drink, her card on the bar. He licks his top lip, thinking, and then simply says, "Yes."

Kateri raises her eyebrows. "Kid in trouble," she repeats. It's clearly more than that.

And Bear cocks his head. "More trouble than he anticipated, apparently."

"Well," she says, "thanks for your time."

"Thank you," Bear says, and it's a little too heavy-handed for her to just turn and walk out. A little too sarcastic, a little biting. He feels jilted, she thinks.

"What's going to happen to the house?" Kateri asks.

"My house?" Bear says. "I'll sell it," he says.

"No, the house on Hidden Drive. The Jenkins house."

Bear shrugs. "Cash sale?" he suggests.

"Keep me posted," she says.

* * *

At home, she opens the sliding door that leads to her small wooden balcony and looks at the sky. There's not a cloud in sight, and yet there are tiny crystal flurries around her face, catching under the light that comes from the window.

He didn't look like anyone else in Spring Falls. Not even like the summer people who came through on their way deeper into the mountains.

And it unnerved her. He was exactly the kind of distraction she enjoyed. Smart but a little sarcastic, just at the edge of being mean. A little bit pretty. A little bit rough.

"Fuck," she says aloud into the night air, and reaches inside for the last of her stashed cigarettes.

He wasn't telling her everything.

Neither was Shannon.

SEVENTEEN: SHANNON

SUNDAY, SEPTEMBER 17

I could see it only with two mirrors. A scar that seared from the underside of my arm, over one shoulder blade, up toward my neck, and into the middle of my spine. In the places where I could reach it, the skin felt different, like it couldn't stretch, like part of me was made of plastic.

I let Bear touch it. And I shivered.

"Does it still hurt?" he asked.

"No," I said, but it wasn't quite true. Sometimes it shot with pain, the skin tight and hot. Sometimes it itched. "It's sensitive," I said.

"This is from the fire?" he asked.

"Yeah."

His finger traced the outline, from my neck and around. "It kind of looks like Canada," he said.

"I always kind of wished I had two," I said, my face sideways on the pillow, watching him.

"Why?" he asked.

"So it would look like I had wings," I said.

*　*　*

There were things I would never tell him. That I'd bought my bike with money I stole from my mother. I had always gotten my own checks and she had always kept them, saving them, she told me, for when I was

153

older, and then I was old enough to care and there wasn't any money. None. Of course they hadn't been saved. She'd spent them as soon as she got them.

So I took a hundred dollars from her drawer, from the envelope where she set aside money for bills, for groceries. She never directly confronted me. We had a standoff in the hallway. The envelope of cash in her hand. Her body already showing her pregnancy with Birdie that we had also never talked about. She glared at me. I pushed past her to get outside. I wanted my own things. I wanted my own means.

The first time I rode that bike, I went halfway to Mount Snow and stopped, breathless at the top of a hill where you could see miles and miles of New York State stretch out below, quilted greens and browns meeting the sky.

I could never tell him how many times I'd wished I had just died in the fire.

Or how sometimes I thought I had. That I'd been a living dead boy all these years, stuck in the house with her.

"You're lucky to be alive," Bear said.

"I don't know about that."

He looked surprised. "You could have died from a burn that large," he said.

"I meant the lucky part," I said.

He touched my hair, and it took restraint not to flinch at his hand. "You wouldn't be here," he said.

I couldn't tell him it was the luckiest I'd ever felt. I didn't want to jinx it.

"How did you get out?" Bear asked me. We sat up in the bed. I pulled the covers up over my chest. I couldn't keep my hand from the hair on his stomach.

"My mom," I said. "She pulled me out with her." That's what she'd told me. I couldn't remember it myself. Sometimes I had dreams about the stairway in the farmhouse, the walls licked with fire, the smoke

154

filling my lungs. I'd feel the slap of flame on my back, hear screaming. Sometimes in the dream it was my dad. He was the one screaming. Most of the time, it was me.

"I was in the hospital for like a month," I said. "Because of the burn, and because of some breathing issues, but I really don't remember it. Bits and pieces sometimes."

"Where was your mom?" Bear asked.

"She was in the hospital too," I said. "I don't think as long. The beam broke part of her back, and she needed surgery. And then she was out, but we lived with my grandparents, and she had, like, a brace she had to wear. And they had arrested Park, and all that happened while I was in the hospital."

"Park is your dad," Bear says.

"Yeah."

"And your sister?"

I closed my eyes. I should never have said anything.

"She's not your dad's," he said.

"No."

He waited, and I felt his ankle wagging under the blankets. I could hear Buddy snoring on the floor in front of the fireplace.

"She's a secret," I said.

He repeated it to me.

"Yeah. I've never told anyone about her. Like, anyone," I said, "ever before. My mom has never taken her to the doctor, never registered her for school. She doesn't have a birth certificate." I rolled my eyes upward. Saying all of it aloud felt like that stairway again, narrow and closing in with fire.

"Why?" Bear whispered.

"She's terrified of my dad," I said. "She's afraid he'll find out—that, that she had another kid, and didn't wait for him? I don't know. She's super paranoid," I said. "But to her credit, he did try to kill us."

"Who's her father?"

"I don't know."

"Where was she born?"

"At home," I said.

"Were you there?" he asked, like he couldn't believe it, and when I said yes, he just said, "Jesus."

This was why I didn't tell. That one word, like it was all too much. To have been burned alive in a fire your dad started. To have watched your mother give birth to your secret sister. It was too much.

The window was open just enough to hear the wind through the pines outside, like a cold, soft whisper. I saw Buddy rouse and lift his nose and sniff the air as it came in. The air was sharp. But the bed was warm.

"You could get out of there," Bear said.

"I've thought about it."

"But?" Bear asked.

"I can't leave her behind," I said.

"Your sister?"

"Yes."

"Your mother did that to her, not you," he said.

"She's just a baby," I said.

"It's abusive to both of you," he said. "It's just as bad to expect you to keep the secret, to live with that, as it is for her to keep her."

I was quiet. I didn't disagree with him; I just didn't know what to say. How do you leave? How do you leave behind that little pudge-legged curly-haired baby?

"What if it kills you both?" he asked.

"It didn't, though," I said. "What was supposed to kill me didn't." I chewed at my lip, thinking. "We should have all been dead," I said. "But we're not. I'm not, and now she's here. I can't just leave her."

He sat up and turned his back to me, checked his phone, then put it facedown on the nightstand. He had million-dollar skin. Not a blemish, not a scar. No one had ever clocked him upside the head or set his house on fire while he was sleeping. I didn't think he had so much as a split end in all that beautiful hair. His teeth were blinding white.

He looked over his shoulder. "I get it," he said.

"You do?"

I'd been braced for rejection. For fury, or coldness, or anything other than understanding. He got under the covers and lay on top of me, his elbows on my shoulders and his arms alongside my face so I couldn't move at all. I jumped, captive. My whole body wired and taut. When I jumped, he said, "I'm not going to hurt you."

I closed my eyes, because it was too much, the sight of him, the proximity, the weight. He kissed me. He put his thumbs at the corners of my eyes and waited for me to open them, to look at him.

"I'm going to help you," he said, and smiled a little, the way he did, like a cat. "It just might not be pretty," he said.

*　*　*

In the morning, I nudged Bear's shoulder in the dark.

"I have to go to work," I whispered. "It's five-oh-five."

"Take the car," Bear said.

"Your car?"

He rolled over. "I don't need it," he said.

I was wide awake, already thinking about the things I had to remember to do at the diner. "Are you sure?" I said.

Bear laughed. "It's just a car."

Buddy knew I was up. He nosed the side of the bed, and I got dressed and let him out the back door before I left. I filled his water bowl and gave him a scoop of food, which he plowed through, his head wagging from side to side, kibbles flying. I wanted coffee but didn't know how to use the machine Bear had. It was like a glass-and-metal sculpture. The only coffee he had was whole, oily beans that he ground fresh for every pot.

I took the key off the hook. It was on a short lanyard with a bear print on it.

I told Buddy to be a good boy. I knew he would bound back to the bed with Bear.

I thought, this is not my life.

*   *   *

After work, I drove home. There were things in Bear's car I didn't know how to use—the sunroof, the heated seats, the electronic adjustments for the seats and mirrors. I sat for a long time moving the seat in tiny increments with a lever on the side. The radio was on North Country Public Radio.

I looked in the mirror before I went inside. I felt different at a cellular level, in my spine, in my bones. I wondered if someone might be able to see it.

But then I jumped out of my skin and whacked the mirror with my hand. I must have looked like an old cartoon cat where the skeleton startles outside the fur.

A sound boomed that set my teeth on edge and filled my mouth with metal like the tip of a pencil. My ears fuzzed over with ringing.

Then it happened again.

I watched a flush of birds scatter over the top of our house, but I couldn't hear them. I just saw their black wings, the sway of branches above the leaves, falling down in their wake.

I went inside the house, working my jaw, blinking hard to try to get my ears open, but it was no use. My hearing was white noise. My mother stood facing the kitchen window, which was loose in its casement like it had been pried out, and Birdie was screaming.

My mother swung around with the shotgun and pointed it at me. I dropped Bear's keys and held up my hands, shouting, "Mom!"

She butted it against my chest, hard, the metal nose of the gun against bone.

What if it kills you both?

"Don't yell at me," she said.

Birdie let out a shriek and ran for my legs, gripped my knees, her face pressed into my thigh.

"Mom," I said, and swallowed. I put my hand in Birdie's hair. I tried to guide the gun away from my heart. I had arrived in a strange car. I was lucky she hadn't shot me.

"You think I have that for nothing?" my mother said, and pointed at the TV. "I know when there's people lurking," she said.

"There are people in the woods all the time. We're on a trail," I said. "You can't just shoot at people going by."

"This wasn't a hiker," she said. "No one hikes in a fucking suit," she shouted.

I let go of the barrel and she let it down, pointed at the floor.

"And I don't know where you decided to sleep last night," she added. Then she looked out the front door at the Land Rover, parked in the gravel, and whipped around. "Who is here?" she yelped. "Shannon, who did you bring here?"

"No one!" I shouted back. "I'm driving that," I said.

She peered again.

"The hell you are," she said. "Whose is it?"

"He's my friend," I said, and hesitated just an instant.

"Uh-huh. Your friend drives a fucking Land Rover?" Her eyes scanned my clothes, but I was wearing my own. "Since when do you have a friend with a Land Rover?"

Birdie sniffled, still holding on to my knees.

"She's scared," I said softly to my mom.

"She should be," she said.

I patted her on the butt, and she headed into my mother's room for toys or books, or maybe to cry herself to sleep, and my mother pulled the gun back up and held it across her chest like a shield.

"What does he know?" she asked.

"Nothing," I said.

"Bullshit," my mother said

"Nothing, Mom," I said. "I haven't said anything."

"You were there all night."

"Yeah," I said. "We spent all that time talking about my crazy-ass mother and my secret sister."

She swung the barrel of the gun at me. I ducked, but I heard it whip past my head.

"You don't remember," she said, "what it's like to have someone try to kill you. Because you were little, because your brain did you a favor and blacked it out for you."

"Mom," I said.

"But you will," she said. "And when you do, remember that I warned you."

* * *

I took the gun with me. I wanted to give her the impression that I was taking care of something. I also didn't trust her with it. I laid it in the back of the Land Rover, tucked under Buddy's blanket, and left the car parked in town. No one hikes in a suit. I knew only one person who even wore a suit.

I walked. It had been warm in the sun, and as it got dark, a sharp wind blew through. The trees shivered with gusts. I pulled my collar around my neck. The flannel wasn't enough.

I was afraid of finding him. Always. Whenever I went there, I feared walking in on something awful. A crime scene. Blood. His body, stiff and blue in the bed.

They had found my great-uncle Marion that way. Hanging from the rafters in the basement of the house we lived in now.

My mother told me his friend found him, days later, black faced and bloated.

Not his parents. Not even my grandmother, his only sister. They were only ten months apart in age. His friend came looking for him.

"Who was his friend?" I'd asked my mother more than once.

"Some hillbilly queer," she said, shooing me away. "Don't get romantic about it."

But now, when I pictured the friend going into the cellar, it was me, cutting the rope that held Baby Jane, holding his blackened face and cradling his head, weeping.

He had a heavy sadness to him. Like an old saint or an icon even, with the big sad eyes and the gaunt mouth.

When I got to the house, there was blood on the doorknob, and it was locked. When I wiggled it, I got the blood on my hands and left my prints on the door.

I could hear movement within. "Baby," I called. "Open up."

I would break in if I had to. I could get the screen out of the window. I could break the glass.

He flung the door open, holding his arm. "Don't," he said.

He was wearing a gray suit jacket that was torn through at the bicep and soaked with blood.

My mother had shot him.

"Why were you at my house?" I asked.

"Where have you been?" he asked in return.

He stood with his feet planted in the doorway, trying to block me, but I pushed past him.

"What's it to you?" I snapped. "Not sleeping on top of the covers," I said.

I pulled at the jacket, and he let it slide off most of the way, until it stuck to the wound. "You need a doctor." I pressed at the tear in the fabric, and the blood oozed fresh.

Baby drew in a sharp breath.

I tried to see. I thought he needed stitches; it needed to be cleaned; he might need antibiotics.

"Don't touch me," he said. He hissed it through his teeth, his jaw tight.

"Don't be stupid," I said.

His face was pale but set. His lips a straight line.

"Sit down," I said. I forced him to sit on the love seat. There was blood on my hands, on my shirt. It had dripped on the floor.

"It's all over you," he said.

"So what?" I said. "My mother tried to shoot you."

"She did shoot me," he said. "She tried to kill me."

"Why were you there?"

"Why weren't *you* there?" he shot back.

"You can't come looking for me," I said. "That's not how this works."

"Wash your hands," he said.

"Why?" I shouted. "This is what you're afraid of?" I took the wet blood from my hands and smeared it on my face. "Who fucking cares?"

"Shannon," he said, shrunk into the love seat. His face was wet with tears but also sweat. "It's dangerous," he said.

I laughed at him.

"I'm dangerous," he said.

"I'll believe it when I see it," I said, and rolled my eyes. He was living like a hermit, like a monk, alone without TV or a phone. And then I thought, so am I.

EIGHTEEN: KATERI

Shannon's prints show up on everything inside the house and out, including the ax. There are hair samples from what looks like both kids, blond and kinked red, and Pearl's. And a fourth that Kateri cannot identify.

She has saved those—fine, straight, and black—bagged and ready for the lab. There are another set of prints in the house that are not quite readable, like they have been left with gloves, smudged with plastic in between. They measure the size of an average man's hand. But they don't leave a whorl.

Hurt says, "They're probably Shannon's. He probably used some kind of gloves, or even just plastic wrap, thinking it would protect his identity."

He hovers his hand over the print, the impression left by the unreadable hand, and it's just slightly smaller than his own.

No weapon has been found near Craig O'Neil. And all of Craig's items—his badge, his cuffs, and his gun—were taken by the killer.

"Why wouldn't he run?" Kateri asks.

They sit at the table in the investigation room, the pictures on the board looking back at them.

"It's a thrill," Hurt says. "Sticking around, watching us try to figure it out. Playing the game."

She's never seen it go that way. Her cases have been rage killings and domestics. Nothing that ever felt like a game.

"You have enough," Hurt says.

She looks at the image of the fingerprints on the ax.

"In the meantime," he says, "let's get a warrant to search Miller's house."

*   *   *

She asks Shannon in to look at evidence. It feels dishonest, leading him there to get him to talk, but both Hurt and Chief Whittaker are breathing down her neck to arrest him.

He leans to the side in the overstuffed chair, his body slack, tired. Lying is hard on the soul, even the body. She's seen suspects fall dead asleep after confessing, so relieved to not be holding it in any longer. The way he tilts his head, she can see his neck better than last time. The bruises are fading.

He complicated everything, she thinks, ahead of herself. Hurt kept telling her not to worry beyond the arrest. The rest is not her job.

She had thought for sure he could get a self-defense plea. She needed him to admit to the abuse. She needed him to talk more about the girl.

But in truth, nothing about the case is simple. There hasn't been enough of Pearl's body found to satisfy Kateri. Her killing and the burning of the body point at premeditation. So does ambushing the cop to get to the girl.

She looks at the hollows of his eyes. She's not convinced he has it in him.

"When's the last time you saw your sister?" Kateri asks him.

"At home," he says.

"You didn't visit her in the hospital," Kateri says.

"I didn't even know she was in the hospital."

"Her legal guardian signed her discharge papers."

"Who the fuck is her legal guardian?" Shannon shouts. "Am I? She's not my kid."

Kateri shrugs, cool, and then Shannon's face turns to fear.

"Where is she?" he asks.

Kateri waits.

"Where is Birdie?"

"I could ask you the same thing," she says.

He stands up, swings, and punches a dent much bigger than his fist into the wall. His knuckle cracks open, bloody.

"I can have you restrained," Kateri says, her voice louder.

"Fine," Shannon says. "Can you find my fucking sister?" He has puffed up and she sees it for the first time, the propensity for rage in his curled fist, his hard breathing.

"Please sit down," Kateri says.

Joel Hurt comes in without knocking, having heard the bang on the wall. He looks at the dent and down at Shannon's hand.

"Should we move rooms?" Hurt asks. "Interrogation B is open."

"I think we're okay," Kateri says. Interrogation B is a windowless, cinder-block room. She will lose him in there.

Hurt stays, though, his back against the wall, leaning, not asking questions, letting Kateri do her work.

"I need you to think, Shannon," she says, "about who your sister might have agreed to go with."

"No one," he says. "Or, I don't know, maybe anyone. She's a little girl," he says. "She's never been anywhere. The only people she knows are my mom and me."

"Are you sure about that?"

His lips part, and his eyes search the ceiling. "I think so," he says.

"How do I know it wasn't you who signed her out?" She's pushing. He doesn't fit the description the nurse gave her, fortyish, dark haired, unless he disguised himself really well. But she wants to see him react.

"It wasn't," he says, point blank.

She pulls out an enlarged copy of the signature on the discharge papers and shows it to him.

"That's not my signature," he says.

"That could be an *S*," she says, pointing to the flourish.

"In the middle," he says. "You think I signed it *Jenkins, Shannon*?" He thrusts the paper back at her. "This is not my signature," he says.

"What about your father?"

Shannon covers his mouth before he starts speaking again. "Well," he says. "If my father broke out of prison to sign my sister—who is not even his—out of the hospital, I would hope you would know about it," he says. "Like, through the police network or something."

"Do you know for sure that he's still incarcerated?"

Shannon's eyes look blank, his lips white. "The last I knew," he says. He holds out his hand. "Can't you check that? Don't you have a database or something?"

"Of course," Kateri says, but she makes no move to make a note or look anything up. "When's the last time you had contact with him?" Kateri asks.

She watches him rub his neck and swallow. "I told you," he says. "Two years ago."

"After she was born," she says.

"Yes."

"Did you tell him?"

"No."

"What about your mother? Did she have contact with him?"

"My mother was terrified of him," he says.

"That could be a reason for staying in touch," Kateri says. "Many women maintain contact out of fear."

"I don't think so," he says. "She didn't leave. After Birdie, she like never left the house. We don't have a phone. We don't have internet."

"Mail?" Kateri asks.

"I don't know," Shannon says.

"What about your father's associates?" Kateri asks.

He says the word back to her. "He didn't work with anyone," he says, confused. "You mean like cousins?"

"Alliances he may have made in prison," Kateri says.

Shannon's face falls, and he looks down at his lap. "I don't know," he says, barely audible. "Not that I know of."

"The remains we found were burned," Kateri says.

"So?"

"Your father is in prison for arson. Arson doesn't just happen to the same people twice," she says. "Could he have put someone up to it?"

"I don't know," Shannon says.

"Could he have put you up to it?"

He looks around the room, like an animal looking for holes in the trap. "I didn't do it," he says finally. "But sure. If you want me to speculate for you, he could have put me up to it. But he didn't. And I didn't do it."

It's Hurt's turn to chime in. "Crimes often repeat generationally," he says to Shannon.

"I know," Shannon says.

"You know?"

"Yeah, every goddamn fire in this town comes back to me," Shannon says. "I get questioned every time."

"Yes, but this time it involves your mother," Kateri stresses. "Are you telling me that a fire happened to your mother twice?"

He looks at neither of them and holds his hands open, an empty offering. He stares at the wall behind them. "Do you want me to repeat myself?" he asks, and then does. "I didn't do it."

Kateri rubs the ever-growing crease between her brows and tries to switch gears.

"Your mother kept you both captive," Kateri says. "Complicit. After your sister was born. You had to keep the secret too."

He nods slightly.

"Where are you staying?" she asks, stretching her neck, watching, to see if he'll unconsciously mimic her. She needs to get a better look at each side, the mark of a thumb and four fingers.

"I don't know why that matters," Shannon says.

"Well, it might matter a great deal," Hurt says, sudden and loud, and Shannon jumps at the male voice.

"Do you have a friend," Kateri asks, "or a coworker, maybe, who might have signed Birdie out for you?"

"No," Shannon says. "I didn't ask anyone to sign her out."

"What about Bear Miller?" Kateri asks.

Shannon blinks, presses his lips together, and looks away from Kateri. "He didn't sign her out," he says.

Kateri cocks her head. "How do you know Bear Miller?" she asks.

"I work for him," Shannon says.

"Is that all?" Hurt asks.

"Does it matter?" Shannon asks.

"Let's say that it does," Hurt says.

"Is it true," Kateri says, "taking back over, that you're staying with Mr. Miller in the model home at the River View site? On Fountain Street?"

Shannon's shoulders sink low in the chair, his neck hidden, his hands laced together in his lap, fidgeting. He wags one foot.

"Why don't you tell me?" he asks. "Since you seem to know exactly what I'm doing."

"How did you get the money to pay for the lawyer when you put the property in your own name?" Kateri asks.

He won't look her in the eye. She hears the click of his teeth.

"If you couldn't pay the utilities," she says, "and the taxes were years behind, how did you manage to pay Dan Sullivan for his services? It must have been, what? A thousand dollars?"

Kateri perches on the edge of her desk. She can wait a long time, but she watches all the small movements that Shannon makes, his fingers, folded, unfolded, his hands in his hair, his bouncing knee.

"Did Mr. Miller pay for it?" she asks.

It takes him a minute to respond. Finally he says, "He has been nice to me."

"Nice," Hurt repeats.

Shannon's face flames up, hot pink spots on his cheeks. He bites his lower lip.

"How long have you known Bear Miller?" Kateri asks.

Shannon shrugs. "A couple of months."

"Do you know anything about him?" Kateri asks.

Shannon's eyes search. "I don't know what you mean," he says.

"Anything about his family? His past? Where he's from?" she asks. "Do you know if he goes by any other names?"

"No," he says, and his chest caves a little.

She tries a little harder. "Michael?" she asks, then, "Bart? Bartholomew?" His face is blank. "Jane?" she says.

He jumps. "What? No." Then he adds, "That's a woman's name."

"Mr. Miller knew your situation at home, correct?" Kateri asks. "He'd been nice to you, as you said. He understood your struggle."

"I guess," Shannon says. "I don't know why it matters."

"Does he know about your sister?" Kateri asks.

Shannon's face pales.

"If he was willing to pay your legal fees," Kateri says.

"He didn't pay them."

"Who did?"

"I did," Shannon says, but Kateri doesn't quite believe him. He's hiding where he got the money.

"He knew about Birdie," Kateri says, and pauses for a long time, watching Shannon get uncomfortable. "Would he also hurt your mother?"

His face begins to look green in the hollows of his cheeks. "No," he says, barely voiced. "No."

"But he knows," she says.

"Yes," he says.

"Who hurt you, Shannon?" Kateri asks.

"What?"

She points at his neck. "Who tried to strangle you?"

"No one," he says.

"You have visible bruising on your neck."

He pulls his collar around him, lowers his head.

"Who did that?"

He looks small in the chair, hiding more than just his neck.

"How often did you fight with your mother?" Hurt asks.

Shannon shrugs.

"Often," Hurt says. It is not a question.

"Sometimes," Shannon says.

"Physical," Hurt says.

"No."

"You just punched a hole in the wall over a question," Hurt says. "You're trying to tell me that doesn't also go on at home?"

Kateri watches Shannon press his lips together, flat, white.

"Did you fight about the house?" Hurt asks.

"Something had to be done," Shannon says. "She wasn't going to do anything about it. We were going to be homeless."

"Did you fight about your sister?" Hurt asks.

Shannon clamps his jaw tighter.

"You were tired of being implicated in her hiding," Hurt says. "You disagreed with the way your mother had chosen to keep her captive all this time."

Shannon looks at Hurt, then looks Kateri in the eye.

"So you confronted her," Hurt says, projecting. Kateri has seen other investigators use this, and she's used it herself. Tell the story the way it might have happened and wait for the suspect to disagree, to begin to tell it right, or to crumple with guilt, or flare with anger at being caught. "It got physical," Hurt says. "You're still badly bruised," he says, and Shannon's hands go to his throat. "And in reaction, in rage, pent up from years of lying, you struck her."

Shannon moves his shoulder a little, shifts against the wall. "Maybe you didn't mean to do that much damage," Hurt says. "But faced with what you had done, you tried to hide it, you destroyed the evidence, and you hid your sister in the safest spot you could find: the closet."

Shannon's nostrils flare, and he draws his lips in so tight they are nearly invisible.

"When you found out your sister was at Mercy, you staked out her guard, attacked him in the parking lot, signed your sister out, and fled."

"Fled," Shannon repeats.

"Did you sign her out?" Kateri asks. "Or did you send someone up? Tag team, so to speak," she says.

"While you ambushed Craig O'Neil in the parking lot," Hurt says. He shrugs, cool. "Maybe you didn't mean to kill him. But he died, bound and drowning in the trunk of his own car."

She watches Shannon swallow.

"We're in the process of searching Bear Miller's house," Kateri says.

Shannon huffs.

"Your prints are on the murder weapon," Hurt says.

Shannon's mouth falls open, and his eyes spring with tears. "I didn't do it," he says. "I didn't do anything."

"Where's the girl?" Hurt asks.

"I don't know," Shannon says.

"Triple homicide is a steep offense," Hurt says.

Kateri watches two tears brim and fall from his eyes. "I would never hurt her," he says.

"I'm sure you didn't mean for it to go this far," Hurt says.

Kateri leans forward on the desk. "Who's the angel?" she asks.

Shannon closes his eyes for a long moment before he looks at her. His eyes have gone dark and searching with fear. "I don't know," he says, but he knows what she's talking about. This is not a new phrase to him. She folds her hands and lets him sit with it, and she notices that he starts to shake, first in his hands, which he clamps together, and then in his arms and across his torso. She has knocked something loose in him.

Hurt nods at her.

"I didn't do it," Shannon cries.

"I have to arrest you," Kateri says.

"Fisher," Hurt says suddenly. "Stop telling him and just do it."

She begins, reads his rights, her own voice wavering. He sobs for a minute—"I have to call Bear," he says—and the break in his voice hits her hard. But then he seems to suck it all in, tight, pale, shocked into silence. He won't meet her eye anymore. He makes the phone call with his back to her, and she can't make out any of the words, and then she has a deputy, a young dad in his thirties, walk Shannon down to booking. He never looks back.

NINETEEN: SHANNON

SATURDAY, SEPTEMBER 30

I'd cut all my hours down at the Hub. Bear wanted me available to begin work on the house, and I'd been working six days a week. I couldn't keep spending so much time with Bear. Not working meant less money. I needed to stay on top of the bills. But I didn't want to be anywhere else.

"How much are you making at the diner?" Bear asked.

"Three hundred," I said.

"For six days?" he said.

I blushed hard. It was unheard of to him. We sat at the kitchen island. The stone always felt cold, even when the house was warm.

"Are you going to pay me?" I asked, when he didn't offer.

He laughed. "You can have whatever you want," he said.

It was hard for me to understand. I didn't know what I wanted. I needed to just rely on regular money in my pocket. Junior gave me cash every week.

"I don't think you understand," I started.

He tipped his head, listening.

"Anything . . . means nothing to me," I said. "It's not a thing."

"Do you want cash?" he said.

"I guess," I said. "I mean, I've always just been paid cash, and that's how I pay the bills and buy groceries. So, yeah, that's what makes sense to me."

"I don't have cash on me," he said, patting his shirt pockets like it might be there. "But I'll take some out tomorrow and I'll give you five hundred dollars."

"I haven't even done any work yet."

He got up and came around the back of me, his hands holding my shoulders in. He put his lips on the top of my head. "It's part of the anything you want," he said.

The next day, he sent me out to buy paint. I'd picked the color myself, a buttery warm beige called D'Anjou, and I used Bear's credit card, even though I protested.

"I can't use your credit card," I'd said to him. He hadn't given me the cash yet.

"Sure you can," he said. "Sign my name."

"I can't sign your name," I said.

"People commit worse crimes all the time. You're spending seventy-five dollars on paint." He handed me a black AmEx card and waved his hand. "Take the Land Rover," he said. "Take the roadster if you want."

"I can't drive a stick," I said.

He laughed. "What are you going to do when we go to Europe?" he asked.

I looked at him like I had no idea who he was. I *didn't* know who he was. My eyes felt huge. Europe might as well have been another planet.

I sat in the parking lot of Lowe's like I was someone else. I parked far away, so no one would ding the sides of the Land Rover, even though I'd seen Bear drive it with total abandon. I had his keys on the bear lanyard and his credit card tucked into my wallet.

I clicked the key fob to lock the car and caught the eye of a woman going in ahead of me.

It's not my car, I thought. It's my . . .

The word I had meant to think of, the word I was having trouble admitting, was *boyfriend*.

But the word that actually came to mind was *master*.

* * *

When I got back, I went into the basement. In the model home, it was just another part of the house, not like the cellar in our house, which was dirt floor and stone walls with spiders bigger than I ever wanted to see again.

This was finished, with dark shining hardwood floors and walls that were flat white with primer. I needed to mask everything down there and get it ready for painting. But before Bear came to see what I was doing, I went into the workroom, where the floors were cement and there was a tool chest, a closet with hooks for hanging hammers and extension cords, and I hid my mother's gun.

It had been in the back of the Land Rover, wrapped in Buddy's blanket, for days. It was like a beating heart out there. I was always aware of it, always afraid Bear would find it and question me.

I thought, I could probably tell him.

But instead, I stood it up in the closet with a broom and mop in front of it.

I moved a box filled with picture frames that still had the fake photos in them. A pretty, copper-haired girl in a white sweater. A baby with creamy, perfect skin.

I laid plastic over the floor—the way you would if you were going to hide a body, I thought. But it was blue masking tape instead of duct tape, and my tools were brushes instead of knives. I anchored the plastic down with tape and the weight of the paint cans, and I stood on a ladder to mask the ceiling. But my hands were shaking, all the secrets coming to the surface—the hidden gun, Birdie. Every day I braced myself for the next thing. A dead body. The police. I kept peeling the tape off and starting over.

* * *

I woke up to an empty house, in the big white bed by myself. I was sprawled in the middle like a starfish, with Buddy curled into my side. I couldn't ever quite stretch out in my twin bed at home; my hands and feet hung off either end. Bear's room was light as soon as the sun came up, but I'd been asleep through hours of sunlight, the room warm and drowsy, the dog snoring.

Apparently, I'd gotten used to taking up space.

I'd had Bear teach me how to make coffee in the high-end machine he had. It produced just regular coffee—nothing fancier than we had at work. I set it up and went out back to smoke a cigarette, standing, because all the patio furniture had been covered for winter.

First snow was possible as early as next week.

I let Buddy out to run in the back, watching his lean, athletic body leap through waves of tall, brittle corn, golden and dry, rustling like paper in the breeze.

The Land Rover was gone.

I was going to try finishing the basement, pull up the masking, touch up the edges where I needed to. The painting calmed me. The clean smell of it. The steady coverage. The straight grid of color going on thick. I imagined staying in the house until work tomorrow, a long free day, an evening with Bear. Maybe a walk with the dog.

But instead I heard the doorbell. And a baby.

I thought, there aren't even neighbors up here.

And then whoever had rung the bell was now trying the knob, knocking it in its casing. Buddy was too far out to hear or care. I left him out there, chasing a swallow that teased him over a flat part of the field, swooping so low it looked like he could get it and then darting swiftly back up again. Buddy leaned and barked. Barked and ran. He would be tired.

I went in, crossing the great room like I belonged there, and swept open the big, heavy front door that had only a small window to peer out of, the window having its own tiny door, like in a medieval castle.

"Hi," the woman said to me, impatient. She shifted the baby on her hip and pushed past me, walking into the open dining room.

She had red-gold hair, pulled up in a perfectly messy bun with soft, curved wisps hanging down at the temples. A sprinkle of freckles. The baby had the same copper hair, pierced ears. A blue corduroy dress.

They were the people in the pictures. The ones I had thought were fake. An advertising family.

I heard the coffee finish brewing. I thought, maybe that's what they are. They are models, and Bear needs to pay them.

"Can I help you?" I asked, soft.

She laughed. "I don't know," she said. "Is Bear even here?"

"No," I said, suddenly glad I was dressed and hadn't wandered into the kitchen in my shorts and T-shirt, one of Bear's flannels over my shoulders.

She swung a diaper bag onto the formal dining room table, the one I'd never seen used for anything other than occasional pieces of mail. It sat eight. She stuck her hand in the side pocket of the bag, digging until she pulled out a small green pacifier and gave it to the baby, who sucked it right in.

"She's tired," the woman said. Then, "I'm sorry; you are?"

I felt like a puppet. Like a rag doll. I said my own name like it was someone else's.

"What are you working on?" she asked.

"The basement," I said. It was barely above a whisper.

Out the front window, her car sat in the driveway by the front sidewalk. A black Mercedes SUV. She had on slim navy-blue pants, cropped above her ankle, and shiny leather loafers.

"I don't mean to keep you from your work," she said, and then touched the side of her head, dumb. "Sorry!" she said, and held out her hand. "I'm Meghan."

"Meghan," I repeated.

The baby fussed and smashed her face into Meghan's collarbone, hungry.

"I'm not staying," Meghan said. "Unless Bear takes a really long time to come back. Do you know where he is?"

"No," I said. I thought, Maybe getting my money.

My breath was coming short and hard, and I had to press my lips together to try to slow down my heart.

"I'm sorry," I said. "I just have only ever dealt with Bear."

"No surprise," Meghan said, and she walked into the kitchen without hesitation, opened the fridge, rooted around. She set the baby on the floor with a soft square toy. The baby scooted around on her butt, pacifier tight in her mouth, bumping the toy, then going after it.

"He's not great at talking about himself," Meghan said. She poured filtered water into a tall glass. "Of course, there's a reason for that. No one else has been here?" she asked, laughing.

I felt my eyes widen. "No," I said.

"No . . . other women?" she asked. "Another wife? Another baby?"

I couldn't stop looking at the baby. Bear's baby. "No, ma'am," I said. "Just Bear."

"And what are you doing?" she asked again.

"Painting."

She looked at my clothes. My own jeans, but Bear's T-shirt. Both clean, both free of paint. I was barefoot.

"Is that it?" she asked.

I stammered. "Unpacking," I said. "Moving stuff." The words felt jumbled in my mouth. I couldn't tell her what I was actually doing.

Meghan nodded and smiled. "You're his minion," she said.

All I could think was that a minion was an animal, a donkey, or an ass. A Sherpa who carries all your shit up a mountain. A minion was something the devil had, to do his dirty work.

"It's okay," Meghan said. In all her perfect, milky-white skin, there was a scar below her left ear. It followed the curve of her jaw, fading. It had healed well, had likely been stitched shut and watched carefully. Nothing like the rippled welts of my scars. When she saw that I noticed it, she touched it, ran her finger down the length of it. She wrinkled her nose in disgust.

"We're not together," she said. "We have an agreement."

I heard the sweep and heavy close of the garage door, and Bear's footsteps in the hall.

"Well, well," he said, his voice echoing.

The baby scooted toward Bear, her arms bouncing, excited.

My stomach felt like it would never uncoil.

"What's the occasion?" Bear asked.

Meghan took a stack of papers from her bag and slapped them on the kitchen island. I tried to turn and duck into the basement, where I'd belonged the whole time, but Bear caught my elbow.

"Stay," he said.

That's it. No introduction. No *This is my minion, Shannon The one who sleeps with me.*

Bear picked up the baby.

"Bee wanted to see you," Meghan said.

"Oh, really?" Bear said. "Did she tell you that?" He flicked his eyebrows at Meghan, but he nuzzled the baby's neck and Bee laughed, mouth open, gruff, from her belly. Then he put her back on the floor with her toy, where she was unsatisfied, scooting, fussing, and jamming her fist in her mouth.

Meghan flipped open the stack of long contract papers. They were flagged in places where Bear was supposed to sign.

"You didn't have to drop these off," Bear said. "But," he added, "you wondered what I was up to."

She looked at me. "I see what you've been up to," she said. I looked away.

"I'll send them back," Bear said.

I could see that the baby, Bee, was about to let out a wail, so I did what came naturally to me and scooped her up, my arm under her butt and my hand in her armpit. She pushed her face against my shoulder, rooting.

Meghan watched me with her daughter. "You could sign them now," she said to Bear. "Maybe he could nurse your daughter."

I hid my face in Bee's hair and tried to shush her. She smelled like clean powdery baby.

Bear showed his teeth. Not exactly a smile. "There's no way I'm signing this without edits," he said. He put his phone, his wallet, and his keys on top of the contract, claiming it, saving it for later. Then he walked to the front door and pulled it open, stood waiting. A sharp wind had picked up, especially up there, on the hill. Leaves turned in circles across the lawn.

I smoothed Bee's superfine copper hair.

"He's cute," Meghan said to Bear, and took the baby from me. "And too young for you," she said. "Not that you care." She took the diaper bag from the table, and the baby wrapped her fist into her mother's hair. Meghan stared Bear in the eye, then shifted to the side and looked back at me.

"He's a piece of shit," she said to me. "There's no way he's told you everything."

"Not in front of Bee," Bear said. "I'm sure that's in the contract?"

Meghan shook her head and didn't look back.

When he was shutting the door behind her, I stole into the basement and stood in a dry corner, where I craned my neck and then smashed my face as hard as I could into the wall without getting a running start.

It lit up all my bones. The hot pain, ringing in my skull. It gave the other pain a place to go. I did it again.

"I'm sorry," Bear said from the stairs. He stood with his shoulders square, his hands open. He hadn't seen me hit my face.

"You should have told me," I said with my back to him.

"It's usually a deal breaker," he said, light.

I turned around, not smiling. When he came closer, he looked at my face, where it was flaming, and at the wall, where my face had left a mark in the fresh paint.

"Were you just not going to tell me?" I said.

"I was," he said.

"When?"

He slid his fingers along my cheekbone, where it pulsed under his touch. And then down the line of my jaw, his thumb over the curve of my top lip.

"Soon," he said, low.

"What else don't I know?" I said.

He leaned in and kissed the skin in front of my ear, not where I'd smashed my face but behind that, a soft, tender spot. My skin prickled with his breathing.

"I'll tell you," he said.

He didn't have his hands on me anymore. Just his mouth. He grazed his lips over the hot part of my cheek, where my face throbbed underneath. I could feel my pulse.

"What are you going to tell me?" he asked. I had to grip his shirt to keep from falling over. My knees were turning to water.

Anything, I thought. Anything you want to hear. He could ask me to kill someone, with his lips on my ear, and I would do it.

TWENTY: KATERI

It's not a jail; it's a justice center. It's where both Kateri and Joel have small offices adjacent to each other, where Chief Whittaker has a large office with a wall of windows, where the deputies have their cubicles. And it's where Shannon Jenkins is held in one of a few small cells. If he is ordered to stay incarcerated after his arraignment, they will move him to a county prison outside of town. If he is convicted on even one count of murder, he will end up in maximum.

He is likely to be charged with one count of second-degree murder in the killing of Craig O'Neil, second-degree murder in the killing of his mother, and first-degree kidnapping.

She can't imagine him in maximum, his thin arms and his soft face.

"I don't think it was forethought," she says to Hurt.

"Really?" he says. He stands with his back to her in her own office, fidgeting with the fat leaves on a jade plant on top of the filing cabinet. "Don't be naïve, Fisher."

"I just don't," she says again, but looks down. It weakens her argument, she knows, but she feels weak about all of it, like she put herself on the line.

"It's an open-and-shut case, Fisher," he says. "All the pieces are there."

"They don't fit," she says. "We can't confirm the murder weapon without a body. A good defense lawyer will eat this case alive," she added.

"That's not our job. Our job is just to arrest him."

She chews her lip, looks at the situation board, the young, scared picture of Shannon from high school.

"I'm going to be out tomorrow morning," Hurt says then. "Unreachable. For a few hours."

Kateri raises her eyebrows at him.

"I have a breakfast." He doesn't want to tell her.

"For the case?"

"No," he says. He stands sideways in the doorway, slim. "With my son," he says.

She tucks her head back, surprised. "Oh," she says. "I didn't realize."

"You don't know everything about me," Hurt says.

"I don't know anything about you," Kateri says.

"He's twenty-two," Hurt says.

"Oh," she says.

"I'll check my messages after one," he says. "Text me if anything new develops." He walks out and then steps back with one foot. "It won't," he says.

But she feels like there's something she's missing. Some other thread that has eluded her, something more complex than Shannon Jenkins acting alone. She misses things all the time. Has no idea what gives someone like Joel Hurt joy, or what has caused him pain, but now there's a full-grown man who belongs to him, who is part of him, and for whom Hurt is taking a very rare half day.

Details, she thinks.

There is something she has not noticed.

Her phone alerts her to a new email, and there's a message from Bear Miller.

I'd like to provide a defense attorney for Shannon Jenkins. Please call me.

She hits reply and types, *Why?*

But then deletes it.

*   *   *

When she visits the cell, Shannon won't look at her. He sits on the stainless-steel cot, leaned forward, elbows on his knees, his face turned away. He looks small in the prison-issued scrubs, his shoulders bony. His long, willowy arms are faintly striped with scars that Kateri recognizes as self-inflicted. Years ago, she thinks. They hold the pattern of purposeful injury.

"Shannon," she says. "I need you to tell me where we might find your sister."

He lets it sit between them, the heaviness of the missing girl, for a moment before he answers. "I don't know," he says, flat.

"The more time that passes," Kateri says, "the more dangerous it becomes."

He looks her in the eye. "I know."

She waits, and he says nothing more.

"A lawyer is being provided for you," she tells him.

"Free of charge?" Shannon says, and then looks at her. His right eye is bruised underneath—again, Kateri thinks, self-inflicted. "I need a court-appointed lawyer," Shannon says. "I can't afford one. Which basically means you can just move me to death row now," he adds.

"There's no death penalty in New York State," Kateri says.

"Oh, well goody," Shannon says.

"Bear Miller is providing an attorney for you," she says.

"Why?" he asks.

"I don't know," she says, and feels catty, and hates that feeling in herself. "He seems to have a soft spot for you," she says.

Shannon scoffs and then laughs, but it's bitter, hard, and there's not a hint, she thinks, of a smile, or any kind of mirth, on his face.

"Great," he says.

*　*　*

The attorney Bear sends is slick. Kateri has seen his type before, in Syracuse. He's not exceptionally good-looking, but his dress is outstanding. An expensive, precisely tailored suit. Immaculate shoes. A heavy watch that Kateri cannot make out the brand of. His hair is dark and well cut, combed off his forehead. He's fit. In fact, his body is perfect, like the only thing he does, other than work, is work out. He might be a machine, Kateri thinks. Or a robot. Or most likely, a sociopath.

He's a different kind of fit than Hurt. She knows that Joel runs, hikes. She imagines him kayaking with a slightly younger version of himself. His body is lean and well used. She wants to think that's what gives him joy. But she detects something hollow and lonely in Joel Hurt. Somehow, the wind blows through him.

"David Brewer," the lawyer says, and shakes her hand. He has dark eyes without smiling.

He is either a freak about cutting his nails, or he gets manicures.

Kateri begins to feel, as she often does in the presence of highly professional men, like she's the help instead of the lead investigator. Like she should be getting his coffee. Or minding his children.

It's the morning Hurt is off. She notices that Brewer looks around for another detective.

She hands him the Jenkins file, which he opens and appears to fall right into. Kateri's handwritten notes. The crime scene photos.

"Excellent," Brewer says, and leaves the file open on a photograph of the burned bones, the delicate curve of spine, the butterfly pelvis. "This is all you have?" he says.

"Nothing else has surfaced," Kateri says. "I think it's all that survived the fire."

She can see his wheels turning as he looks at the bones.

"DNA match?" he says.

"Not to Shannon," Kateri says. "I can put you in touch with the medical examiner. The blood found on the murder weapon matches what was in the house."

"Does the blood match?"

"Not Shannon," she says again.

He straightens up, like his job just got easier.

"His prints are all over the weapon."

Brewer looks at the photo of the bones. "How do you know that's the weapon?" he asks.

"It was with the bones."

"Hmm," he says, dissatisfied. He slaps the folder closed and looks first at Kateri's chest before meeting her eye. "I'll see my client now," he says.

She can't do it. It's a small team. She could walk down the hall, make small talk, usher him into the interrogation room. Make eye contact with Shannon to make sure he's okay with all of this. But she steps out of her office and motions to Dawn, the fiftyish mother who works for them as a receptionist.

"Dawn?" she says. "Would you escort Mr. Brewer down to Interrogation B, please? And have a guard fetch Mr. Jenkins?"

"It's a pleasure," Brewer says. It's then that he smiles.

"No problem," Kateri says. She folds her arms and retreats to her office.

* * *

She passes by twice, hours apart, and can see from the window in the door and from the two-way mirror in the observation room that David Brewer sits with Shannon Jenkins for more than three hours. He takes notes on a yellow legal pad, his handwriting slanted and hard. Some items are underlined, others starred. She catches a glimpse of Shannon's face, lit up with recognition, and then he shakes his head.

But I didn't, she imagines him saying.

She's not sure why it makes a difference to her at all.

She watches Shannon move his hands around the table, plotting out, she thinks, the layout of the house, the kitchen, Pearl's bedroom, Birdie's safe spot in the closet. She wants to tap on the glass. You have to tell the truth, she thinks. Tell him everything.

He was a soft-faced boy, she thinks, the first time she talked to him. Soft and scared. And now something has crept in at the edges, has hardened the bones in his cheeks and jaw. Something has left a shadow under his eyes and around his neck like long fingers.

She looks at the way the bruises are disappearing on his skin. Where the thumb would have gone. Where the fingertips were. She puts her hand to her own throat and feels, recognizes what it was that unsettled her before.

There's no way Pearl Jenkins's hand was that big.

* * *

On her way back from Interrogation B, she swings by Hurt's office to see if he's in yet. It's past three. His office is still generic, still like he's using borrowed, temporary space. The chair pushed in, the computer monitor off.

She walks around the desk and opens a side drawer, not sure what she's even looking for.

A lint roller. A small paper copy of *Be Here Now* with an ornately illustrated cover. A river stone. She closes the drawer abruptly, and when it slams, she jumps.

On her way out, she glances at the reception desk.

"Any word from Detective Hurt?" Kateri asks, her phone buzzing in her pocket with a text message.

"No, ma'am," Dawn says.

She turns her back to Dawn's desk as she reads the message.

It's an unknown number: *Envious of the person who does get to have a drink with you, Detective. Maybe we can fix that.*

Kateri stands still in the middle of the reception area, Dawn answering the phone, keyboards clacking away, the printer whirring and spitting out pages.

Bear? she types and sends, and regrets immediately not using a more formal tone.

What big . . . eyes you have, he answers.

She laughs aloud, but it's tight and nervous.

She deletes the messages, her hands jumpy. And then regrets that too.

TWENTY-ONE: SHANNON

TUESDAY, OCTOBER 10

He finally told me. I was afraid to ask, and threw myself into work—shifts at the diner, work in the house—and it took more than a week before I could ask anything. What did she mean? What didn't I know? I couldn't even begin to explain what I did know.

I could hardly listen. I watched his face, his hair, his eyes, his hands. The way he breathed. His mouth.

They got married when he was thirty.

She wanted a baby. He didn't.

He hadn't really even wanted to get married.

They'd been living apart since before Bee was born.

"Bee?" I asked him.

"Like a bumblebee," he said.

"Like a birdie," I said.

"Or a bear," he said, getting closer.

I thought it, or rather saw it in my head, the sentence, typed out and lit up, but it was Bear who said it aloud: "We belong to each other."

*　　*　　*

We sat on the bed with the dog. I had never finished the basement after I hid the gun and uncovered the photos. After I smashed my face into the wall. I had a tender spot that would turn green in a day. I'd left the basement half done, partially masked, the coat uneven. I started upstairs instead, painted a gray bathroom, a green bedroom. I asked Bear to explain the business to me. I asked him what else he had done, what he had kept a secret.

"It's my mother's company," he said.

He was such an adult to me, I had never even imagined him with a mother. Or a family. I stopped him.

"Are there more of you?" I asked.

He laughed. "There's only one of me," he said.

I stumbled. "I mean, you know, brothers and sisters."

"No," he said. "Just me, and my mom, who took over my dad's company after he died."

"Do you work for her?"

"Sort of," he said. "I invest her interests."

"Right," I said, faking it. I'd been making seven dollars and fifty cents an hour for four years.

"It's a complicated web of transactions right now." He pressed his lips together.

"Is that the secret?" I asked. "That you don't really work for her? It's just like, money?"

"No," he said.

"What is it?"

He took his hand from mine and tucked his hands between his knees. "I got in trouble as a kid," he said. The dog stretched between us, his frog legs out behind, his head ducked underneath a pillow.

"Legal?" I said. I couldn't imagine him committing a crime. Stealing. Why would he steal? Then it occurred to me. I could imagine him raping someone. I thought about the power he held when he leaned over me. I held my breath and waited.

"Yeah," he said, "although nothing ever really came of it. So," he said. "I don't have a record."

"Were you arrested?" I asked.

"Yes," he said, "but it was all expunged."

"What happened?"

"I got in a fight," he said. "The summer right before I went to college."

"That's it?" I said, waiting.

"No," he said. I watched him blow out a long breath. "The other kid died."

"How?" I yelped. "From the fight?"

"Yeah," Bear said.

"How?"

He seemed to hold his breath. I had never seen him stressed, not even when Meghan was there. And I wasn't sure he was now. He might be pausing for effect. But I was on edge, listening to the story, waiting.

"I hit him," he said. Then, "With a bat."

It was so quiet I could hear the refrigerator come on in the kitchen. "You killed him," I said.

"I was seventeen," he said.

"And nothing happened?"

"No," Bear said. "I mean, a lot happened, but my father's lawyer took care of all of it."

"If anyone knew I even thought about killing someone, I would be in jail," I said.

"I know," Bear said. "It's a terrible misuse of privilege. But that's what happened. That's the thing. That's the secret," he said. "Meghan likes to hold it over me."

"The secret is that you killed someone," I said, my voice high, on the edge of hysteria. I got up off the bed.

"Shannon," he said, trying to appeal to me.

I couldn't stop the words from coming out of my mouth. "You killed someone," I said. "You killed another kid."

"Shannon," he said again.

I covered my own mouth. I thought I might scream.

"I'm not telling you to scare you," he said. "I'm telling you the truth. I'm not dangerous," he said. "I was a stupid kid. It was an accident. I meant—I meant to knock him out," he said. He held his hands open, palms up, waiting for me to take them. "I'm not going to hurt you," he said.

I was shaking inside.

"Listen," he said. "I could have told you anything, but I told you the truth. I could have made something up, right? The secret could have been that I cheated on Meghan."

"You are cheating on Meghan," I said.

His voice was low and determined. "I told you the truth." He made his face softer, his eyes bigger, his mouth loosened so it wasn't so rigid. "Please," he said.

"Please what?" I said.

"Come back here," he said, holding his hands out.

I was still standing in the room, wringing my hands. Buddy rolled over onto his back, and Bear slapped his belly. The dog groaned with pleasure, his lips loose, his eyes half closed.

I got back on the bed, the dog between us, and I sat quiet for a few heavy moments, until Bear put his hand behind my knee, fingers moving in the crease. The dog snuffled back under the pillows, and I thought that maybe there would be a million things running, manic, through my mind, but all I could see was his face telling me: the other kid died.

I thought about Meghan saying they weren't together, that they had an agreement, the long stroke of her finger down her jaw. "What happened to Meghan's face?" I asked him.

"We were in a car accident," Bear said.

"Really?" I asked.

He took his hand away. "You can believe me or not believe me. I didn't hurt her. Or I did hurt her, in many awful ways, but that was not one of them." He pushed the dog off the bed with a sweep of one leg, and Buddy stretched on his way, his hind legs hooked on the mattress, dragging. "If you don't believe me," he said, "this will never work."

I sat, small and dumb. "What will never work?" I asked.

He came toward me on all fours. "You and me," he said. He took my face and kissed me. "I'm not lying to you," he said. "And I'm not trying to hurt you. I want you to trust me."

The room felt like a vacuum. Everything felt different—his hands, the way he moved me around. Like I could feel his fingerprints on my bones. And nothing outside that room was real.

It was hard to pay attention. I kept thinking of the dead kid, bleeding out, his head bashed open. Maybe it hadn't been that hard. Maybe his death was delayed.

My distraction stopped him.

He stopped. In the middle of kissing me, when he had already pushed the covers on the bed down to make a space for us, had already gotten undressed. He stopped, leaned over me, and I snapped my eyes open, like I was coming back from the dead, like I was coming up for air.

He leaned into my neck. "I want you to trust me," he said.

"Okay," I said. It was empty.

He ran his hands along my collarbone, up, onto my neck. And then pressed his thumb into the side of my windpipe, his fingers tight.

"Do you?" he asked.

"Yes," I whispered.

"Things are going to scare you," he said. "But it's okay. I'm not dangerous," he said. "You think the wrong people are trying to hurt you."

He tightened his hand, and he thrust hard into me so that my whole body was jolted with a shot of pain. My mouth opened, and I gasped.

"Now?" Bear said.

I shook my head. I didn't know what he was asking.

"Do you trust me?"

My air was tight. My chest panicky. My heart raced hard, and a fine sweat broke out along my shoulders, down my back, across my forehead. He squeezed.

"Tell me," Bear said, between his teeth as his back arched and pumped. "Tell me."

My eyes streaked pink with shooting stars when I came. My head was like a pounding balloon. My vision began to darken from the outside in.

"I trust you," I mouthed. But my limbs were weak. My voice gone.

*   *   *

In the morning, I leaned into the mirror, inspecting my own face. Normally, I avoided it. I was disappointed by my own mediocrity. My left eye was bloodshot in a way that was different from smoking or drinking. The redness was heavy in one spot, with a streak of blood. Underneath both my eyes were dark freckles, not pigment but blood, rising up from underneath the skin.

It hurt to swallow.

My neck was shadowed with the shape of Bear's hand. A deep, dark thumbprint along my windpipe and a stretch of fingers around the side.

I thought: He's going to kill me.

Just like he killed that other kid. And some expensive lawyer is going to erase me from history. Like I never was.

Worse, it was going to feel so good I wouldn't stop it until it was too late.

*   *   *

Bear was in the kitchen, making breakfast, bacon and a diced-up potato, and when I came out from the master bedroom, showered, dressed, and feeling like someone else in a clean shirt and dry socks, Bear added an egg to the skillet and fried it over easy.

He put the plate in front of me and poured me a mug of coffee. I followed a vein of quartz in the stone counter top.

Things were getting away from me. At an alarming speed. The house, my mother, what to do with Birdie. I had wanted Bear to be a safe port, and I was beginning to question everything.

But even though I was the one who felt unmoored, I decided to turn it around on him. I wanted to see if I could get him to talk.

"What are you thinking?" I asked him.

"About what?" he said. He had a way of concentrating, looking down, his brows knit tight, his mouth a straight line, and then looking up and grinning like a fool, showing all his teeth. It was on the edge of cruel. I realized that part of his catlike quality was the potential to pounce.

I shrugged. He chuckled, like an adult humoring a kid. Then he said, "I don't want you to go back there."

"Home?"

He tipped his head to the side, leaned on the island, and took a potato off my plate with his fingers. "I don't want you to stay there anymore," he said.

I sipped the coffee, clenching my teeth to get past the ache in my throat. The coffee was better when he made it. He ground the dark oily beans and brewed it extra strong. But I missed the way my mother made coffee, with a cheap can of Bustelo, brewed in the percolator on the stove, mixed with just a hint of cinnamon.

"Well," I said, my voice husky. "What are you asking me?"

Bear opened his hands on the counter, an offering. "I want you to stay here," he said.

I started coughing. I felt a sharp piece of bacon in my throat and took a hot gulp of coffee.

Bear came around behind me and kissed the top of my head. "Do you want me to get you a ring?" he joked.

"You're still married," I said.

His hands moved down my sides, over my ribs, pressing. I couldn't answer. I couldn't say what was needling me: the wife, the baby, the dead boy. What I might have to do with Birdie, and when. I drummed my fingers beside the plate but didn't notice until Bear put his hand on top of mine.

"You're safe here," he said. "You know that."

I nodded.

"Let's figure out what to do with your house," he said.

"Like what?" I asked.

"Why let it go to auction?" he said. "You could sell it."

"It's not worth shit, Bear."

He shrugged. "Somebody always wants real estate. Even if they don't want the structure, they'll want the land."

My toes bounced on the rung of the stool. "You'll never get my mother out of that house," I said. "Not with Birdie." I shook my head. "It's . . ." I searched. "It's her place," I said. "It's all she's got."

I couldn't even begin to think of what I would tell them, how I would say that I was leaving. That I would live over here now.

Why? My mother would ask. Because he's rich?

"Just . . . try to trust me," he said, like he knew he'd get me to come around. He stroked the side of my neck with his finger, tracing the places that ached.

* * *

After breakfast, we put Buddy in the Land Rover, and Bear asked me what I needed from the house. Buddy butted his nose against the window in excitement. He knew we were headed toward the woods.

There wasn't much. A few books, I thought. Some clothes. I wanted to check on Birdie. I needed a moment alone with her, wanted her on my lap, wanted to rough up her curls, get her to belly laugh. I needed to know that I could see her whenever I wanted. What I really wanted was to take her with me. I would send her to school. Set things right for her. She still had a chance.

I told Bear I just needed to check on her.

"Of course," he said. "You should."

We parked in the lot and opened the door for Buddy, who tore off after a rabbit in the field.

"I want you to come here as often as you want," Bear said.

"Okay," I said.

"I'm not trying to take you away."

"I know."

He turned the engine off and just sat, looking at me.

"But," I prompted, because I sensed it, that he wasn't saying something.

"But I want you in my bed every night," he said. He wasn't smiling. It wasn't flirtatious, and it wasn't *our* bed. It was a demand.

I felt myself tremble. I clamped down. He cupped my knee and shook it. I tried not to think of what he might look like in a rage. Or with a bat in his hand. Or what I might look like with my head bashed in.

TWENTY-TWO: KATERI

TUESDAY, OCTOBER 31

Sometimes she wonders about her ex, Andrew. Her grandmother knew his mother, and Kateri can remember him as much as a little boy as she can a man. He knew all her shit. About her mother, about her father. When they got to nineteen and they were both done with the family drama that was no longer theirs, they got married in a courthouse, by a judge. Kateri wore a yellow dress and put flowers in her hair. His mother was there, with her grandmother, holding hands.

It lasted five years.

She had started college without him, commuting in her grand-mother's rusted-out Toyota with peace signs on the bumper. She hated it—the classes, the other kids, the delayed adulthood. She was eager to work, to start living. So she joined the force at twenty-one and was ready to make detective by the time their marriage was over. Andrew thought she was single-minded and selfish. She thought he wasn't single-minded enough. She wanted him to be independent, for them to work hard, side by side. But she earned the money, and he resented that. They drank a lot. And fought. Or cried.

When he moved out, she helped him. They picked out his new place together, and she brought over boxes in her car.

"I'll see you in ten years," Andrew said.

"For what?" Kateri asked. She lived less than a mile away.

"Everything will be different then," Andrew said.

* * *

Afterward, she didn't date. She didn't then, and she still doesn't want a boyfriend, although she misses the feel of another body, the weight of someone, the thrill in a deep kiss. She craved the exhaustion of sex, some use for her body that wasn't work related. She sometimes didn't even tell them her name. Or she said her name was Kate, or Katie, depending on the guy. She didn't want to be traceable. She wanted sex as a physical transaction between bodies. When it was over, it was over, and it wasn't bogged down by love and drinking and crying and trying to make a life together. She thought she loved Andrew. She did love him. But when she moved to Spring Falls, she came without any attachments, certainly not a boyfriend, not even a cat. Her last living relative had died. She felt unmoored and unattached and empty, like a good strong wind might blow her away. She took a sunny upper apartment in a farmhouse outside of town, with bright oak floors and white walls. She brought things that reminded her of her grandmother's home: a dream catcher, river stones, candles.

When she was a rookie cop, the older men would hit on her. They liked her thick hair, her skin, the way her uniform stretched over her body. She had a burn on the inside of her wrist from when she was fifteen. Her mother's boyfriend had caught her coming in after two in the morning and pressed the hot crown of his lighter into her flesh. He was younger than her mother. He wasn't even thirty. "Next time," he said, "your neck." She'd been out with Andrew.

* * *

Halloween falls on a Tuesday. She stays late in an office filled with pumpkins and skeletons and then stops at home to change before she drives out to Mount Snow for a slow walk through an empty Walmart.

She's eager to be off duty. To be in regular, comfortable clothes, to shop anonymously. In the store, the costumes are picked over, half on the floor, ghoulish heads and witch hats strewn in the aisle. She buys one bag of candy, for herself, and some new candles, including a seven-day Lady of Guadalupe. No kids will come to her house. She leaves her porch light off. Cemetery Road is forty-five miles per hour, and people tend to go much faster. The kids in Spring Falls trick-or-treat in town.

She comes home after nine, when most of the town's kids have gone in for the night, chilled to the bone and sugared up. There are trails of toilet paper in the trees, silly string on the stop signs, but the town is quiet. On Cemetery Road, one small car is parked off to the side, broken down, she guesses, or maybe it's a couple. She catches it in her headlights when she pulls into her own driveway.

She hasn't gotten used to the country dark. She catches herself squinting when she drives at night, or wide-eyed, searching for the shape of the road in front of her. The fields on either side could be anything—ocean, sky. She comes up the stairs in the dark, feeling her way, wishing she'd left the light on. Over the railing, she sees the field next door, hears the whisper of cornstalks farther away, the rush of the river. And a voice.

"Detective."

Her heart spasms hard in her chest, leaving her breathless. It's Bear Miller, in the shadow beside her door. He has a bottle of Angel's Envy rye. When she sees him, he moves over, his arm across the threshold of her door.

She lays her hand over her heart, willing it to slow, and drops the bag to the porch floor. "How did you find out where I live?" she says. She tries to stay smooth. Tries to hide the panic in her voice.

"In this town?" Bear says. "You just have to ask the right people." He tips his head to the side, blinks slow. "I brought you something," he says, and holds up the bottle. "Some of it's already gone."

He holds the bottle to his lips, drinks, and then tips it toward her.

"No," she says.

"What did you think of Brewer?" he asks.

Beyond the porch, the wind whistles through the cornfield. Far off, she sees the orange light of a bonfire.

She exhales slow, her breath a long visible line in the cold air. Her entire body is taut, on guard. "How long have you been out here?" she asks.

Bear shrugs.

"What did you think?" he asks again.

"I thought he was slick," she answers. "But quite possibly what Shannon needs."

"What Shannon needs is a miracle worker," Bear says. "A guardian angel." He laughs, his mouth wet and open. "An act of God."

"Then why'd you hire him?" she asks.

Bear shrugs. "He's the best there is," he says.

"What do you care?"

A gust comes off the field and whips her hair over her face. Bear takes the opportunity to brush it away from her eyes, off her lips. He holds a hunk of hair in his hand, over her shoulder, and moves so that his body is in front of the door, more in the light. He's wearing a knit hat and a leather jacket, the same as last time she saw him. A flannel shirt. An erection is visible through his jeans.

Her phone is buried in her bag. Her keys are in her hand. She can't call anyone for backup, and she's unarmed.

"You need to leave," she warns.

He plants his feet and braces himself against the door.

"Or?" he says. He swipes out at her waist, and she jumps away before he can reach her. She's not sure what he was grabbing for. The pocket of her jeans? The belt loop? Something to hook her and bring her closer. When he misses, he leans forward and laughs, takes another drink.

He nods at the door behind him. "Go in," he says. He moves his hand down the front of his jeans, stroking.

"Not until you leave," she says. She watches his eyes dart.

"The keyhole's right there," he says, and traces his finger over it. "Go ahead."

She looks down the stairs. She could just leave. Get back in her car, drive to the station, make Hurt come back with her. Except that she's incensed at having Miller at her own house, blocking her door. She was off guard. She wants into her own home.

Instead, she tries to leave, her purse on her shoulder, the Walmart bag on the floor, but when she turns just a fraction, he hooks his finger into the back pocket of her jeans and pulls her in, switching their spots, Kateri with her back against the door and Bear in front of her. He holds her hand that has her keys, by the wrist, hard. When she wiggles her fingers, he presses on her tendons and her arm shoots with pain, but she won't let go.

He pushes his knee between her legs and has her pinned against the door. She can feel him against her leg. She turns her face away, her eyes on the pines across the street, her hand going numb, his whiskey breath near her ear.

"You're strong," he says. She feels his tongue along the folds of her ear. Her stomach tightens, her spine stiff.

"Fuck off," she says, flinching away.

"Don't be coy," he says.

She gathers strength like a coiled spring, appearing to soften beneath him so that he presses harder against her. He pushes his lips into her collarbone and inspects the scar under her chin.

"What's this?" he asks, and runs his cold finger along it so that she shivers.

"What didn't kill me," she says.

He sniffs into her hair. "Did it make you stronger?" he asks.

"Try me," she says.

205

Then, "I can smell that you want it."

She lurches and pushes him back. It might be just enough to let her duck and run, she thinks, just enough to break the spell and give her a chance to get away. But when he steps back to regain his balance, his foot lands on the candle, the cylinder rolling, shooting his leg out in front of him, throwing him off, sending him in a tumble down an entire flight of porch stairs.

She unlocks the door, slips inside alone, and turns the bolt.

She covers her mouth, trying not to scream in anger, to release some of what has built up in her racing heart, and she hears him in the driveway, yelling, "Fuck. Fuck you, Fisher," he yells. She barely breathes, trying to listen for the sound of his feet in the gravel. She doesn't know if he's hurt. He yells it again, and then after a moment she hears the roar of the engine of the small car that was parked alongside the road. His. She didn't realize. She thought he drove something more substantial.

She peers through the side of the curtains, watches the lights as he turns the car around and then speeds down Cemetery Road, leaving a patch of rubber on the pavement. And then she unlocks the door just enough to reach outside for the bottle of whiskey. She sees the bag. The spilled candy crushed underfoot when he fell. The Lady of Guadalupe on her side like a rolling pin.

* * *

She takes a long drink from the bottle, and as soon as the warmth hits her throat, down, into her belly, her face floods with tears. Everything that has been held so tight, so hard, rushes out of her, and she doubles over onto the living room floor. She drinks again.

Her phone buzzes deep inside her bag, and she assumes it's him, it's Bear Miller, taunting her now via text. She digs it out and sees instead a text from Hurt. *You still in the office Fisher?*

"Ugh, fuck you," she says at the phone. What she wants is a girlfriend, another woman whose house she can go to and stay up all night in, cry in if she feels like it, yell if that's better. She has never been good at keeping women as friends. They compete. She's threatening, or she's threatened, and a man gets in the way. She closes her eyes and thinks there's nothing more she wants than to see her grandmother one more time, to sit across from her at the kitchen table, for her to say complete bullshit to her like everything's going to be fine, just so Kateri can hear her voice.

She lets herself sob for a minute. Then she gets up and checks outside to make sure he's really gone, and by then, her phone is buzzing again.

It's Hurt, and he's calling.

"Yeah," she says.

"Anyone come to your door?" Hurt says, and for a moment she stiffens with panic, thinking that Hurt was in on it somehow. That he set her up for a test she didn't see coming. That somehow, in addition to her accident and her drinking, he found out about the men she'd slept with in Syracuse, that he was trying to tempt her to ruin everything.

"What?" she snaps.

"Kids," he says. "Trick-or-treaters."

"What?" she says again. "No."

"You sound weird," Hurt says. "Where are you?"

"Home," she says.

"Are you okay?"

"Yeah."

He pauses. "Are you drinking?" he asks.

"Yeah, Hurt." She rolls her eyes, even though he can't see it. "I'm fucking wasted," she says. "I have to go."

"Fisher," he says, sharp.

She inhales a raggedy sob.

"Do you need me to come by?" he asks.

She feels the yelp come out of her like it's a stone, projecting from her mouth. Her legs collapse on the floor, and she sits, unable to answer him.

"I'll be right there," he says.

*   *   *

She opens the door again, because she wants to hear him coming, wants to see that it's his car and not be surprised by a knock on the door after ten o'clock at night, in late October, when the whole town is reveling in dead things and darkness.

"Aren't you cold?" he says when he comes up. She's on the couch with her arms crossed and her knees up to her chest.

"I don't need you to save me," she says.

He frowns and shakes his head. "Wasn't my plan," he says. He looks at the bottle, the amount that is gone, or rather the amount that is left. "Company?" he says.

"I actually don't want to talk about it," Kateri says. "You should go home."

He shakes his head again. "It's late," he says, but she can't tell if he's agreeing to leave.

"Were you ever married?" she asks.

"Was your ex here?" he asks her.

"No, no," she says.

"Yeah," he says.

"What happened?" she asks.

Hurt sits in the chair opposite the couch and settles a minute before he answers her. "She died," he says.

"Oh fuck," Kateri says. "Really? Because now is not a good time to fuck with me."

"Fifteen years ago," he says.

"How?" she asks, and then she says, "Sorry."

"She had breast cancer," Hurt says.

"Joel," she says, and tilts her head to the side. "I'm sorry."

"Thanks," he says. "It's still hard," he says.

She remembers his son, now a grown man, but he must have been just a little boy when his mother died. Hurt must have raised him alone. She doesn't feel drunk anymore. She doesn't feel anything but empty and clawed at. "How old are you?" she asks Hurt.

"Forty-five," he says.

"She was so young."

He nods and then stands up. "You want some tea?" he asks.

And she sees him all at once, what it is that blows through him, the hollowness about his soul. She nods her head, because she's afraid if she speaks she'll cry, and she hears him go into the kitchen, fill the kettle, look in the cupboards for things that will soothe her instead of make her into his prey. He brings her a steaming mug of orange spice tea, and he's put honey it in because he's seen her do that at work, and he stays in the chair across from her, doesn't sit next to her or try to get close to her at all.

"I'll stay out here," he says, "if you want to go to bed."

"I won't sleep," she says.

He shrugs. "I'll stay out here anyway," he says.

But sometime after two, her body gives in and she curls onto her side on the couch, exhausted, cried out, and Hurt stays there in the living room, awake all night, sitting in the chair, and then sitting on the floor with his back against the couch while she sleeps. He watches the TV with the volume on about three, and she can't comprehend how he can even hear.

When she wakes up at seven, the *Today* show has started.

"Have you been there all night?" she asks.

"Yeah," he says. He gets up, stiff, and twists his back.

"You didn't have to," she says.

"Yeah, I did," he says. "Coffee?"

TWENTY-THREE: SHANNON

SUNDAY, OCTOBER 15

People walk dogs off leash in the woods all the time. You aren't supposed to. And mostly it's fine, but sometimes a runner will complain, or a hiker will call a dog vicious. I was afraid of having Buddy loose. His look scared people—his big square pit head, his strong jaw. Even though I knew him to be nothing but gentle, he had a prey drive that made me nervous. He'd lunge unexpectedly. I'd seen him kill a squirrel in the yard, his head whipping back and forth, the squirrel screaming.

When it was dead, he dropped it, and then rolled it over with his nose, trying to coax it into playing with him.

I didn't want Bear there. I could do it alone. It was better alone. Gathering my things, explaining things to Birdie in a way she would understand. She always understood more than I gave her credit for.

But I couldn't get away from him. His hand, even, steering my neck as we walked. I was afraid my mother would notice.

Inside the woods, Buddy bounded off, straight toward the house, and I was afraid that he'd overpower Birdie if she was out. Not that he'd hurt her. But he'd knock her down for sure. He might frighten her.

But the dog stopped on the porch, hovering near the door and barking. He leaned forward, front paws outstretched, not in play, and barked over and over, sharp, staccato warnings.

"Buddy," I said. I was glad then that I'd taken the gun and hidden it. The last thing I needed was to have my mother shoot the dog right in front of me. Or Bear. Because maybe this time she'd hit her intruder dead on and kill him.

"Buddy," Bear scolded the dog, calling him back, but he wouldn't budge, not even then, and he was usually scared of Bear. He just stood in the doorway, braced and barking.

The door was wide open, the screen bent backward, flat against the clapboard, and I could see the shadow of a bird inside, banging against the window, trying to find its way out.

"There's a bird," I said to Bear, and pointed at the dark form fluttering on the other side of the glass.

"Buddy," Bear called again. He got close enough to pat the dog on his side, a thick, closed thud.

"I can get it," I said. I'd done it before. The last time I'd tried guiding the bird out with a book, waving at it, but it just confused the bird, so I got close enough to cup its tiny, beating body. It was a catbird. A small, round, gray bird with a nearly transparent beak and tiny, sharp claws.

Bear pointed at Buddy and told him to wait. Buddy bared his teeth as he barked, snapping. I'd never seen him like that. Bear crossed the threshold into the house and stepped inside, looking for the bird, back and forth from room to room, but then stepped out.

I thought maybe it was a bat, but it was midafternoon.

"No," Bear said, and took my shoulders, hard. "Don't," he said.

Buddy kept on barking. I heard the clamp of his jaws each time. The bird battered itself against the glass.

"I can get it," I said again. I'd liked the feel of the bird in my hand for those few seconds, before it realized it was free. Before it took off.

Bear put his hands on the sides of my face. "Shannon," he said, stern. "What happened?"

My stomach turned. "What?" I asked. "I don't know what you mean," I said. I tried again to get past him and into the house.

Bear started to walk me backward up the gravel path. "Buddy," he called, sharp. "Come."

I had to fight to get his hands off me, but I found that I couldn't. He was stronger than I thought, and determined. "Let me go," I said.

I thought, maybe they're gone. Maybe the house is empty and a bear has come through, ransacked the cupboards, the stinking refrigerator. I thought of her traveling on foot through the trees with Birdie on her back, disappearing into Canada. Changing her name.

My father had been in jail for fifteen years. No one had told us when he might get out. I wondered what she knew.

I ducked under Bear's stiff, outstretched arm and made for the doorway, past the still-barking dog.

At first sight, the house was a mess, but nothing more than normal. Shoes and clothes on the floor and dishes on the table. There was a high cloud of cigarette smoke, and underneath that, a dark and metallic smell. Not like food. Not even rotting food. It smelled like blood.

There was blood on the walls, the cupboards, the ceiling, and a puddle on the floor, with the drag of a body through it.

I couldn't breathe, my throat sore and contracting. I ran from the house back outside, fell to my knees and vomited up everything I'd eaten. It was so violent I could barely take a breath back in. I opened my eyes wide, like I was drowning, and sat up, arched my back, wheezing in air, my chest tight and panicked.

"Shannon," Bear said behind me. The dog was still barking, but he had circled over to me and my vomit and was sniffing us both out.

I gasped for breath, my nose flaring.

It came back to me all at once: the feel of smoke, burning my eyes, constricting my airway, the desperate crawl through the farmhouse while the beams fell, flaming. "Mom," I yelled, and in my head I heard my little-kid voice, calling for her, but I was saying it now. "Mom," I called.

"Shannon," Bear said again, in the same voice he used on the dog. I half expected him to say, "Come," and for me to do it.

The trails were wet and cold, even in the sun. A couple of runners called out to us from the path. They'd heard me scream. They saw me on my knees in the gravel.

"Everything okay?" the guy yelled.

"Yeah, yeah," Bear answered. "Dead deer," he said, and then waved them on.

"Shannon," he said to me, quiet and terse.

My throat felt like it was bleeding. He pulled me to standing. My head was light and I had to hold on to his arms, he had to hold me upright.

"What did you do?" I said.

"What did I do?" Bear asked, sharp. I watched behind him as the dog went back to the door but was quiet. He sniffed, his head low and cautious.

"Did you do this?" I said again, my voice like it had razors in it. "What we talked about," I said. I held my hand out toward the house. "The house," I said. "The boy," I said. "The one who died," I whispered. I felt crazy. Like I was putting together pieces of a bad dream.

He put his hands on my shoulders, heavy, and I felt like he was pressing me into the ground, or like he was the only thing holding me to earth. "Do you think I'm out of my fucking mind?" he asked.

"Yes," I said, my eyes wide. I gasped again. "You want the truth?" I said. "Yes, I do. I'm fucking terrified," I said.

I started to scream again, and I thought he was going to hit me, but he covered my mouth. Behind his palm, my face broke open and all that came out was crying, my cheeks wet and my mouth open. When he let go, my belly caved in, and I fell up against him.

He held me for a moment, just his arms around my back, his hand rubbing. Then he picked my face up.

"Did you?" he asked.

I felt hollow. I thought the answer was obvious, but I'd done so many strange things since I'd met him, I wasn't sure of anything.

"Me?" I said.

"What happened?" he asked again, as if I knew. Then he said, "It's why I told you. I can get you out of it," he said. "If you did."

"I didn't do it," I said.

He looked hard at me.

"I was in your bed all night," I said, and he nodded, but his eyes were sly, shifting. "So were you," I added, but I knew, as soon as I said it, that when I finally fell asleep, I'd had no idea if he was there or not. And the same was true of me for him.

"Listen to me," he said, holding my face. "Listen."

There was so much blood. I looked, panicked, at my own shoes, but it didn't look like I'd stepped in it. I screamed for Buddy not to go in. I couldn't imagine getting blood off his white paws. I thought of him leaving prints all over the model home, the floors, the white bed, of my mother's blood.

I tried to get free to go back into the house.

"Shannon," he warned.

I wailed under his grip, and he put his hand over my mouth again, even tighter. My nose flared and I reeled it in. His stare was hard. His eyes a weird bright green in the forest light.

"I am going to make a call," Bear said. I felt like I was choking. "And then we're going to leave."

"Where is she?" I asked, frantic.

He shook his head. "I don't know," he said. It felt like frost coming from his lips.

"How am I supposed to know that you didn't do this?"

"Shannon," he said. "I was with you." He took my face. "I was with you," he said again. "Say it. I was with you. You were with me."

I swallowed hard and saw a flash of light behind my eyes from the pain. "I have to get Birdie," I said.

"Listen to me," Bear said, his voice so calm it felt blue to me, like a blue light, shining through dark water.

"She can't be in there with that. She can't be alone," I said.

His look had changed. It was hard, searching. "She's not there," he said.

"She's probably in the closet," I yelped. "That's where my mother puts her." My mind raced, and my body was sore, from retching, from tension. I looked at my hands, my own skin, for freckles of blood. I didn't know who to trust.

"She puts her in the closet?" Bear asked. I thought: I am insane. This has made me insane.

"Give me your phone."

He looked afraid. For the first time ever, I looked at his face and thought he looked scared. Not of everything that was happening, but like he was scared of me. What I might do. Like he might be next. It filled me with enough rage that I thought he might be justified. I noticed the toes of his boots were soaked in blood.

"No," he said, when I held my hand out, and tucked the phone away.

"So I can use the flashlight," I yelled.

I pointed at the hose on the side of the house.

"What?" he said.

I made him hose off his boots, pink water running off the soles.

"Come on," I said, when the water finally ran clear.

*   *   *

Outside the Land Rover, I made him take off his boots.

"I washed them," he said.

"Give them to me," I said.

He seemed alarmed at my directness. He bent and unlaced the boots, took them off, and then I said, "Socks too," and he did as he was told.

"What are you doing?" he said.

I walked them over to the dumpster behind the pavilion and threw them in. I took mine off and did the same. He stood there barefoot in the parking lot.

"Those are five-hundred-dollar boots."

"So?" I said. "You don't have another five hundred dollars? You want to get into your car with my mother's blood on your boots?" I asked. "Are you crazy? Trash comes tomorrow," I said.

He narrowed his eyes. "How do you know that?" he asked, like I'd been scheming.

"I live here," I shouted. I gripped and released my hands, trying to remember anything.

I got into the car barefoot, and Buddy jumped into the back seat. The dog leaned over my shoulder and panted, his nose wet and his breath hot. I felt like I'd been hit over the head and stunned. My body ached. My throat was sore. I watched Bear, pacing in the grass, phone cupped in his hand. I watched his shoulders hunch while he bent at the waist, yelling something I couldn't make out.

Buddy nudged the side of my face, hungry, impatient.

The dog didn't know the difference. He'd forgotten the trauma of the blood. I was just his other owner, the one in the passenger seat, the one on the left side of the bed.

My mother's truck was parked in the last spot, under a pine tree. I fished my keys out of my pocket and walked over to it, while Bear put his phone away and called out to me.

"What are you doing?" he asked, suspicious.

"Taking my own car," I said.

When he looked at me, blank, searching, I said, "I'll meet you there."

* * *

I went around the park and drove slow up and down the hill of Mill Street before I went up Fountain. Baby Jane's remained closed up tight, the way it had been the last time I was there. The blinds without an inch of light coming in or out, the yard neat and empty. A newspaper sat, damp and rolled, on the concrete step.

Back at his house, Bear asked me to make him a drink.

"Of what?" I asked. My head felt stuffed with cotton.

"Whiskey," he said.

I stood in front of the bar. There were three different types of whiskey and a variety of glasses. I always drank straight from a small, plastic bottle. Usually Canadian Club, usually with Baby Jane. I picked up a bottle called Angel's Envy and poured it into a heavy-bottomed glass.

"Make it how?" I asked, stupid.

Bear hunched over his phone on the island. "Just put ice in it, honey." He was texting quickly, with both thumbs, and then swiping over the glass, deleting as he went.

I put the drink on the island. "What's going on?" I asked.

"Nothing," he said, and frowned before he looked up. "Meghan," he said.

I was about to ask him how often he saw Bee but couldn't get the words out of my tight throat. I plunked down on the stool across from him and held my head.

"What am I going to do?" I asked.

Bear pushed the drink at me.

"You're going to take a drink," he said, "and a deep breath, and relax."

I didn't know who he'd talked to or what he'd said. He'd made the phone call far away from me, with his shoulders hunched and his back turned.

"What did you tell them?" I asked.

"Who?" he said.

"Nine-one-one," I said.

"Just to check the welfare," he said.

"What does that mean?"

"You know," he said. "If you haven't seen a neighbor or you think a kid is at home alone. You ask the police to come check the welfare of the occupants."

"Did you say that?" I asked. I felt my hair stand on end. "Did you mention her?" They were going to find her. It was going to be over. I had no idea what that meant for me. Or her.

"No," Bear said. He held up his hands in surrender.

"But they know it was you who called," I said.

He shrugged. "I'm just a bystander," he said.

I stared at him. "But you're not."

"There were lots of people in the park today," he said. "Anyone might have called."

"But they know it was your phone," I said.

"It doesn't matter," he said.

"They can trace you to me."

His mouth was tight, and he closed his eyes for a moment before he said anything. "I didn't use my phone," Bear said.

I felt in my pocket for mine, confused. "Whose phone did you use?" I asked.

"A burner," he said. He shook his head a little. "I threw it out."

"Why do you have a burner?" I asked. The whiskey was hitting me hard. I'd poured enough for him, which was too much for me.

"Look, it doesn't matter," he said. "Lay low. And I'll take care of it."

"I didn't do it," I said, full of confidence in that one second. "Did you?"

He looked at me hard, eyes blazing. "Oh my God, Shannon," he shouted, and I ducked. "No," he said.

"Why do you have a burner?" I hissed.

"Sometimes I need one," he said, showing his teeth, the way he had with Meghan.

I tried to believe him.

"There's nothing else for you to do right now," he said.

219

TWENTY-FOUR: KATERI

WEDNESDAY, NOVEMBER 1

At the station, Kateri makes another full pot of coffee and goes into her office alone. Hurt went home before he came in, to shower and change, and she won't blame him if he's taking a quick nap. She can't believe he was up all night.

She logs in to the state database and does another search for Bear Miller. Again she finds nothing out of the ordinary. He attended the University of Vermont. Is still listed as legally married, though she's never seen or heard anything about a wife. She doesn't know why she thinks she'll find something this time when she didn't last time. But part of her feels certain there's something not there, something redacted, something sealed.

She could press charges.

On what? she thinks. The threat? He'd say she pushed him down the stairs. And probably have the bruises to prove it.

She wants to walk down to Shannon's cell and ask him outright, "Did Bear Miller kill your mother? Did Bear Miller kill the cop? Did he take your sister? What has he done to you?"

But she knows he's tight-lipped and protective of Bear.

If she arrests Bear, who will pay for Shannon's defense? It's a sure bet that without it he'll be convicted. Of something he probably didn't do. Possibly something he was forced to watch someone else do.

Joel Hurt opens her door without knocking and she jumps, and he jumps. She spills coffee down her work pants and grabs a handful of tissues to mop it up.

"Someone spotted the girl," he says, and hands her a report. "And your report came back. There's blood that's not a match for Pearl or Shannon or the girl."

She throws the tissues into the garbage can under her desk and then moves her coffee cup away from the computer keyboard. "Where did they see her?" she asks.

"Dirt road near Star Lake," Hurt says. "Beside an old Buick."

"Alone?" Kateri asks.

"No description of the driver," Hurt says.

"Fuck," she says. She needs to get a DNA kit on Bear Miller.

She presses her fingers into her lips, and Hurt asks her, "Are you okay?"

"How can I see if someone has a sealed file?" she asks.

"Shannon Jenkins doesn't have previous," he says.

"Not Shannon," she says.

"You need an order," he says, and shrugs. "It's not hard. Who?"

"Bear Miller," she says.

She's afraid he will go straight to last night, but his head is in the case. "What makes you think?" he says.

She presses her mouth closed and shakes her head. "A feeling," she says, annoyed, and disappointed that it's the best she can offer.

She holds up her hand. She was grateful for him last night, for his sitting up, waiting, making her tea. But right now she doesn't want a work lecture on how feelings affect cold analysis.

"Let me figure it out," she says.

He backs down. "Okay," he says. Then, "I trust your feeling. I've had the same one," he says. "Well, maybe not exactly the same."

She gives him a look. "Can we get an APB on the Buick?"

"Already done," he says, and leaves her with the evidence report and damp pants.

222

* * *

The judge sets Shannon's arraignment for November third with no bail. The closest local news stations come to perch on the lawn in front of the justice center, reporting on the arrest of Shannon Jenkins and the continuing searches for Pearl Jenkins and a small child. It makes Shannon sound like a serial killer, and Kateri thinks, he'll never get a fair trial in this town. Photographers from the paper flash lights in Kateri's eyes when she goes in to work.

Brewer comes in every day. She begs him to please not talk to the news.

"I might suggest the same to you," he tells her. "The less info we have out there, the fairer a trial this kid gets."

Nothing in this kid's life has been fair.

Brewer wants the charges reduced. He tells Kateri that Shannon shouldn't be charged with murder at all but manslaughter self-defense, and adds that Shannon keeps fighting him on it because he insists he didn't do it at all.

"She was abusive," Brewer says to Kateri.

"I know."

"Did you see the bruise on him?"

She thinks before she answers. "I did," she says.

"I don't know why he won't trust me," Brewer says. "I can get him off."

"Because he didn't do it at all," Kateri says, against her better judgment. "And because he's probably been raised not to trust people in authority. His father's incarcerated," she reminds him.

Brewer shakes his head. "Sometimes it's in the blood," he says.

He slides into his suit jacket, which is black and shiny like it's coated in oil. "I fucking hate these white-trash cases," he says. He leaves the door open when he goes. Outside, there's a flutter of flash as he gets into his car.

Kateri feigns working late. Hurt comes into her office at six and asks if she wants a beer, stammers, and adds, "Or whatever," as she clicks away on her keyboard without actually typing anything. She looks up from the screen. "Nah, I need to follow this thread," she tells him.

In fact, she's sure there is a thread she should be following, and she has a feeling it goes back to Park Jenkins and Pearl's desperate fear of him. She wishes there were an easier way to take their fucking white-trash case and zoom out—to the county, the state, the nation. Something that might illuminate the connections for her. Might light up a line whose hook ends in Bear Miller.

They have an all-points bulletin on the Buick. There are Amber Alerts for Sparrow Annie Jenkins, age five, 38 inches tall, 38 pounds, blue eyes, red curly hair, mixed race. No one is sure what she's wearing. Or if it matters.

Kateri tries first to narrow the number of old-style Buicks on the road. Hurt told her it was an early-'90s model. Old, but not that old. Just enough to stand out. No one got plates. And there is no telling if the plates might be New York or Vermont or even Ontario or Quebec. Searching is slow and turns up a lot of nothing.

"How's it going?" Hurt asks from her doorway.

"Not great," she says without thinking.

He leans in, and his body softens, his eyes warm. "It's the course of the case," he says. "It's what happens. People get tired and discouraged."

"Is that how I seem?" Kateri asks.

"Not in a bad way," Hurt says. He comes all the way in and takes the chair across from her desk, sits with his ankle crossed over the opposite knee.

Kateri looks at the ceiling, thinking.

"I brought you something," Hurt says then, beginning to smile.

She jumps, and her phone clatters from the desk to the floor. She's wary of men bringing her gifts. "What is it?"

He places a fat folder on her desk.

"It's Bear Miller's sealed file," he tells her.

*   *   *

It's from the mid-'90s. Kateri goes through the slick, damp-feeling fac-simile pages and behind that finds a handwritten report from an officer in Vermont. Bear Miller was arrested at seventeen for assault on another boy, also seventeen.

It's written in careful cursive. Began as a fight. Boys were acquainted. Happened in the parking lot of a Kinney Drugs. Miller swung a bat in self-defense. This part is underlined. The other boy, Beaulieau, was knocked out.

Charges were dropped.

She looks at the date, and the town and the county, and opens her laptop. There must have been something else. Drugs. Money. A girl, maybe. Someone knows the rest of this story, she thinks. Otherwise, why seal it? It seems incomplete. Petty, even.

She searches through the local files for Beaulieau. There are many, including other arrests. Burglary, assault, DUI. When she scrolls through the death records, there are Beaulieaus of all ages. An infant, the grandfather patriarch. And James Beaulieau, seventeen, of South Burlington. She pulls up the death certificate.

Cause of death: cerebral apoplexy, secondary, hemorrhage in brain. The death is ruled natural.

"Natural?" Kateri says aloud.

The date is five days after Bear Miller's arrest.

Kateri covers her mouth. She wants to run down to Shannon's cell. It took him five days to die.

*   *   *

After nine, it's just her and the guards and the officers who are on duty overnight. She takes her key fob and lets herself into the wing where

225

Shannon's cell is. There are empty cells, ones they use mostly as drunk tanks, or when they pick up a guy on domestic and let him sweat it out in there, sappy and apologetic by the time someone finally comes to get him hours later.

Shannon is at the end. The cell has a wired, tempered-glass door. Inside, the light is on, and Shannon sits on the bed. They've let him have a book.

Kateri knocks on the glass and then uses the fob to let herself in.

"Hi," she says, soft. The room, the whole corridor, is eerily quiet.

"Hello," Shannon says. He puts the book flat on the metal bed, its spine cracked open. They've given him an old paper copy of *Shane*.

"I hate this book," he tells her.

"I haven't read it," she says.

"There's no dad, and then the guy who could be the dad just takes off." Shannon rolls his eyes.

"How's it going with Brewer?" she asks.

Shannon shrugs. "He wants me to plead guilty and say it was because she abused me. Self-defense."

Kateri leans on the wall. There's a stainless-steel toilet between them.

"I didn't do it," he says. He looks her in the eye.

"I know," she says.

He shakes his head, his eyes wide. The bruises on his neck have all but faded. "I can't say that I did it," he says, "just to get off. I'm not saying I did that," he repeats. "That I killed my own mother, and then, and then, and then burned her body? I was in a fire," he says. His voice goes up, shrill, tense. "Why would I do that?"

"Well," Kateri says, "the prosecution will likely argue that that's exactly why you did it."

"They won't let me go," he says. "They'll never let me go, even if I say I did it in self-defense."

"Who did?" Kateri asks.

His lips are a flat line. "I don't know," he says.

"Let's look at our options," Kateri says. "You didn't," she repeats.

"No," he says.

"What about Bear Miller?"

His jaw tightens. "He didn't," he says. She watches him press on his teeth from behind.

"Are you sure?" she says.

"He was with me."

"When?" Kateri asks.

"When . . . it happened," he says.

"How do you know that?" she asks. "We're not exactly sure when she was killed."

"We went to pick up some things, and the kitchen," he says, "it was full of blood."

She waits, and her own heart fills up her ears, beating. "You have to tell me what you know."

"That's all I know," he says.

He has trusted Bear with everything. She sees it now. Behind her, the faucet in the stainless-steel sink drips, a soft patter that after days would drive anyone crazy.

"What happened during the fire? When you were little?"

"I don't remember," he says.

"You were hurt, though."

"Yes," he says. "I have a burn scar." He turns his arm over, and she can see the edge of it, coming out from underneath his short sleeve.

"And your mother?" she asks.

"She broke her back," he says. "That's why she always has pain meds."

"Where on her back?" Kateri asks. She pictures the bones on Elise's table, the pelvis with the birth scars, the knuckles of spine.

"Low," Shannon says. "We were crawling to get out, and a beam hit her. By her waist," he says.

"Are you sure about that?" Kateri asks.

"Yeah," he says. "She has a scar. She had to have surgery on it."

The sink patters away. She needs to look again at the bones as soon as possible. She takes her phone out and checks for messages. Then she asks, "Does Bear know about your sister?"

"Yes," he says. Then he adds, "He doesn't have her." He folds and unfolds his hands, switching the lace of his fingers each time. "Aren't you looking?" he asks.

"We have a substantial lead," Kateri says. "She's been seen."

He presses his fingers together and steeples his hands in front of his face. It's too late for her to try Elise Diaz, but she can get Hurt, and she can get there first thing in the morning. She notices the relief in Shannon's shoulders.

"Who's the angel?" she asks him again, and this time he looks her in the eye, waiting. "The tall man," Kateri adds. "In the suit."

"Did they see him?" Shannon asks.

TWENTY-FIVE: SHANNON

MONDAY, OCTOBER 16

It was my turn to leave him in the bed. I got up while Bear was still sleeping and crept through the house. I looked in all the drawers; I tried to open the computer. It was password protected. I couldn't think of anything he might use as a password, and my guess was that he was really good at coming up with something obscure. Like IWasATeenageMurderer.

I almost typed it in, but the sound of Buddy's feet from the bedroom made me jump, and I slammed the laptop closed.

I let Buddy out, then shooed him back into the bedroom and closed the door most of the way. But before I did, I looked for a long time at Bear, asleep on his stomach, his arm stretched out where I had been, his face slack, the whiskers on his chin coming in gray.

I looked in boxes in the basement and boxes in the garage. I didn't want to open anything that had been sealed. I found a lot of nothing. Camping supplies. Books. A set of dishes. I figured anything important was sealed, or wasn't even here.

So I drove out to Mill Road by myself. I couldn't risk taking the dog, and it had sounded like he'd settled in on the bed with Bear anyway.

It was early, and I wasn't working. Junior had hired fucking Kyle Metzger to replace me. Kyle was just a shitty version of me. All I could think was that Kyle was lazy and stupid, and Junior had said he'd knocked up his girlfriend, so I guessed he needed to work. Every time Junior called to ask me if I wanted a shift, I turned him down. If Bear was in the room when I answered and I said "Tomorrow morning?" to Junior, Bear would shake his head, and I'd decline. I didn't even know if I had a job anymore.

I parked in Baby Jane's empty driveway, under the shade of pines and out of view from the road, where I saw two, then three cop cars go by, lights flashing, toward the park.

But Bear had called yesterday, I thought. They should have found her yesterday. I tried to think of where Birdie might be if she'd been locked in the closet this whole time. Who might have come in to bash my mother. Bear kept telling me it was okay. That it was going to be okay. That he was on my side and he had resources. But it was a blank spot in my memory. A plain white wall. I'd fallen asleep. I could only remember being in bed.

I went around the back of Baby Jane's house. I had come prepared, with a screwdriver, thinking I might be able to pop out the screen and slide in through the window. But the kitchen door was unlocked.

Inside, all the shades were drawn. There were sheets thrown over the couch and the chair in the living room. The bed was neatly made with the white chenille bedspread. Everything was gone from the bathroom. No suits hung in the closet.

It smelled faintly of Pine-Sol, with just the lingering hint of cigarettes. I lay down on the bed, and that's where I caught the smell of him, of whatever it was he put in his hair, a tonic, something old-fashioned like linden water, or bergamot. He never smelled sharp, but he always smelled clean. I thought about the hollow gauntness underneath his eyes the last time I'd seen him.

"What could kill you?" I had asked him. I had resigned myself to the truth of it. He certainly had.

"Something opportunistic," he said. "An infection. A fever. Meningitis. Pneumonia."

We sat in the car. It might have been the last warm evening. It smelled like pine needles and smoke and lingering whiskey. Leaves were falling, one by one, bright gold, around us.

"Why did you stop taking your meds?" I asked him.

He stared into my eyes. "Because I was done," he said.

"Done living?" I asked. I felt stupid and afraid.

"Yes," he had said. "It was just more complicated than I knew."

I thought about the blood in his cabin, the gunshot wound from my mother. Birdie's shriek.

Where were you before this?

Jail.

I rolled onto my back on his bed. He knew she was there. He'd known all along. *Tell your mother*, my dad had said, *that I know every goddamn thing she does.*

Everything rushed at me at once.

They were going to find my mother dead. They were going to either find my sister or find out about her, and someone was going to be charged with kidnapping her. The house was going to be closed off as a crime scene. I was undoubtedly going to be arrested for some or all of it.

I lay still with panic, my chest heaving, my hands shaking. All I could do was trust what Bear had said. That it would be okay. That he could save me. My mother was dead. I didn't have anyplace else to go.

TWENTY-SIX: KATERI

WEDNESDAY, NOVEMBER 1

"I need to see Diaz again," Kateri tells Hurt. "I'd like you to go with me."

He looks only mildly surprised.

"Find something?" he asks.

"Not yet," she answers. "But I'm confident I will."

They drive out in her car, and the sky is cut in half, along the horizon, bright blue and above that a sharp line of heavy gray snow clouds. It's forty-eight degrees and dropping. The radio warns of freezing rain.

She knows no plans have been made to release the remains or to have them processed in any way. There is still some slim hope of finding more of the body.

In the lobby, the receptionist picks up the phone, and Kateri can't hear what she's saying. When she hangs it up, she says, "Dr. Diaz isn't expecting you. Is there something I can help you with?"

Hurt stands at her side, looking up at the art on the walls. Lithographs that look arty and Eastern, maybe Persian.

"I need to reexamine the bones in the Pearl Jenkins case," she says.

The receptionist comes out from behind her desk, and Kateri sees that she's in a well-cut pantsuit, with a white blouse that is open quite a ways, but it doesn't seem to matter because the woman is thin and fairly flat chested. Kateri shrugs her own shoulders forward, caving her chest in.

233

"Let me see if I can interrupt her," the receptionist says.

When Elise Diaz comes out, she's wearing a white medical coat and has just taken off surgical gloves.

"You didn't tell me Detective Hurt was here," she says.

Kateri fights rolling her eyes.

"All Fisher," Hurt says.

Diaz looks up at him, coy. "You're not coming?" she asks. She's about to lead them into the basement.

"No, I'm coming," he says. "But it's Fisher's lead."

* * *

In the exam room, Diaz pulls out the specimen drawer and lays the bones on paper, where they can examine from all sides.

Kateri leans but doesn't touch. "Can you explain the birth scars to me again?" Kateri asks.

Dr. Diaz pulls on fresh gloves and turns the pelvis over. The burn marks are surface stains, the way smoke leaves a trail up a wall, curling and sheer.

"Birth is a trauma to the body, Detective Fisher," Diaz says. She points to several pits in the bone. "These here, along with these depressions, indicate a body that has given birth—at least once," she says.

"Is there any way to tell if there were further births?" she asks.

"No," Diaz says. "We can generally tell if a body has never given birth, or if it has. It's more difficult with cesarean deliveries."

"And what about the spine?" Kateri says, looking at the other knuckles of bone. "How hard would it be to tell if a bone had been broken?"

Hurt paces around the table while the women stand still, heads bent.

"Oh, quite easy," Diaz says. "A fractured humerus, or a femur, for example, shows postmortem."

"Would a fractured spine?" Kateri asks, without looking up.

"Mostly likely. Maybe not in the case of a hairline fracture."

"No," Kateri says, "a compound fracture, in vertebrae L3 and L4. Which," she says, looking up at Elise Diaz, "we have here."

Diaz draws in a sharp breath. "These have not been broken," she says.

Kateri looks at Hurt. "It's not her," she says.

"How do you know?" he says.

"I pulled her medical file from Mercy Hospital. When the fire burned that house down, Pearl Jenkins broke her back. She had surgery on it. She was in recovery for months. It was probably never the same. I have the summary that describes the fractures to L3 and L4."

Diaz looks at Hurt and raises an eyebrow, but the conversation is between him and Kateri.

"When's the arraignment?" he asks.

"Friday morning," Kateri says.

"And no further sighting of the kid."

"No," she says.

"Let's search Miller's house," he says.

Kateri looks to Elise Diaz, who looks down at the bones on the table and not at Kateri. Hurt, meanwhile, leans in very close to the bones, without touching.

"What else could these be?" he asks Diaz. "Besides human."

"There are several animals similar in size," Diaz says. "The DNA is not back on these yet."

He takes a pen from his pocket and tips the piece of pelvic bone over on the table.

"What is it?" Kateri asks.

"I think it might be a bear," Hurt says.

*　*　*

They rush back to the car as a sharp wind whips through the trees behind the building. What leaves are left are quickly falling, raining down on the cars.

"Did you look at Miller's file?" Kateri asks Hurt.

"Yeah, it's definitely a cover-up," he says. "He paid to get out of something."

"He killed that kid," Kateri says.

"Did you find that?" Hurt asks.

"Well," Kateri says. She has a hard time keeping her eyes on the road because she keeps looking over to Hurt in the passenger seat. "The death was deemed natural," she says.

In town, they get stuck behind slow-moving construction trucks, headed up to Fountain Street, where Bear Miller's house is. She pulls off abruptly and takes a side street toward the station.

"You okay?" Hurt asks when he regains his balance.

"Let's take a squad car," she says.

*   *   *

"This is a pleasant surprise," Bear says when Kateri comes to his door this time, but he stops smiling his wide, eerie grin when he sees Joel Hurt behind her.

Kateri holds up a warrant from the judge. "I have a warrant to search your property, Mr. Miller," she said, "based on evidence that Shannon Jenkins was staying here."

"Mr. Miller," he repeats, and then laughs.

Hurt comes around to Kateri's side and takes in the expanse of the house and the yard.

"You can cooperate," Hurt says, "or you can wait in the car with me while Fisher does the search. But that'll take longer."

"I don't get to wait in the car with Fisher?" Bear asks. He's standing barefoot on the Persian rug in the great room. The dog—the same dog that has been riding around with Shannon—runs out back.

"Not an option," Hurt says.

*   *   *

Kateri starts in the back bedroom, the master. She takes both tooth-brushes from the en suite bath and a razor she finds in the trash bin. She grabs a book from the nightstand that she suspects is Shannon's. *The Weekend*. She remembers then the books in his bedroom at his own house, the book he has in his cell. This kid reads, she thinks. She can't decide whether or not it's unusual, given his circumstances. He didn't finish high school. He was working as an unskilled laborer. But he's smart. She doesn't know what to expect anymore.

Hurt stands looking out the back window while she bags things and labels them.

"Jesus Christ," he says, at the pool, the tennis courts.

"Is this the only bedroom?" Kateri asks.

"No, there are like seven bedrooms," Hurt says.

"I mean, the only furnished bedroom," she says. "The only one being used."

He looks at her bags of toothbrushes, the book.

"Shit," he says. "That's too weird."

"Why?" She leans into the white pillows on the bed and plucks one of Shannon's shorter, blond hairs. She threads it into a smaller bag. Then she grabs a longer, golden-brown hair and bags that.

Bear leans in the doorway behind her. "You could just ask me," he says.

"Ask you what?" Kateri says, without turning to face him.

"If we're sleeping together," Bear says.

She presses the seal on another bag and hands it to Hurt, who collects them all in a large container.

"It's pretty clear," Kateri says.

"Do you need physical evidence?" Bear pushes. "That I've been fucking him this whole time?"

"Do you want to wait in the car?" Hurt asks Bear.

"I'm not sure why it matters," Bear says. "Except maybe personally," he adds.

"Don't be an asshole," Hurt says, and brushes past him into the hall. "It makes you a potential accessory, at the very least," he says. "And a possible suspect."

The rooms upstairs are empty. Kateri moves from bedroom to bedroom, through the other en suite baths, checking empty closets, the laundry chute, the back playroom. For one second she imagines Birdie there, on the floor with dolls, this one room more vast than anything she's ever seen in her five years.

In the basement, she finds tools, items she is sure will show Shannon's prints, and she bags them all out of protocol. A hammer, a screwdriver, a drill, paintbrushes. Nothing looks out of place, stained, or unusually clean either.

"I should have brought a team," Kateri tells Hurt in the basement. He peers into the back room, an unfinished workroom with a bench and fluorescent lighting. There are saws in there, both hand and power.

"We should luminol that room," Hurt says.

"Do you think it's here?" she says, heart hammering. "The real body?" she asks. Her eyes widen. "Hurt, who placed those bones?"

"We've got more to investigate," he says, "that's for sure. Do you think . . ." He hesitates, and Kateri thinks he's about to speculate on whether or not Bear Miller has killed more than one person. "Do you think they're gay?" Hurt says.

"Joel," Kateri says. "We have unidentified bones," she whispers. "And a missing girl."

But his face is perplexed. It's a detail he can't get past.

She opens a utility closet in the workroom. "And a shotgun," she says.

*   *   *

Bear is sitting on a stool at the kitchen island when they come up. Hurt carries a box of bagged evidence out to the squad car, and Kateri goes out the back door to do a preliminary search of the veranda, the storage boxes, the pool house, the work shed. She orders a team. And cadaver dogs.

She stoops and takes a picture of a boot print in the shed. It's unusual, and one she's seen before, inside the Jenkins kitchen. It doesn't have the normal zigzag or tire print of a work boot. It leaves a sort of fleur-de-lis in the dirt.

Hurt is in the garage with Bear. He has gone through the cabinets and taken apart the Land Rover. There are cigarettes in the can at the back of the driveway, which Hurt has bagged, but Kateri already knows they match the ones she picked up in the park.

"Any Luckys?" she asks Hurt.

He looks in the bag. "No."

Bear rubs his eyes. "There are yellow American Spirits," he says, exasperated. "And some cheap white Indian cigarettes. They're mine and Shannon's," he says. "No one smokes Lucky Strikes." He laughs at her.

"Oh, someone does," Kateri says. "They're in the evidence bin." She holds out the picture of the boot print. "Where are these boots?" she asks. She looks at the ones on his feet, but when he holds them up, the soles don't match.

"Those?" Bear says.

"Yes, these," Kateri says. She's tired of his stalling, of everyone's efforts to distract her, to lead her in a different direction, to confuse her with things that don't matter, reluctance to just tell her the goddamn truth.

"I left them," he says.

"Where?"

"At my wife's house," he says. "In Vermont." He waits a moment and then adds, "Surely you knew I had a wife."

"I did know," Kateri says. "When's the last time you were there?" she asks.

"Last weekend," Bear says.

She nods to Hurt. She needs to get her hands on those boots, and whatever else might have evidence from the crime scene on it.

Bear leans on the rail of the step that goes back into the kitchen. "You can't put me on trial," he says, "for having a consensual affair with a boy who's of age."

Hurt tips his head and slips into the kitchen again for one last sweep.

"It wouldn't be for that," Kateri says. "It would be for plotting to and/or helping him kill his mother. The affair is just icing," she says.

"Why on earth would I kill his mother?" Bear says.

But she doesn't get a chance to answer, because Hurt comes back into the garage and takes the evidence bags from Kateri, adding them to his growing collection kit.

"Thanks for your cooperation, Mr. Miller," Hurt says, curt. "A separate forensics team will be out this afternoon to conduct a more thorough search."

He walks briskly away from the garage and motions for Kateri to follow.

"We'll be in touch," Hurt says over his shoulder.

Kateri, follows, flummoxed, and gets into the driver's seat.

"I don't care if you drive," Hurt says, "but please stop for coffee."

She drives out of the new development, back into town, and gets two sugary, creamy coffees and a bag of doughnuts from a non-chain place in town, where the doughnuts are heavy grease balls covered in granular sugar and cinnamon. They sit in the parking lot before going back into the office. The sky is a blinding bright blue behind trees that are nearly bare.

Hurt pulls an evidence bag from his jacket and waves it at Kateri.

"What's that?" She licks the sugar off her fingers.

He has bagged a piece of mail. An envelope from Kerpak Industries to the auction house. It's stamped, but it's not canceled. Outgoing mail.

Hurt waits while she registers the name, the context, and then puts it back in his pocket.

"He wants the property," Hurt says.

"That's it?" Kateri asks.

"I don't know if that's it," Hurt says. "There's clearly some other shit going on. But that house is standing in the way of Bear Miller making a fuckton of money."

"On what?" Kateri asks. "The house is worthless."

"The land," he says. "He wants to develop the land. The Jenkins own a big chunk of it," he says. "I guarantee you when we open that, it's a preempt. A hefty offer prior to auction."

Kateri leans back in the driver's seat. "Who would go that far?" she asks. "To get property?"

"It's worth millions to him," Hurt says. "And he's a sadist. Any other businessman would just offer the kid money and buy him out. Not Miller," he says.

"That poor kid," Kateri says.

"Well," Hurt says.

"Miller is providing his lawyer," she says.

"Yeah," Hurt says. "That kid's fucked."

TWENTY-SEVEN: SHANNON

THURSDAY, NOVEMBER 2

Brewer slams around when he comes to visit. It's like the chair isn't enough to hold him. He's not a big guy. Not much bigger than me, but he takes up a lot of space. He asks questions like an annoyed school psychologist, like some kind of shrink, hoping to blame it all on my mother.

"What are you doing?" I ask him finally. I'm tired of wearing prison scrubs. My feet feel clammy inside the rubbery crocs they issued me to wear over these awful scratchy white socks. The seams of the scrub shirt rub under my arms and leave my skin red and raw.

"What do you mean, what am I doing?" Brewer asks.

He's not attractive. I mean, I'm sure someone finds him attractive, like maybe a woman who wants to be told what to do without ever being looked in the eye. He's too perfect. Not a hair is out of place. Bleached teeth. It's repulsive. His eyes are bright but creepy. His shirt, underneath his suit jacket, is so starched it's like heavy paper.

I motion at the notes he's always making. "With this," I say. I just want to lie down, on a real bed. On the white bed, with Bear, and Buddy curled behind my knees. It's been hard to sleep at all, and I'm always tired, frayed, fuzzy at the edges. If I didn't know better, I'd swear it was a tactic.

"I'm building a character study," Brewer says.

"On me?"

"And your mother," he says. He moves his feet noisily on the concrete floor, and it echoes in the room.

"Is she on trial?" I ask. I want to goad him. I feel like a brat.

"Kind of," Brewer answers. "I have a better chance of proving you not guilty if I can paint an accurate picture of her."

"You can never paint an accurate picture of her," I say. "She's more complicated than one thing," I say. "Was," I add.

"Not without your help, I can't," he says. He drums his fingers hard on the table. His hands are big, with squared-off fingers and short nails. "This is difficult," he says to me, "and I apologize."

I shrug. I'm not even sure what Brewer might find difficult. Lifting, maybe. Having a pimple.

"Were you sexually abused by your mother?" he asks.

"No."

"Someone else?" he asks.

"No," I say.

"How often did your mother abuse you?" he asks.

"I just said she didn't," I say.

"Physically," he says. "Hitting, kicking, et cetera." He waits.

"I don't know," I say. I was hit a few times, in the midst of bad fights. It wasn't what I would call abuse. It was fighting. Abuse is when you hit a kid who can't hit back, when you beat someone with something. A bat.

He writes on his pad without looking at me. "Did your mother try to strangle you?" he asks.

"What?" I say. "No."

But Brewer points at my throat.

"I know it's hard to admit." He tries to be soft. "It's very important," he says. "It's recent. And it incited you to take action. In reality, you might not even remember it correctly," he says, "like the crime itself."

My hand goes to my neck.

"I do have photographs," Brewer says, shuffling through a fat folder, "that show the bruise at its worst, which will help. Can you do your best to describe the scene to me?"

"What scene?" I say. All I can do is whisper.

Brewer puts his pen down. "When she tried to strangle you," he says. His eyes are heavy, with thick, dark lashes.

"She didn't," I say.

"Shannon," Brewer says, and he leans back in his chair, puts his foot up on the opposite knee. "This isn't the time to defend your mother, okay? It's time to defend yourself. It actually should be easier than this," he says. "But you're making it very difficult."

The scene, I think, and I remember the glint in Bear's eyes, the feel of his hand around my windpipe, the flash of stars, of gasping for breath finally, with my whole body in a flush of euphoria.

I trust you.

"I need a minute," I say, and swallow. I really, really want a cigarette.

"Sure," Brewer says, and stands up, the chair rattling backward. He stomps around in a circle. "I'll step out," he says. "I need to make a call."

"Can I speak with Detective Fisher?" I ask.

"Without me?" Brewer shoots back.

"Yeah."

"It's not smart," he says. He leans down on the table. The table is a metal mint green with crosshatched lines, like the teachers' desks in elementary school. I remember standing at those desks, telling one teacher after another that my mother couldn't make the conference. She's working, I'd say. Everyone knew she didn't work. I wouldn't even tell my mother about the conferences. I didn't want her to show up high.

"I am your best defense," Brewer says. "I want you to tell me every-thing you even think about saying so that I can say it for you, because everything you say will be used against you. Can you understand that?" he says. "You're not in a position of power here. You're very vulnerable."

"I can speak for myself," I say.

"You can also go to prison," Brewer says. "For murder. What do you have to tell Fisher that you can't tell me?" he asks. "Kid, you're not going to confess, are you?"

"I didn't do it," I say. My insides hum, little fried nerve endings vibrating. I wonder if someone, a dog maybe, can hear that sound. The sound of my body singing at a high frequency. Buddy. I miss the feel of his lean.

Brewer stretches his hands behind his head, his elbows out at angles, and he blows a long breath through his lips.

"Okay," he says. "I'm stepping out. I'll give you a minute to think," he says. "Think hard."

*　*　*

I pace until Detective Fisher comes in. I ramp up faster than I realize, and when she comes in the door, there's the vacuum rush of air and I spin around, panting.

"Have you found my sister?" I ask.

"There's been a sighting," Kateri says. "We're getting closer."

"She's with someone," I say.

Kateri says, "She was spotted in a car."

"What kind?" I ask.

"A Buick," she says. "Does that sound familiar?"

"No," I say. I can't think of anyone who's driven a Buick ever. "I can't do this," I tell her.

"You can," she says. I like the sound of her voice, even in that closed room. It's soft, like it has round edges.

"I'd rather just be dead," I say. My head feels like a whirlpool.

"Sit down."

"I've been sitting down," I say. All I do is sit down. I'd do anything, I think, to get into the woods, to feel the wind on my face, hear the creak of the trees.

"Do you want a Pepsi?" she asks me.

"Yes."

She comes back in with a tall plastic cup filled with ice and a can of Pepsi. I crack it open and pour, watching the haze of effervescence. It fizzes at my nose when I drink it, and it smells like summer to me. "I need to talk to Bear," I say.

"I'll see what I can do," she says. "Is there anything I can help you with?"

I look over my shoulder, even though there's nothing behind me but a blank cinder-block wall.

"I want a different lawyer," I say. "How can I ask for that? I didn't ask for this one. I can't pay for anything," I say. "I'm going to lose everything."

"The court will appoint you a lawyer," Kateri says. "That doesn't mean that the court lawyer will be bad. Sometimes they're great," she says. "What don't you like about Brewer?"

"He's like . . . making it up," I say. "Because he says it's what I need."

"Well," Kateri says. "That's the nuance of a defense. Sometimes you have to trust that he can tell the story in a way that's favorable, in a way you maybe couldn't yourself."

"No," I say. The Pepsi seems loud between us. I wish again for a cigarette. "I don't know what happened to my mother, okay? But I know what didn't happen. I didn't kill her because she tried to strangle me. I didn't kill her at all."

Kateri puts her fingers to her lips, thinking, or avoiding.

"Who did?" she asks.

"I don't know," I say. "I swear to God, I don't know who killed her."

"No," Kateri says. "Who . . ." Her hands go to her own throat. "Who tried to choke you?"

247

"It doesn't have anything to do with this," I say.

"You don't know that," she says.

"Yes, I do," I say. "I did it. Myself."

"You did it to yourself," she repeats.

"I caused it to happen."

She shakes her head and sighs. "No, Shannon," she says and stands up. "This is what I mean. You need a lawyer to hear this."

She turns toward the door, about to summon Brewer back in there, and he is the last person I want to say this to.

"Bear did it," I say.

Kateri turns around with the door still shut. Her face is pale. "Did he attack you?"

"No," I say. "The opposite."

"The opposite?" she says.

"You know." I roll my eyes and flash back on the scene. The room, the bed. My skin blushes from my collarbone up to my eyes. "We were in bed," I say.

"Shannon," Kateri says. She comes back and sits across from me, but I can't look at her. The blush is so hard it almost hurts. My eyelid twitches. "Just because something happens during sex doesn't mean it happens out of love," she says.

"I know that," I say, and my throat locks up.

"He hurt you," she says.

I bite my lip and try to listen to the diminishing Pepsi instead of her voice. "I need to talk to him," I say.

"So do I," she says.

"Don't," I say then, pleading. "Don't. He didn't do it either," I say. "I swear."

"Do you know that?" she says. "For absolute sure?"

I feel like I'm drowning. Like water is rising up from my lungs and flooding me from the inside out.

"Why would he?" I whisper.

Kateri taps her fingers on the table, thinking. "Let me get Detective Hurt, okay?"

"Why would he kill my mother?" I say again. I can't stop seeing his face when he bares his teeth, the pure anger, like a white fire behind that.

*　*　*

Kateri comes back in with Hurt and Brewer, who sits down across from me. Brewer clicks his pen a few times, and Hurt puts a small digital video camera on a stand and turns it on. He announces who's present into the lens.

Hurt has a look. A kind of dad look, but not an out-of-touch dad. More like a dad who cares what his daughters think. A dad who can cook, maybe. I don't know anything at all about him. I've barely talked to him. But it's a feeling I get. The way he wears a suit, if he does. There's something soft, something still about him. Calm. He stands close enough to Kateri that their sleeves touch. I wonder about that.

"Has Bear Miller ever talked to you about your mother's house?" Hurt asks me.

"Yes," I say, before Brewer can stop me, and he huffs about it.

"Please, please," he says. "Look at me before you answer, okay?"

"What was the status of your mother's house when you met Mr. Miller?" Hurt says.

I look at Brewer but answer at the same time. His eyes flash with anger. "It was about to be seized for taxes," I say. Then I add, "These are just facts," to Brewer.

"Did Mr. Miller help you with that?"

"Client declines to answer," Brewer says.

"Why?" I say. "Why does it matter? I was trying to save the house."

"Have you heard of Kerpak Industries?" Hurt asks me.

"No."

"Has anyone ever contacted you about the house?"

"The county," I say.

"I'm not sure how any of this is relevant," Brewer says.

"Anyone offering to buy it from you?" Hurt says. "For cash, maybe?"

"No," I say. "Who would even want it?"

But I think about Bear. *Someone always wants real estate.*

"Client declines to answer," Brewer says, before I can open my mouth.

"Have you seen his house?" I say. "He doesn't want mine," I say. "He told me to sell it."

"Stop talking," Brewer says.

"To who?" Hurt says. I watch his eyes narrow. I want to know what he knows, or what he thinks he knows.

I shrug. "Just to sell it," I answer. "Why?"

"Did he give you any indication as to why that might be a good idea?" Hurt asks.

"Before it went to auction," I say. "He said I could get maybe ten thousand dollars for it after everything—you know, once the taxes were paid."

"Ten thousand dollars," Hurt says.

"Yeah."

Hurt looks at Kateri, who looks at the floor.

"Why?" I ask.

Brewer leans back in his chair again, his ankle crossed over his knee. He smells like a harsh cologne, grassy and acidic.

Hurt nods to Kateri.

"Shannon," she says. "Your house is on a piece of land that is very, very valuable to Bear Miller."

"What?" I say. My eye twitches again. "How? That doesn't make any sense at all," I say.

"Do you know what he does for a living?" Hurt asks.

Brewer holds up his hand to silence me, and I push it away from my face. It's a reflex, a hand coming at my face, and even though he doesn't touch me, I smack him away.

"Dude," Brewer says, and stands up. He shoots a look at Hurt and says, "Can you do something about this?"

"Real estate," I say.

I invest her interests.

"For?" Hurts says.

"His mother's company?" I say. I've never actually seen him work. I had no idea what he was doing. "But not my house," I say. "There's a huge difference, if you haven't noticed. Like a billion-dollar difference," I add, which makes me sound like a stupid kid, and Brewer laughs at me.

Kateri draws a calm breath before she starts talking. "Kerpak Industries is developing luxury real estate," she says. She nods at me. "That is his mother's company."

"Yeah, okay," I say, "up on the hill. Not by my house."

"Actually," Kateri says, "they are. But they can't build where your house is because your family, the Jenkins family—you," she says, "own the land now."

I shake my head. My stomach turns sour. "No," I say. And I can't think of anything that might disprove her, so I just say it again. "No."

Hurt adds, "Well, he's not officially doing that. He's not officially doing anything," he says. "He's not even drawing a goddamn paycheck from Kerpak. Who knows how they distribute the wealth."

"He invests her interests," I say.

"Exactly," Kateri says. "Your property is of great interest."

I look at Brewer, who just shakes his head.

"Did you know about this?" I ask, annoyed.

"No," he says. "I don't know what the fuck they're talking about, or why it makes a difference."

"Oh, come on," Hurt says.

"It totally makes a difference," I say to Brewer.

"Would you excuse us?" Kateri says to Brewer.

"I'm not leaving my client alone with you," he answers.

She looks at me.

"Just go," I say. "Like, for good, okay? Call Bear and tell him I fired you."

"Against my recommendation," Brewer says, but he snaps his pad into his briefcase.

"I'll take my chances," I say.

*   *   *

Only Kateri stays in the room with me. We sit there at the table for a long, silent moment.

"We took some evidence from the model home," she says finally, "that proves his interest in the property. I don't know yet if he's willing to cooperate with us."

"I need to talk to him," I say.

She takes me out to the lobby to make a phone call and lets me call Bear from the office phone, not the pay phone.

All it does is ring. There's no voice mail. It rings fifteen times, with me just holding the receiver, listening while Kateri stands a few feet away, watching.

I shake my head and put the phone down.

I had no idea I had anything of interest, anything that was worth anything to someone other than just us. It was just our house. I never thought beyond that. And I was stupid enough to think I was the thing he wanted.

When she walks me back to my cell, Kateri gives me a Twix bar she got out of the machine.

"Are you going to arrest him?" I ask.

She presses her lips together and nods.

Two hours ago I would have said he didn't do it. I swallow, my throat still sore. "I just want my sister back," I say.

Kateri touches my shoulder then, and I don't mean to, but I crumple up against her, and for just a second she puts her arms around my shoulders and cups the back of my head like no one has hugged me in a long, long time. I smash my face into her collarbone. She smells like sandalwood, like soap my mother used to use. Then I jump away abruptly and wipe my face.

"He has more of a motive than you do," Kateri says.

I look at the floor. "Did Brewer know that?" I say.

She tilts her head. "It's likely," she says. "Bear's been controlling more of this than anyone knew."

"It's all different than I thought," I say. "I can't trust anyone."

"You can trust me," she tells me. "I promise."

TWENTY-EIGHT: KATERI

THURSDAY, NOVEMBER 2

"I don't know if they can convict him," Hurt tells her. "He's slimy, and I'm sure he's got resources. But you definitely have enough to arrest him."

They sit side by side in an unmarked car, not Kateri's and not Hurt's, but a squad car. A big, gray sedan.

"He's capable of anything, Fisher," Hurt says, as if she needs reminding. It will be a long time, she thinks, before someone touches her and she doesn't think of his urgent, searching fingers.

Hurt drives this time, stuck in traffic in the small town, where the road slows to fifteen miles per hour in front of the school. Kids come out. Kids close to Shannon's age. Boys, laughing. They drive trucks and smoke cigarettes and call out to girls who walk over to Stewart's.

"Don't second-guess it," Hurt says. "My gut is that we'd better act quick."

"Do you think he'll flee?" Kateri asks.

"I hope he hasn't already," Hurt says. "He's got places to go. He could disappear pretty easily."

She feels wired taut, trembling. She's afraid of what Bear will say and is sure that he's a sociopathic liar, that he'll implicate her, that he'll retell everything in his own best light. And her worst. She leans her head back against the passenger seat. I should have said something, she thinks. I should have recused myself the second it happened. But she couldn't. She'd been waiting for months for a decent case to come along, and she'd be damned if he was going to ruin that for her.

When the traffic frees up, Hurt turns the car onto Fountain Street and heads toward the developing tract of houses, on the corn hill that sits above town. It looks down onto the village, over the train tracks. Over the ravine and over the park, which sprawls to the north of town where the house that Shannon still owns sits, empty and cordoned off, tainted with blood and tissue.

She got him to say it.

She watched Shannon steel up, his jaw clenched, his face blank of emotion when she knew inside he was crumbling.

"What exactly did Bear say to you?" she asked. It was late. The camera ran in the corner, and he didn't even seem to notice anymore.

"That he could get me out of it," he said. "He kept talking like I had done it, like it was obvious, but that I had blacked it out or whatever. I didn't remember. So he kept saying it would be okay. I just needed to trust him."

"He said he could get you out of it," Kateri repeated.

"Yeah," Shannon said. His lips were white around the edges. Pressed. Tight. "Because he had gotten out of it before," he added.

He knows, she thought. She waited for him to go on.

"He's done this before," Shannon said. "He killed someone," he said, and his voice broke. "You know this, right? And they covered it up—it was sealed, or whatever that means."

"It was sealed," Kateri said softly.

"You know," Shannon said.

"I do," Kateri said.

* * *

From the hill, the town looks like a postcard. The steeple and the school tower. The green grass replaced with colored leaves. From Fountain

Street you can see the Hub, where by now another blond boy, similar in size and shape to Shannon, has replaced him. The justice center. The train, barreling through, filled with freight.

Hurt leaves the squad car at the foot of the driveway, with Bear's monstrosity of a house looming above. The lawn is fresh and clean, not a leaf out of place, the edges sharp and the driveway blown out.

"Not a good time," Bear says, a little louder than Kateri expects, when he opens the door. They don't even ring the bell; he just sweeps it open and shouts.

"It's never a good time," Hurt says, and pushes his way past Kateri into the open great room. There are tools on the kitchen counter, a paint can, a roll of blue shop towels.

"Do you have a warrant?" Bear asks. "I'm kind of busy." His hair is loose and sweaty, his face flushed with anger. His eyes dart in agitation. Kateri swallows, watching him. He seems coiled and ready, like he will strike at any moment.

Hurt humors him. "Doing?" he says.

"The work that Shannon's not here to do," Bear says.

"Oh yeah?" Hurt says. "Can you suck your own dick? Actually, don't answer," he says, holding up a hand. "I'm sure you've figured it out."

"Hurt," Kateri says, trying to shut him up, but she sees it happening, Bear's fist as it clenches, the knuckles white, the spring of his arm as he pulls back and clocks Hurt cold. She can't stop it, and Hurt can't get out of the way fast enough. The punch jolts his jaw upward; she hears the smack of his teeth and the knock of his head on the marble floor of the entryway.

Kateri stands still for a moment, staring down at Hurt on the floor, and realizes that in the action, as a reflex, she has drawn her gun. Bear looks at her and laughs, his teeth bared and his face devoid of humor.

"Let's not get dramatic," he says.

"I have a warrant for your arrest," she says. Her heart pounds in her ears, and her armpits start to itch.

"For what?" Bear shouts. He is still smiling his mean grin, not mirth but rage. He massages his knuckles where he connected with Hurt's face. His shoulders square up; his chest pushes out. He makes himself bigger than he is, and he comes toward Kateri.

"For the murder of Pearl Jenkins," Kateri says. She has to clench her arm, deep in the shoulder socket, to keep her hand from shaking. A bead of sweat rolls down her back, collects at her waist.

Bear creeps closer, his eyes bright and intent, and he shakes his head. Kateri knows she needs to call for backup, but she can't take her gun or her eyes off him. She needs Hurt to get up.

"Don't come any closer," she warns.

"Or what?" Bear says. His eyes flash.

She steadies her gun on him, suddenly settled, still at her core. Her arm is rod straight.

"You don't have any evidence," Bear says, turning the power play against her.

"I do," Kateri says. She hears Hurt stirring on the floor, his limbs slow, his head, she's sure, ringing from the inside out. She's been punched like that. Once. By a woman whose son Kateri was arresting. It made her head feel like a bell.

"Why would I kill Pearl Jenkins?" Bear asks.

"Because you were tired of waiting for Shannon to do it," she says. "Like you wanted."

She puts herself between Hurt and Bear while Hurt rolls over and pushes himself to standing. He leans on all fours for a minute, still steadying himself. She watches bloody drool drip from his open mouth. With her free hand, Kateri unloops the cuffs from her belt.

"No cuffs," Bear says. He keeps his shoulders wide and open and keeps stepping toward her, the way a cat creeps through grass when it stalks.

"Not negotiable," Kateri says.

"You're an idiot," Bear says, suddenly louder. He laces his fingers together, gripping. "You're in so far over your pretty little head," he hisses.

She sees Hurt wipe his mouth. He straightens up, draws his weapon, and nudges his elbow at Kateri. "Cuff him," he says, his mouth wet and slurry. "Let's go."

"Is that what Shannon told you?" Bear asks, taunting. Of course she believed the kid. It's her weakness.

"We can add resisting," Hurt says.

"Did Shannon tell you," he shouts at Kateri, "that I told him to kill his mother?"

"We can go over the details later," Kateri says.

"Shannon couldn't kill a dog," Bear says. "Shannon couldn't even throw a punch," he says.

"That's why I'm arresting you," Kateri says.

"Do you think I would have actually done it myself?" Bear asks. "I don't even sweep my own floor. I'm not getting my hands dirty over Pearl Jenkins. Shannon's a stupid kid," Bear says. "Delicious," he adds, with another menacing grin, "but poor, and stupid."

His eyes lock on Kateri's, like he's trying to outstare her and he's winning. "He's not so different from you," he says.

Bear steps closer, his hands open, his body like it's gliding through water.

"Stop," Kateri says, holding her arm taut.

"You've never shot anyone," Bear says. He moves slowly, and she watches every inch, his feet as they creep closer. He catches her eye and holds her attention, and then in a snap motion, he grabs the nose of her gun.

She sets her jaw and fires, afraid for a split second that she saw it wrong, that she imagined his quick grab at the barrel of her weapon. It doesn't matter. Her shot knocks Bear to the floor screaming, and she fires again. Her ears fuzz over with the noise from the gun, and Hurt is yelling, his mouth moving, but she can't hear his words.

"Jesus Christ, Fisher," he says. He pulls her toward the door and yells again, and this time she can hear him. "Jesus Christ."

Hurt steps out onto the sidewalk and backs Kateri up against one of the huge pillars holding up the second-floor balcony on the house. "Stay there," he says to her. She watches him pace the sidewalk and then go back into the house, calling for medical, for backup.

Kateri's arm shakes clear up to the socket, her teeth on edge, her mouth filled with metal and blood from biting her tongue. Her hand, sore and cramped from clenching the gun, is spattered with a fine spray of blood.

Around them is nothing but open lots, poured basements, phases of construction, all of them stalled. Razed land and stubbled grass. The cellars are like graves, waiting. Foundations behind orange plastic fences. Beyond that the cornfield, moving in the breeze, a sound like paper crinkling.

She doesn't know if he's dead.

From the back of the house, the dog comes bolting toward her, stuck with burdocks, his mouth stained with blood. He leans down and barks at Kateri, but when she crouches, he comes slinking forward, his head low, and his whole backside wagging.

She can hear sirens from town.

"Fucking Christ, Fisher," Hurt says from the doorway, the hot smell of gunshot lingering inside.

Kateri stands and keeps petting the dog, to stop him from going inside to Bear. She tries to answer Hurt, but she cannot unclench her teeth, and her insides vibrate like a motor. She stays there while Hurt goes back inside, and she hears an animal wail from Bear.

"Where did I hit him?" she whispers when Hurt comes back out. Her head is so filled with static she doesn't know if the words have any voice to them. She hates herself for bringing her own fear, her own feeling into it. She thinks, I would have shot him anyway. I wanted to shoot him.

Hurt looks down at the dog, slumped against Kateri's leg.

"Where should you have hit him?" he asks, and then adds, "Fisher, you're not a rookie."

"I know," she says.

"Your arm jumped," Hurt says. "You hit his neck." He spits blood onto the grass and watches behind her, at the activity in town.

She gasps hard, all at once, like she has not been breathing for a long time.

* * *

She takes the dog home. She asks Hurt if he thinks anyone will notice or care, and he says no, not in the face of everything that has happened. She takes the dog home first, lets him into her apartment, and leaves him with a bowl of water and a soft blanket, which he seems to settle down with in a patch of sun coming in her back window.

The ambulance sped off toward Mercy Hospital. The voices a blur of commands. Blood pressure. Oxygen. Intubation. Kateri stood on the sidelines, dazed.

In the office, a mountain of procedure. Interviews, paperwork. Statements.

She hears Hurt in his own interview. "We were both threatened," Hurt says. "I was out cold for a few minutes. He grabbed Fisher's firearm," he says. She repeats this over and over herself. Grabbed. Ambushed. Reached for my weapon. It was what she was trained to do. She's not sure who she's convincing anymore. Other than herself.

It feels like the longest day of her life. Longer than when she crashed her car, which she mostly doesn't remember. She can't remember her own ride in the ambulance; she remembers the days in the hospital bed as faded, gray. Without the blur of booze, the drip of narcotics, this day feels sharp, long, torturous.

It's midnight before the chief, Bill Whittaker, tells her she did a good job and that she should go home, that she should rest, and that he's recommending time off.

She is stunned when he says it was a good job. She'd thought for sure he was calling her in to fire her.

"You broke this wide open," Whittaker tells her. He's a man in his fifties who looks like he was thin in his twenties but now bears the barrel chest of administrative work. He wears horn-rimmed glasses and has a buzz cut like someone from an earlier decade.

"And Miller?" she asks.

He shakes his head. "Didn't survive the surgery."

She feels a chill up the back of her neck, into her hair, tingling. "He's dead," she says.

"Good job," Whittaker says.

"Sir," she says.

"We'll see this through," Whittaker says. "But for now, you should take some time."

"I can't," Kateri says. "The Jenkins arraignment is tomorrow morning."

"It's not a suggestion, Fisher," he says.

"Oh."

She stands and undoes her belt, releases her firearm, and leaves it on the table.

"You can be at the arraignment," he says. "But Hurt will close the case."

* * *

She can't tell Shannon. She can't leave him with the knowledge that Bear has been shot dead—by her—the night before he sees the judge. She calls Brewer to plead with him not to tell Shannon. But when she reaches him on the third try, close to one in the morning, he tells her he quit the case.

"When?" Kateri asks. She remembers Shannon saying, *Tell Bear I fired you.* She sits in her office in the dark, just the glow of her computer and the light from the hallway.

"This afternoon," Brewer says. "I can't work with that kid," he says. "And he doesn't want me. Trust me, he says it was mutual. What the fuck happened up there?"

Kateri leans into her hand. "What have you heard?" she says.

"Standoff. Shots fired."

"I may need you for questioning," Kateri says.

"Well, fire away," Brewer says, "but I don't know anything."

"I thought he was your friend," Kateri says.

Brewer laughs. On the phone, his voice is low, gravel but sharp. It's a sexy radio voice. A good phone voice. "Bear Miller is no one's friend," he tells her.

"I thought he hired you," she says.

"He did," Brewer says. "And I've known him for fifteen years, but you're a fool if you think he's a friend to anyone."

"I see," Kateri says, completely unmoored by what is happening, how things are revealing themselves.

"He's a sociopath." He laughs again. "He always has been."

"I'm sure someone would like to get a statement from you," Kateri says.

Brewer breathes into the phone, a low hum. "Shit sure is wild," he says.

* * *

At home, the dog has chewed through her hiking boots. When she opens the door, he lies with his head flush to the floor, in a land mine of leather and rubber debris.

"Oh, no," Kateri says to him, and he shifts his body onto his side, his belly exposed, his tail thumping weakly.

"Buddy," she says.

His back legs flail. If she's not careful, he'll start to pee.

She picks up the scraps of leather and gets the dog more water, her body slow-moving and stiff. She's sitting on the floor with the dog pressed into her when Hurt calls.

"Buick spotted near Brasher Falls," he tells her. "Side roads," he continues.

She feels empty, raw. Her jaw is tired from clenching. The dog smells like a velvety biscuit.

"Did you send anyone?" she asks.

"Stopped at a Stewart's, paid cash," he says. "Kid in the front seat. Driver bought her Skittles. Security footage from Stewart's shows the kid clear as day," he says. "Driver in a flannel shirt and a knit cap. Kept their face down the whole time."

"Is it Park Jenkins?"

"He hasn't been released," Hurt says.

"You checked."

He laughs a little. "It's the first thing I checked, Fisher."

"Did you run the plate?"

"Either they wrote it down wrong or it doesn't exist."

"No record?" she asks.

"None. We put deputies on 374, and there are road blocks on 30 and 11," Hurt says. "But there are so many back roads, it's hard to say. They won't get past us," he adds.

"Unless they do," Kateri says. She's weary down to the bones, her shoulder still ringing from the kick of her weapon. She looks at the map of the roads winding through the mountains, many of them not even marked. An email comes in from Hurt, who is still on the line with her. It's the surveillance screen grab of the little girl, her face turned up to the camera, her hair in two puffball ponytails. She holds on to the shirt of the person who pays, her little hand tucked into the hem.

TWENTY-NINE: SHANNON

FRIDAY, NOVEMBER 3

I lean my head against the glass door. No one is around. I know that it's Thursday, because the arraignment is set for tomorrow, on Friday, when the judge will decide what to do with me and then set another date. Everything inches forward.

I want to know what Kateri knows.

Why won't Bear answer?

I tried him twice, with no pickup, no voice mail, nothing but endless ringing.

I imagine him back where he came from, in the mountains, in a smaller but even nicer chalet in the woods.

Why did he just leave me here?

No one else is here. The cell sits at the end of a mint-green hallway, chilled with cement and stainless steel.

I eat a bologna sandwich and drink a carton of room-temperature milk. Then I lie flat on the metal bed with the book open on my chest, but I don't read. I close my eyes and try to imagine something of comfort. What do normal people think of? Their mothers? I'm haunted by the kitchen, and by the image of a boy I didn't even know.

I can't even cry. I've cried so much I was a dried-out shell, brittle and pearlescent.

I don't know when I finally fall asleep, the black-and-red scrunch of my closed eyes easing into a heavy, sinking dream.

But when I wake up, I'm covered with a rough, warm blanket. It smells just like clean fiber, a cottony, woolly smell. My feet stick out the bottom, still in their socks, but the rest of me is blanketed, held down, warm, safe. I try to remember anyone coming in, the heavy chunk of the cell door opening. Anyone, tucking me in, watching, praying, the way a parent or a guardian angel might. But I can't.

* * *

In the morning, I attend the arraignment in scrubs. I get a shower, and a clean set, with new socks. Kateri comes in with another officer I've never seen, and I ask her if I should change into regular clothes, or a suit, even though I don't have one. She says no. I didn't come in anything particularly nice, and I don't know where those clothes have gone.

There's a tense hush in the building, down the corridor, into the offices and the courtroom. There's some discussion between Kateri and the new officer—a young man, not much older than I am, but baby clean and buff, his hair like white down on his head. He asks her if I should be shackled, either by hand or by foot or both.

"Don't be ridiculous," Kateri says.

She wears a suit, and her hair is down, long, to her midback, and a rich dark brown that is scattered with something warm and nearly red.

"I could walk him in myself," she tells the officer, "but they're making me take you."

He flicks his eyebrows and won't look at me.

They have barricaded off the lobby, and through the windows I can see that the press has gathered outside—TV cameras, reporters, photographers. There are guards at the door, not letting anyone in, but people outside hold up cameras, iPhones, and a reporter from Watertown with a microphone shouts over the top of the crowd.

There are JUSTICE FOR CRAIG signs everywhere, and that unsettling American flag that's black and white with a blue stripe through the middle.

In the precinct office, Kateri talks with the newly appointed lawyer, a woman with a girl's face and a mother's body.

Kateri says, "This is Mandy Donovan. She's been brought up to speed on your case."

Mandy shakes my hand and smiles, like she's half surprised that I'm a normal person, a kid, not a deranged killer. She has strawberry-blond curls, freckles, a kelly-green suit.

They walk me down the windowed hallway to a small courtroom, and I wonder, for just enough of a second that it gives me a prickly nausea, what it would be like to be walked to a death chamber.

We don't have the death penalty in New York.

Even if they convict me, it won't happen. I'll have years to sit it out.

I'm not the only one in the courtroom for arraignment. There are two other cases before me, a DUI and a domestic assault. The woman with the DUI pleads guilty, and the judge sets a further court date in December. The domestic case involves a restraining order and supervised visits with children. It's a man in his thirties, with short hair and thick arms. He too gets another date. This is how it goes. They inch you along with further dates.

Where is Bear?

I wanted him to be here. I want to look over and see him, in a suit, his hair knotted behind his head. Wearing a pair of shoes that shine, that click on the tile floor. Watching me, believing in something. I just wanted him to be the thing that stops it all from going any further. The thing that saves me. The thing that causes the judge to say I'm free to go.

But there's no one else here. No one but Kateri Fisher believes in me. After the first case, Detective Hurt comes in and leans to say something in Kateri's ear that I can't hear except for the word *Buick*.

I sit between Kateri and the lawyer, and I turn my head for just a fraction toward Kateri and say, "It's him." I say to her, "I'm sure of it."

I hear her breathe through her teeth.

I feel like I'm at the very edge of a cliff and someone I can't even see is about to push me off. I'll fall and fall, and when I hit the bottom it'll feel like falling into bed, except it will break all my bones.

She turns in the chair to face me, her legs crossed, and beside me, Mandy is struggling to hear us.

"Shannon," Kateri whispers. "Does he smoke?"

"Yes," I say. And the memory of it is suddenly sharp with fragrance, from the cigarettes, the whiskey, the smell of the pines underneath the wheels of the car, the damp smell of leaves. "Luckys," I say. I feel my gut rising up against my lungs, shortening my breath.

"He has her, doesn't he?" I say, a little too loud. "He has her."

Kateri stares at me and hushes me. I notice the darkness under her eyes, that she has covered it with makeup. Her lashes are stiff and curled with mascara. Her eyes deep, deep brown.

"Do you know who he is?"

"Yes," I say, and my hands tremble. "And no," I say. "I don't know anything about him."

Mandy pats my unshackled hand. "It's going to be okay," she says. Then, "I wish we'd had more time to go over this."

Kateri turns forward again but keeps talking to me, barely moving her lips. "Is there any chance Bear could have hired someone to kill your mother?" Her voice is hoarse, raspy.

"I don't know," I say, and I feel like all my hair is standing on end. "He could hire anyone to do anything. Couldn't he?"

She closes her eyes and shakes her head. "I don't know," she says. "I don't know anything anymore."

When the judge calls me up, Mandy goes with me, and Kateri stays behind on the chair that is linked to all the other chairs and bolted to the floor. I stand a few feet back from the bench and say my whole name, Shannon Lee Jenkins, and then repeat my date of birth and social security number into the microphone.

There's a bustling of whispers behind me, and I hear Kateri's voice, and I wish it were her standing up here with me, but she says, "No, no cameras," and then I hear Detective Hurt's voice telling someone to get out.

The judge shuffles a stack of papers, straightening them, and then reads the charge:

"One count second-degree homicide in the killing of Craig John O'Neil. One count," he continues, "of second-degree homicide in the killing of Pearl June Jenkins. One count, kidnapping and endangering the welfare of a child under the age of eight," he says.

I shoot a look at Mandy, and she twitches her head, as if to say, hear him out.

The doors swish behind us. The previous arraignments are allowed to leave, and there's a gust of warm air, and more voices, more of Kateri's voice, and a kid's voice even, which makes me think the domestic case dragged the kids in on one parent's behalf or the other's.

"Mr. Jenkins," the judge says. "You have the right to a speedy, public jury trial. You have the right to representation, which I see has been provided for you. Miss Donovan," he says.

"Good morning, Your Honor," Mandy says.

The judge must be seventy. He looks like I imagine a professor would. Longish white hair, a white goatee. There's a looseness in his arms, the way he leans, that I don't expect but makes him seem more likable.

"Miss Donovan," he says again, and smiles brightly at her. She's cute, in her suit, with her gingery hair. "Do you have any question, or doubt in your mind, that your client is fit, mentally or otherwise, to stand trial in the charges placed against him?"

"No, sir, I do not," she says.

"Is the defendant ready to enter a plea?" the judge asks.

"Yes, Your Honor," Mandy says.

"Mr. Jenkins," the judge says, "how would you like to plead to the charges listed against you?" It takes him a minute to look up from the paperwork and at me. When he does, when I have his eye contact, I answer.

"Not guilty," I say into the microphone, and it echoes in the courtroom. "Your Honor," I add, forgetting.

"Do you understand the charges brought against you?" he asks, and Mandy is about to answer for me when I say, "No, Your Honor."

I don't know what Brewer was working on, or how much of it was directed by Bear. I thought he was trying to reduce something, but the judge said homicide anyway, not self-defense, and there was the cop, and Birdie, and all I can think of is that I will never, ever get out of this. I am about to spend the next thirty years in jail. Just like my dad. Just like any other Jenkins.

Where the fuck is Bear?

The judge looks at Mandy, about to ask her more questions.

"Miss Donovan," he says, "it seems to me here that the charges are pretty straightforward. I'll ask you again if you have any doubt in your client's ability to stand trial for the charges that have been brought against him."

"No, Your Honor," she says. "However, we have just met."

"Have you discussed the charges with the defendant, Miss Donovan?"

"No, Your Honor. I was brought up to speed yesterday," she says. "The original attorney recused himself from the case," she says.

"I see." He watches the back of the courtroom, behind me, over my head, while again there's a whip of air as the door buzzes open and closed.

"Pardon the interruption," the judge says, and then calls to the bailiff, "What in the hell is going on back there?"

THIRTY: KATERI

Kateri stands when she sees who they have—that they have brought Pearl Jenkins into the courtroom, alive, beaten, and bald.

She has a few weeks of hair growth on her head. Longer than a buzz cut, and fiery red like Birdie's. The hair has grown into and around the wounds to her skull, the worst at the very back, where the skin has not come together right and where the bone has been broken. Her clothes hang on her, damp and filthy, but when she looks up at Shannon before the judge and then at Kateri, her eyes are bright, sharp.

"He didn't do it," Pearl says.

Little Birdie lets go of her mother's shirt and runs toward Shannon, who cannot embrace her with his hands shackled. Instead, she leans into his leg, and he says, "Hey, Bird," with a catch in his throat.

Pearl Jenkins has a long but seemingly shallow cut along the left side of her head, dried with blood, caked over with dirt and scabbing.

The judge raps his gavel once. "Detectives," he says, unaware that Kateri has been placed on leave, "please conduct your investigation outside my courtroom. This has clearly taken a turn."

"Why'd you come back?" Shannon asks his mother, while Hurt puts cuffs on her and Mirandizes her.

273

Pearl hangs her head, her teeth clenched, possibly in pain, Kateri thinks, looking at the wounds on her head and hands. Defensive wounds.

"I heard about the arrest," she says. "I couldn't." She stops and coughs, and then straightens her back to look up at her son. "I couldn't let you go down too."

* * *

The judge, with his eyes on Pearl Jenkins, alive and harmed but here of her own free will, tells Shannon that he accepts his not-guilty plea and will release him on ten thousand dollars' bond.

Shannon weeps, his mouth open, his eyes raw.

"There's money in my car," Pearl says. "From him." She does not elaborate; she just looks at Shannon.

"Where did you get the car?" Shannon asks.

"From Jane," Pearl says. "You know him."

"The car's a piece of shit," Birdie says, and Shannon unexpectedly laughs.

"It kept overheating," Pearl says. "It would just turn off. And we'd have to wait. We didn't make it to Canada," she says. "And then I heard the news."

They take them in separate directions, Pearl off to booking and Shannon to a holding cell, while the cash is extracted from the Buick and his release paperwork is processed.

They send Birdie with Kateri.

She is not assigned to the case any longer, and the chief made it clear that Hurt would close it. There was no plan made for who would take custody of the child if Pearl came back alive, but Kateri tells the judge she should be with her family.

"Her family?" the judge says.

"Her brother," Kateri says.

The judge frowns, shuffling papers. Nothing is in place. He grants temporary custody and sets a date for family court in ten days.

It's Hurt who walks Pearl down to an interrogation room. When everyone else is dismissed, Kateri takes Birdie by the hand and meets Mandy Donovan in the hallway.

Kateri stops her. "Please," she says, and "I'm sorry," handing Birdie off to her. "Just for a while, here in the building," she says. "I need to be in that room."

* * *

Hurt doesn't give Pearl the benefit of the softer room with the stuffed chair and the bookshelves; he takes her straight to Interrogation B, with its metal table and cold cinder blocks. Pearl is quiet, compliant. She flinches when the guards come to take her clothing, when they strip her naked and search, when they shine a light into her mouth and inspect between her legs. She's covered in stab wounds on her body and defensive slashes on her arms.

"Who gave you the car and the cash?" Hurt asks Pearl, before he asks her anything else.

"He goes by Jane," Pearl says.

"Did he attack you?" Hurt asks.

"No," she says. "Kyle Metzger tried to attack me."

Kateri leans over the table. "Ma'am, he did some significant damage," she says.

"You should see him," Pearl says, smug.

Kateri is afraid of pushing her. Pearl is beaten, dehydrated, exhausted. But Hurt keeps going. He just hammers her with questions so she has little time to think in between.

She was attacked by Kyle Metzger, a kid the same age as Shannon, who she bought drugs from, who she'd known since he was eight years old. She didn't owe him money.

"I didn't owe him a fucking thing," she says to Hurt, her eyes wide and indignant. "He had no reason to come there the way he did."

Hurt points to the defensive cuts on Pearl's hands and forearms. "And then?" he asks.

"I beat his ass," she says. "I fought back. I'm not going down for Kyle fucking Metzger. They were coming for my house."

"Who was?"

"The county. I needed to get out of there, so I took advantage of the situation."

"How so?" Hurt asks.

She rubs her nose with the back of her hand and then coughs, and Kateri pushes a plastic cup of water toward her so she can drink.

"I wanted to make it look like he killed me," Pearl says.

"Inside the house?" Hurt asks.

"No, with the bones," Pearl says.

"You planted the bones," Kateri says. "And burned them," she adds. "Where did they come from?"

"From Jane," Pearl says. "I don't know what they are. I thought they'd be unidentifiable. But you know," she adds. "Suspicious. Maybe enough. Enough for me to take Bird and run."

Hurt scribbles away on his open pad, his handwriting urgent, slanted, but small and neat. Kateri thinks of the map. Pearl and Birdie got as far as Brasher Falls, which is almost to Canada. She could have parked the car, crossed the border on foot through the woods. There are plenty of unpatrolled places to cross over.

"Why did you come back?" Kateri asks. It's almost a whisper. She can't imagine what this woman was thinking, so close to her own freedom with her little girl.

"Fuck," Pearl says. She cranes her neck back, looking at the ceiling, and when she comes up again, she looks like she'll black out from the rush, like she's ready to collapse from the physical beating, the stress, the fleeing. "Fuck," she says again.

"Pearl," Kateri prompts. She refills the plastic cup from a larger plastic bottle.

"I saw it on the news," she says. "At a Stewart's, where they had the TV on behind the ice cream counter."

"Your disappearance?"

"Shannon's arrest," she says. "I can't," she says then, and her face breaks, and Kateri thinks she will start to cry, but she doesn't. She can't be broken, Kateri thinks. Kateri watches her chew at her lip, mouth folded in on itself, and Pearl says, "I couldn't let him go to jail for something he didn't do." Her shoulders go soft all at once, like she's deflating. "I did it to Park," she says. "And I couldn't do it to Shannon."

Hurt drops his pen on the table, and the clatter in the quiet room makes Kateri jump. "Did what to Park?" Hurt asks.

"Let him take the fall."

"For what?" Hurt asks.

"The fire," Pearl says. "The fire at the farmhouse when Shannon was little." Hurt lets her wait, and Kateri watches her face closely. Her eyes well up finally, then, when she talks about her son. "I just wanted to end it," she says. "I hated all of it. The shitty house, living with Park, and taking care of a baby. I was twenty years old," Pearl says, "with a three-year-old. Shannon didn't have shit to look forward to," she says. "In this town, with no money. But then we made it out. He kept screaming for me, but it was Park who pulled him out, and I crawled after him, hurt but alive, and when the cops came to investigate, I . . . I blamed it on Park. I let him take the fall," she says. "And let Shannon think it was Park who tried to kill us."

"But it was you," Kateri whispers.

"It was me," Pearl says.

* * *

They find the man that Pearl calls Jane at his listed address. He opens the door without question, wearing a soft dress shirt, open at the collar, gray dress pants, and black shoes. He moves aside to let them into the kitchen, a small room, tidy and bright, with a bouquet of bird feathers on the table and some sun-bleached animal bones. Kateri recognizes the mandible of what looks like a deer and the stump of an antler. She nudges Hurt's arm, juts her chin in that direction. Jane pauses; it seems to catch his breath, though he's barely moving. Kateri thinks he looks weak, diminished. She noticed how thin his wrists are, how the bones of his face are all visible underneath his sallow skin.

She shouldn't be here. She should have stayed home the way the chief instructed, but when Hurt left in a squad car to talk to Jane, she rushed after him.

"Fisher," he warned.

"I have to," she said. She slid into the car without asking.

Now, in Jane's kitchen, she lets Hurt take the lead.

"Sir, we need to ask you some questions regarding the disappearance of Pearl Jenkins, the abduction of her daughter, Sparrow Annie Jenkins, and the murder of deputy Craig O'Neil."

"None of this is Shannon's fault," Jane says.

"He's being released," Kateri says.

Jane sinks into a kitchen chair, deflated, exhausted. "Thank God," he says.

Kateri sees Hurt jot something down on a plain white notepad, but she can't make out what it is.

"You were released from Clinton Correctional in May," Kateri says. "Did you come right to Spring Falls?"

"I don't have any family," Jane says.

"But you knew Park Jenkins," Hurt says. "Did you know Park Jenkins before you were incarcerated at Clinton?"

"No."

"You must have become quite close," Hurt says. "To move to where his family lives. Were you expecting his release?"

Jane crosses his legs and folds his hands on top of his knee. "I expected to die first," he says.

Hurt scribbles more on his pad. "Dramatic," Kateri answers.

"Is it?" Jane asks.

"You helped Pearl escape after she was attacked," Kateri says, and he nods. "Did you sign Sparrow Annie out of Mercy Hospital?"

"Yes," he says.

She runs her finger along the smooth edge of the jawbone on the table. "Where did you get the bones?" she asks.

He motions out the window, and she knows the woods are full of bones. Off trail you might stumble on the entire skeleton of a deer, a bear. You can buy pelts and bleached, preserved skulls in some trading shops. Mounted antlers, a completely taxidermied fox.

"She wanted to throw them off her trail. If it looked like she was dead, she'd get farther," he says. "She planted the bones, the shoes, the bracelet. She thought they'd catch Kyle and she'd be gone."

"Why help her at all?" Kateri asks.

"It wasn't about her," Jane says. "I wanted—" he begins, and stops to cough, a deep, dry, burning rattle in his chest. "I wanted to set Shannon free," he says.

"From his mother," Hurt fills in. "From the secret kid and the paranoid TV screens."

"Yes," Jane says.

"Why, though?" Kateri asks.

His cheeks color, the redness out of place on his pale skin. "I was quite fond of Shannon," he says. His mannerisms are genteel, his voice soft.

"Did you kill the cop?" Kateri asks. "In order to get to the girl?"

His face falls, then, and he rubs his fingers along his brow, shading his eyes. Then he sweeps his hair off his forehead with his fingers, blinks, looks Kateri in the eye when he answers. "I didn't see another choice," he says. "I regret that. The cop had nothing to do with this. You can arrest me," he says, and Hurt laughs a little at his permission. "But you need to arrest Bear Miller as well," he says.

Kateri is about to answer when Hurt asks, "Why?"

"He sent the kid to attack her," Jane says. "He paid Kyle Metzger to kill Pearl."

"Why?" Kateri asks.

"You'll have to ask Miller," Jane says.

"Miller is dead," Hurt answers.

Jane smiles slightly.

"Hiring a hit man to kill someone is capital," Hurt says. "So is killing a cop."

"I already have a death sentence," Jane says.

Kateri perks up, alert, the second time he says it. She watches his face, the way the sun through the kitchen window catches his blue eyes. His skin is sallow, his upper lip sweaty. He folds his hands, and his fingers are like bones, laced together.

"What do you mean?" she asks. She narrows her eyes and cocks her head, listening.

"I'm dying," he says, and looks her in the eye. His eyes are sharp, the brightest thing about him. "Do you want the details on how and why? I don't have anything to lose," he says, suddenly fired up. "I couldn't get to Birdie any other way. I'm sorry for that."

Hurt huffs. "Yeah, sorry's not going to be enough," he says.

"You can do whatever you want with me," Jane says. "I'm done."

* * *

They book the stranger for murder, kidnapping, and endangering a child. Kateri walks him down to his cell after, where he refuses to eat but asks for an extra blanket. His head is sweaty, his hair damp, and his lip trembles. Kateri watches his face, and he appears to breathe rapid, shallow breaths.

She wonders for a minute if she should call medical, have him transferred to the hospital with Pearl, but before she asks him, he answers her.

"I'm fine," he says. "Just leave me alone."

She hands him the blanket—a rough gray wool blanket like you'd keep in a car for sitting on the ground, nothing that gives any comfort—and he wraps it around his shoulders.

"Listen," he says.

She waits at the door.

"The law office in town has my will," he says.

"Okay," she says.

"I left everything to Shannon. It's not a small amount. I don't have any family. I want to take care of him."

She feels a cold weight in the room, a heavy energy that appears to be filling the space.

"Just make sure he knows," Jane says. "I don't want to be left on a shelf."

*   *   *

It's Hurt who goes to arrest Kyle and finds him not at his own address but at his father's house, which is a single-wide trailer with a large addition on it. Kateri has seen it. She's heard calls there for domestic. It's a dirt yard with dogs and baby toys, a plastic pool in the summer, a rusted-out swing set. Kyle's father, Tim Metzger, is still in county waiting for his own arraignment.

She's surprised that he looks a bit like Shannon. They are similarly built, but Kyle is wiry where Shannon is lithe, Kyle's hair is a dirty dark blond where Shannon's has a reddish hue. He's the youngest of the five Metzger boys, who mostly grew up without their mother, who died when Kyle was still a baby.

He doesn't want to talk. It's late by the time Kateri meets Hurt back in the investigation room, the camera running again. Hurt announces who's present and why they are interviewing Kyle Metzger.

"You knew Pearl Jenkins," Hurt says.

Kyle nods, tense. He seems literally reluctant to open his mouth. "You were selling her oxycodone," Hurt says. "How did you meet Bear Miller?"

Kyle purses his lips before he starts talking. "He came into the diner," he says, slurry, and that's when Kateri notices that he's missing two teeth, recently, to the left of his front teeth.

She points to his mouth. "That happened during the struggle with Pearl," she says.

He appears to bite down on his tongue and nods.

It was Kyle's tooth they found, not Pearl's.

"What happened at the house?" Hurt says.

"I couldn't do it," Kyle says. He slouches back in the chair, his knees wide.

"Couldn't do what?"

"I was supposed . . ." He stops. "I can't," he says.

Kateri leans forward on the table. "Did Bear Miller hire you to kill Pearl Jenkins?"

"The money is gone," Kyle says. "I have . . . I have a kid on the way."

She hears Hurt let a long breath out. "What happened at the house?" Hurt says again.

"I just couldn't." He ruffles his hands through his hair and then over his face, and Kateri sees that his hands are rough, dirty, like he has always worked outside with machinery. "I see Pearl all the time," he says.

"Because you sell her drugs," Hurt says.

Kateri nudges him under the table. She's curious to hear this kid's answer and she doesn't want Hurt to deter him.

"She's like . . . I don't know," Kyle says.

"Your mom died when you were little," Kateri says, soft.

Kyle nods. "I just couldn't. She's like, the same kind of—" he says. "I mean, she's a mom. The kid is still little. The girl," he says.

"How much did Miller give you?" Kateri asks.

"A lot."

Hurt says, "Miller was killed."

"Oh," Kyle says. "Oh, wow."

"Were you friends with Shannon Jenkins?" Hurt asks.

Kyle huffs. "No," he says.

"You were in school together," Kateri says.

"I'm not friends with fucking faggots," he says.

"But you'll accept money," Hurt says.

Kyle stands up, and his metal chair knocks over behind him, and all at once Hurt is on his feet. "It's gone," Kyle says. "I'm not giving it back."

"Did Bear Miller ever come on to you?" Hurt asks.

"Fuck no," Kyle says, and spits, there in the room, onto the shined concrete floor.

"No more cursing," Kateri says, and points for Kyle to sit back down. "And do not spit in here." She looks to Hurt.

"Excuse us," Hurt says to Kyle, who shifts in his chair, panicky.

"I have a kid on the way," Kyle says again.

"Not a great time to make mistakes, then," Hurt says, and they duck out into the hallway, where one long fluorescent light is half out and half blinking, leaving the corridor to look like the way into a haunted house.

Kateri swings her workbag onto her shoulder and then pats the outer pocket.

"Come have a cigarette with me," she says to Hurt.

*　*　*

They stand outside the back door, facing the lot where the staff park, underneath a sickly yellow light. Beyond them, in the lights that hang over the cars, the tiniest snowflakes gather, fluttering around each other but not coming down. The wind has a bite. Kateri leans her back against the brick wall and watches Hurt as he takes his first drag in years.

It goes smoother than she expects, and he smiles a little. "You don't forget," he says. She shakes her head and thinks that not drinking will be easier if she can just have the crutch of a cigarette.

"It's debatable," Hurt says then, "that if they took Miller to Upstate instead of Mercy, he might have made it through surgery."

He also tells her that lesser gunshots have killed people instantly.

Hurt shrugs. "He was unusually strong," he says.

"So was Pearl Jenkins," Kateri says.

"Strip search found deep wounds on Metzger," Hurt says. "Poorly stitched and healing badly. Probably because he was afraid to report it."

"There was definitely a struggle."

"From blunt force," he adds, "and stabbing."

"All that blood," Kateri says.

"He came to attack her," Hurt says, "and she kicked his ass."

* * *

The following morning, Meghan Miller arrives, shining like a girl from a magazine, Kateri thinks, in her cashmere sweater. She seems neither distraught nor surprised. Hurt takes her to the room where they interrogated Shannon, which seems rural and shabby and run-down all around Meghan. She barely sits in the flowered chair, her slim bottom just perched at the edge of the cushion.

"I'm sorry to inform you of your husband's death," Hurt says. "I'm very sorry for your loss."

Meghan nods, her jaw tight, her lips straight.

"If you're ready to speak with us," Kateri says, "we're hoping you can shed some light on the situation."

"It's fine," Meghan says. She shakes her hair back and lifts her chin. "I knew Bear wanted the property in the woods," she says. "It's a huge piece of land; he was going to make millions off of it. I didn't know he had plotted to kill someone over it," she says. "We're not exactly in touch," she adds.

"You're not aware of any connection between Bear and Pearl Jenkins?" Kateri asks.

"Not other than the land," Meghan answers.

"What about Shannon Jenkins?" Hurt asks.

"Is that who he is?" Meghan asks, and then offers a dry, bitter laugh. "Of course," she says.

"Why of course?" Kateri asks.

"It's just like him," Meghan says, and shrugs one delicate shoulder. "He can't just have what he wants. He knows he can have anything. He can buy anything," she says. "He's got to make someone else pay, though," she says. "It's never a straight shot with Bear."

Kateri watches Hurt write something down in a slanted, practiced cursive.

"Where is he?" Meghan asks.

"Released on bail," Kateri says.

Meghan rolls her eyes. "He didn't do anything," she says.

"Do you know that?" Hurt asks her.

"No," Meghan says. "I don't have to. I know what Bear's capable of. I saw that look in that kid's eye the second I met him. He fucks you into submission and he keeps you there with money and trinkets and cars," Meghan says. "Except that poor kid probably actually had feelings for him."

The room goes quiet, and Kateri can hear the tick of the wall clock, Hurt's breathing.

Meghan closes her eyes, then, and covers her mouth with her hand, on which she still wears a large, elaborate wedding ring. Kateri sees a sheet of tears slip from under Meghan's eyelashes and wash down her face.

"Mrs. Miller," Kateri says, and tries to offer her a box of Kleenex in support, but Meghan swats her away.

"Don't *Mrs. Miller* me and pretend you have any idea what this is like," Meghan says. She straightens up and swings back her hair. Kateri has backed onto the desk, farther away.

"Are we done here?" Meghan says to Hurt. "I have to pick up my daughter. I have to make arrangements for her father's funeral." Her voice is gravel and harsh, the sound of the cry still lodged in her throat.

Hurt presses his lips so that they disappear. "Yeah," he says.

* * *

It's Hurt who walks her out and Kateri who stays several feet behind, pretending to pay attention to a file in her hands. When Meghan leaves, Hurt comes back and stands close to Kateri, not touching.

"It was him," he says.

She just looks at him. It was him in so many ways, she thinks.

"At your house," he adds.

"Yeah," she mutters.

"He was trying to subdue you. If not by seduction," Hurt says, "then by force."

"Apparently," Kateri says. She feels far away and empty.

"But he got neither one," Hurt says.

The memory of it, so recent, rattles her core, turns her insides to a running motor, rumbling. She thinks of his face in hers, his snarl. The roll of his foot on the candle and the tumble of his body down the stairs.

"How'd you get rid of him?" Hurt asks.

"I pushed him down the stairs," she says.

Hurt smiles and looks her in the eye. "Yeah you did," he says.

* * *

The stranger doesn't last the night. It's Kateri who goes in early the next morning, after she has taken the girl back to her own apartment, nestled her on the couch with Shannon. She lets herself into the cell wing before five in the morning, when the light is just a lavender glow coming over the tops of the trees.

She finds him curled on his side like a shell. Brittle, intricate, empty.

She sits for a moment on the steel bed and puts her hand to his cool face. She feels for a pulse, but knows without searching. He is still. It may have been an hour or more. His face, pale and bluish.

His knees are tight, his arms close to his chest, and his hands folded under his cheek.

She tries to pray, but her mind is empty, white, quiet. She studies his face instead, the dark fringe of lashes, his soft mouth gone tight and rigid in death.

He had nothing to lose.

THIRTY-ONE: SHANNON

FRIDAY, NOVEMBER 3

When they hand me back my possessions in jail, they're in a plastic bag marked INMATE PROPERTY. The keys to Bear's house and the Land Rover are in there. I have my learner's permit from when I turned sixteen, already expired, half a pack of cigarettes, a lighter, and ten dollars.

Kateri walks me to the front door and out onto the sidewalk, where it's bright and cold. They keep Birdie for a few more questions with a caseworker and a child psychologist.

"Where am I supposed to go?" I ask. My own house was a crime scene, and now Bear's is as well.

"Shit," Kateri mutters.

They wouldn't let me see Baby Jane. I only knew he was in the same line of cells I had been in. The same metal bed. The same cold walls.

Kateri holds up her finger for me to wait and then steps down the hall to another office, where she leans in. When she comes back, she hands me her house key. "Cemetery Road," she says.

* * *

She apologized this afternoon. When she told me, she said it generically: "Bear has been shot." Passive. The first thing I asked her was, how? And then, by who? And then, why?

She told me in her office, where I had my regular clothes back on. She had Hurt wait outside her door.

I felt my head fill up with cotton, muffling other sounds. I thought of him struggling, writhing in pain, and I could barely picture it. He seemed so strong, so invincible. My feet and hands went cold and numb.

"You did it?" I asked her.

"I did it," she said. "I am so very sorry to tell you."

"Did he . . ." I started.

"He grabbed my gun," she said. "It's what I was trained to do." Then, "Your mother has identified her attacker as Kyle Metzger."

"Fuck Kyle Metzger," I said. It was nearly a howl. "Why?" I said. "Did she owe him money?"

Kateri holds up her hand, asking me to wait. "He'd been hired," Kateri said. "By Bear."

"Fuck," I said. "Did you shoot Kyle?"

"No. Kyle is in custody."

It was all I could do to stand up and walk out of there. Outside her door, Hurt was standing with his hands behind him, looking at his feet.

"Did you know?" she asked me at the door.

I shook my head. She just blinked, like she believed me.

I leave there on foot with my plastic bag of things and Kateri's key. The justice center sits on the edge of town, and I walk toward town, through the center of the village and past the Hub and then up Cemetery Road, maybe five or seven miles altogether. The village square and the storefronts have been decorated for Halloween, the town filled with skeletons and tombstones. Part of the park is made up like a fake graveyard, with hands coming up out of the dirt. A straw body in a stuffed flannel shirt lies on the lawn of the bed-and-breakfast, its head in a chair beside it. Rubber bats hang from the trees.

But I'm the one who feels like a monster. Like at any moment the villagers might come after me with torches.

* * *

I wake up with Birdie in The Nest. I'm curled on my side on Kateri's couch, and Birdie is sitting in the triangle of my bent legs, happily watching TV, singing, playing with a stuffed bear. My body jolts, and then when I notice her, I settle. I reach for her arm and wrap my hand around it. She pushes my hand away like everything is normal.

I sit up but keep the blanket over my lap, and outside the sky is heavy and dark with coming snow. Birdie leaps off the couch and runs into the kitchen, where Kateri is bringing me a cup of coffee.

"What time is it?" I ask her. She looks different off duty. Relaxed. Her hair is down, her clothes are normal. She looks young and at ease with Birdie's energy.

"It's three," Kateri says, "on Saturday."

"Wow," I say.

"You slept hard," she says. "It's good. I'm sure you needed it. There are some things you need to know," she says, sitting across from me. "When you're ready."

"I'm ready," I say, and sip the coffee, aware that I'm probably not ready. I rub my eyes and ruffle my hair. I think I would love a long hot shower, but all I can think of is the white glass shower at Bear's, and all at once it comes back to me that he's gone, that he's dead, and I almost spill the coffee, doubling over.

I feel Birdie get up, nervous, and I hear Kateri take her into the kitchen, get her a juice box, murmur something to her. She lets me sob for a minute, and then I sit up, empty. Everything feels unreal.

"I'm sorry," she says to me. Birdie has gone off to play in the bedroom, the door closed most of the way.

"I'm so stupid," I say.

"You're not," Kateri says. She pushes a box of tissues at me, and I dab my eyes, blow my nose. My heart feels like a crater in my chest.

"Kerpak is standing by the offer on your property," she tells me.

It takes me a minute to reconcile what she's saying. Kerpak Industries. Bear's mother's company. "I didn't know there was an offer," I say.

"Bear had written an offer," she says. "Before."

I hold up my hand. I don't want her to say it. "Is it enough to pay off the taxes?"

"It's two hundred and fifty thousand dollars," Kateri says.

My throat tightens.

"Why couldn't he have just done that?" I say. My voice breaks, and I feel like I'm swallowing rocks. *What are you going to do when we go to Europe?* How could he have been faking all of it?

"I don't know the answer to that," Kateri says. "Some people," she starts.

"Don't," I say, and shake my head. "Don't try to explain him."

"I'm sorry," she says. "There is also," she continues, "money for you in the estate of Michael Jane."

"Baby Jane?" I say, and she nods.

"I don't know how much," she says, "but he made it known to me that you are his sole benefactor."

I don't ask. I hear the word *estate* and I know. But I already knew it inside, that part of the empty well in my gut is that he is gone and my body felt it. In fact, that may be what I have been feeling all along. His fading, his absence.

Kateri pours me more coffee, and I hear Birdie start on "I've Been Working on the Railroad," with commentary from the stuffed bear in a different voice. It's hard not to smile. She seems so resilient now, I think, and I hope she maintains it.

"The court has granted you temporary custody of your sister," Kateri says.

"Temporary," I say.

"They'll reevaluate. There's no reason for them to revoke it," she says. "But they have to state it as temporary."

"Okay," I say.

"And your mother has offered a full, signed confession," she says.

"She tried to kill me," I say. "In the house fire, when I was a kid."

Kateri nods.

"All this time I thought it was my dad, and he didn't even do it," I say. "It was her."

It feels like ash in my mouth.

*   *   *

Later, I sit on the floor with my back against the couch where Birdie curls up and sleeps, her hair a wild mess and her thumb tight in her mouth. I had started to doze, my head back on the soft cushion, the TV on low, but I felt something near me, a hand on my shoulder. I checked on her, but she was in a ball at the other end, and the hand I'd felt was bigger, warmer, something protective, and there were lips, near my ear.

Get up.

I heard the voice, and then it was gone.

The light is bright outside, and I can hear the loud scrape of snow-plows moving along Cemetery Road. I turn the TV to a local channel.

And I lean back on the couch, my shoulders cocooned in a white down comforter, watching the radar of a line of snow moving across the Great Lakes, into the North Country, over to Vermont. A dappled line of white and pink. Twelve, eighteen, twenty-four inches of snow.

Outside, it has started, the sky a swirl of white, the grass blanketed, the roads deep and slick. I hear her stir behind me, her mouth sucking like the baby she still is but her body warm and safe and whole. Both of us, whole. By morning, everything will be covered in white, everything hidden under a deep layer of cold, hard sparkle, everything dormant, everything erased, what is buried waiting to rise again. Clean.

ACKNOWLEDGMENTS

There are many people to thank in the making of this book, beginning with my stellar agent, Wendy Sherman, and my editor and woman-who-truly-gets-me, Jenny Chen. I'm grateful to them both for their patience and their keen vision in bringing *The Watcher* to light. I'm also indebted to the many friends who offered me time and space to write: Georgia Popoff, Shanna Mahin, Kristen Sullivan, Tatyana Knight, and Jane Springer. Their generosity and their company during a solitary process meant the world to me. I'm grateful for the many readers and other writers who encouraged me along the long way to publication, but especially Wendy Walker, Danielle Girard, A. F. Brady, Vanessa Lillie, and Lena Bertone, whose daily text messages kept me afloat and continue to highlight my day.

This book was made fully possible by a six-week residency at Virginia Center for the Creative Arts in the fall of 2016. It was there that these characters took shape, and I am forever grateful for the opportunity to be housed, fed, and well companioned amid the mountains and the Osage oranges.

Everything I am and able to do is because of the love and support of my family: my sons, Kieran and Liam, who encourage me daily by becoming the creative and amazing people they are, but especially my husband, Geoffrey, whose grace, patience, and love are my life's blood.